Praise for *Stars and Bones*

"Gareth Powell drops you into the action from the first page and then Just. Keeps. Going. This is a pro at the top of his game."
John Scalzi

"An interstellar intelligence has a plan for Earth's future, but is humanity a part of it? Fast-paced and thoughtful, *Stars and Bones* leaves the reader well-fed with hearty helpings of mystery, suspense, adventure, and terror."
Marina J. Lostetter, author of *Noumenon*

"Gareth Powell's *Stars and Bones* is shocking and beautiful—an electric, epic, and sometimes gruesome look at humanity facing its biggest challenge yet. Powell keeps the pressure on and doesn't let go. I enjoyed it immensely."
Karen Osborne, author of *Architects of Memory*

"A headlong, visceral plunge into a future equal parts fascinating and terrifying." **Adrian Tchaikovsky**

"A gripping, fast-paced space opera that poses the unique question: what if instead of saving humanity, aliens decided to save the Earth?" **Stina Leicht, author of *Persephone Station***

"A grand scale adventure packed with fun banter, snappy prose, and masterful science." **Essa Hansen, author of *Nophek Gloss***

"A vividly imagined, propulsive read. Filled with a loveable cast of characters. Powell's writing creates a rich tapestry of their voices and inner lives. I think readers will be thrilled by this story."
Temi Oh, author of *Do You Dream of Terra-Two?*

"Big ships, big ideas and big emotions. Thrilling space opera which is epic in scope, yet always rooted at the human level, as all the best sci-fi is." **Emma Newman, author of *Planetfall***

"An interstellar collision of massive ideas and startling originality."
Zack Jordan, author of *The Last Human*

"*Stars and Bones* crafts a future that finds hope in dark places."
Valerie Valdes, author of *Chilling Effect*

Also by Gareth L. Powell and available from Titan Books

Embers of War
Fleet of Knives
Light of Impossible Stars

GARETH L.
POWELL

STARS AND BONES

A CONTINUANCE NOVEL

TITAN BOOKS

Stars and Bones
Print edition ISBN: 9781789094282
E-book edition ISBN: 9781789094299

Published by Titan Books
A division of Titan Publishing Group Ltd
144 Southwark Street, London SE1 0UP
www.titanbooks.com

First edition: February 2022
10 9 8 7 6 5 4 3 2 1

This is a work of fiction. All of the characters, organizations, and events portrayed in this novel are either products of the author's imagination or are used fictitiously. Any resemblance to actual persons, living or dead (except for satirical purposes), is entirely coincidental.

A CIP catalogue record for this title is available from the British Library.

Printed and bound in Great Britain by
CPI Group (UK) Ltd, Croydon, CR0 4YY.

For Edith and Otis, with all my love.

“No single thing abides; and all things are fucked up.”

PHILIP K. DICK

PROLOGUE

The ship fled between the stars.

Before the massacre of its crew, it had been scouting the territory a dozen light years in advance of the main body of the Continuance. Its mission had been to prospect for useful resources and forewarn the fleet of any potential threats. Unfortunately, on the last planet it visited—an unprepossessing rock known only as Candidate-623—it stumbled onto something that fell squarely into that latter category: a threat the like of which it had never encountered.

At the bottom of a steep ravine in the mountains, something had killed its crew. They awoke an entity in that gorge, and it dismembered them. Whatever that invisible presence was, it reached through their suits and flesh and wrenched the skulls, pelvic bones and femurs from their thrashing bodies. It burst their eyes from their sockets and cut short their hoarse screams as it tore away their jawbones and slopped their steaming viscera onto the rainswept ground.

Like every other ship in the fleet, the Couch Surfer *was dream-linked to its navigator, whose name was Shay, and so had to endure all the confusion and terror the poor woman felt as her ribs snapped and were twisted from her chest. It shared her pain and sorrow, and the unbearable stab of loss that pierced her heart as it was ripped from her. And now, as the ship ran through the emptiness of interstellar space, Shay's absence hindered it. Without a navigator, it couldn't accurately traverse the substrate. It couldn't plot a course, but the imperative to warn the fleet remained deeply ingrained in its core programming. It was duty-bound to alert the Continuance. It had to send a signal, but protocol demanded it distance itself from the hostile force before broadcasting, to avoid the possibility of its message being tracked. The last thing it wanted to do was to lead an attacker back to the fleet, and the billions of civilians contained in its arks. So, the ship flipped and spiralled through the stars, blindly hurling itself through half a dozen random and potentially dangerous substrate jumps in an effort to throw off any chance of pursuit. Despite being unable to accurately navigate without a human mind on board, its only purpose now was to survive long enough to make its report to the Vanguard.*

Something bad was down there. The Couch Surfer *had no idea what that something might be—its crew had seemed to spontaneously burst apart like flowers opening to the sun—but the ship knew it had to relay news of the thing's existence to its human masters before anyone else fell victim to whatever it was. Everything else, up to and including near-fatal engine degradation, came secondary to that objective. And so, it pushed itself harder and faster than it had ever pushed before, weaving an erratic course, no longer caring for its own physical survival. All that mattered now was the data it had collected, and the forewarning implicit within.*

It was almost three light years from the site of the massacre and preparing to broadcast its message when, without warning or preamble, the same invisible presence that had dismantled its crew began now to reach into its mind…

PART ONE

BLUE ARMS CAUGHT ME

"Quantum theory provides us with a striking illustration of the fact that we can fully understand a connection though we can only speak of it in images and parables."

Werner Heisenberg

CHAPTER ONE

DREAM-LINKING

ERYN

"They get everywhere," the *Furious Ocelot* moaned, speaking to me via the main console rather than through a physical envoy. "And you should see the state of some of their quarters. Clothes and empty plates all over the place. It's disgusting."

The *Ocelot* was a trailblazer. His job was to scout a path for the Thousand Arks of the Continuance. He was not—and he had taken every opportunity to point this out over the past few days—a *passenger vessel*. Usually, it was just the two of us out here among the unnamed stars, exploring the territory ahead of the main fleet. Having another three bodies aboard made the place seem overcrowded. Once we'd located Shay and her ship, I wouldn't be sorry to say goodbye to this crew and reclaim my solitude.

From my seat on the *Ocelot*'s bridge, I stared out at the swirling, unreal light of the substrate. I knew Shay was out there somewhere, and I was going to find her. In the days since her ship's disappearance, I'd lobbied hard to be allowed to lead this follow-up mission. I'd called in favours and banged on desks, and finally been given the assignment—on the strict condition I also bring a team of experienced search and rescue personnel. But the *Ocelot* didn't like hauling passengers, and he made no secret of the fact.

"I'll have a word with them," I promised. "And ask them to pick up after themselves a bit more."

"Please do."

Green readouts on the windshield told me all the ship's systems were operating within normal parameters. Despite his bitching, the *Ocelot* and I were still in synch. We were still functioning as an effective partnership. He remained the same old ship I had known for so long. I revelled in the familiar smell of the grease on the hydraulic arms supporting the cargo ramp, the clang of our footsteps on the metal gratings set into the decks, and the ever-present grumble of the engines.

The evening before our arrival at the *Couch Surfer*'s last known position, we gathered in the *Furious Ocelot*'s crew lounge for a final briefing from Tom Snyder, the ranking leader of the expedition. Food printers and a sink were set into one bulkhead, and a large screen into another. The rest of the wall space had been given over to equipment panels and overhead lockers. A hexagonal table took up one corner of the room. It doubled as an eating space and conference table. I sat with my hands curled around a coffee cup. The *Ocelot*'s envoy sat to my left. He was a heavy-set, bald, blue-skinned man in a three-piece suit the same colour as his complexion. Although physically human, he had no independent mind of his own, and it was the *Ocelot* that looked out from behind those cobalt eyes. The xenologist, Li Chen, sat beside him, with her back to the wall. She was somewhere in her twenties, and slightly built, with purple hair and contact lenses to match. Alvin Torres, the skinny paramedic, sat opposite me, and Tom Snyder occupied the stool to my right. With all five of us in there at once, the lounge felt cramped.

"Okay, listen up, folks." Snyder had dark skin and a grey beard. "As you know, six days ago, one of our long-range scouts went missing. What you don't know is that according to its last transmission, it ran through an emissions shell originating in this system." The table surface cleared to reveal a map of nearby space. Snyder tapped one of the points of light. "More specifically on this planet here, which we've designated 'Candidate-623'. It went to investigate, and it hasn't been heard from since. Our job is to locate the missing ship and retrieve its crew, including Eryn's sister."

The *Ocelot* put his pudgy hand over mine. The others wouldn't meet my eyes.

After an awkward moment, Chen cleared her throat. "I'm sorry, did you just mention an emission shell?"

Snyder enlarged the picture of the planet. "It's coming from a single source, located in the southern hemisphere."

"One of ours?"

"Not as far as we can tell."

"Then what is it?" Torres demanded.

Snyder shook his head. "We have no idea. But I guess we'll find out when we find the *Couch Surfer*."

Torres was about to respond but Snyder held up a hand to stop him. "You're all here because you're the best in your fields," he said. "I've seen your work. You're conscientious, highly knowledgeable, and still young enough to be open-minded."

"But why didn't you tell us this was more than a straight rescue?" Torres was clearly unhappy. "Why weren't we told up front about this signal?"

"Because the Vanguard decided to keep this mission as classified as possible. It didn't want any rumours leaking into the general population, in case anyone else decided to hop in a scout ship and come trampling all over our investigation."

"And Eryn?"

Snyder glanced at me, and then looked away. "She's here because her sister was on the ship that made the discovery, and because she called in a lot of favours to be assigned."

My head felt hot and dizzy. My pulse thumped in my ears. I pushed the coffee away, feeling suddenly woozy. "So, they haven't just disappeared? Something might have got them?"

Snyder looked uncomfortable. "Yes."

"And you didn't tell me?"

"I wanted you to be able to concentrate on your job."

I opened and shut my mouth. Certain things were only now falling into place. For instance, the journey to the *Couch Surfer*'s last reported position had so far taken four days, and I'd spent most of that time hoping I might receive a substrate message from Shay saying she was back on our home ark and fine. When the signal didn't come, I had resorted to touring the ship, inspecting all the fixtures and fittings. The *Ocelot* had just undergone an unexpected refit, so there were new scuffs and scrapes on the walls and equipment; a new aircon system had been bolted to the corridor ceiling; and the rusty ladder from the cargo bay to the crew area had been replaced with a bright new one.

The *Furious Ocelot* was a blunt-nosed wedge with large engines and four sturdy, retractable landing legs equipped with heavy-duty shock absorbers. Following the refit, a cluster of new blisters disturbed the lines of his lower hull. One housed a full-spectrum mil-spec sensor suite, which had been installed to aid our search for the missing ship. If there was anything larger than a hydrogen atom floating around out there, we were going to be able to spot it. The other blisters contained ship-to-ship beam weapons, and a complement of semi-autonomous combat drones.

When I'd first seen them, I had been confused. "That's more firepower than I expected."

The *Ocelot*'s envoy dabbed his forehead with a blue handkerchief. "It's just a Vanguard thing. They want us to be prepared for all eventualities, however unlikely."

And now I suddenly understood what those eventualities were.

Snyder said, "You're upset."

"Of course, I'm fucking upset. You just told me my sister vanished while investigating an alien beacon. Now, I don't know what to think."

"My apologies."

Fighting my queasiness, I watched dust motes drifting through the beam of an overhead spotlight, borne aloft on the warm air. "Tell me what happened. I want to know everything."

"I can't really say. We don't know much, and what we do know is classified. All I can tell you for now is that they put down on the planet designated Candidate-623, as I said, and we haven't heard from them since."

"That's pretty fucking vague."

"At the moment, vague is all we have."

Into the ensuing silence, Torres said, "You knew there was a possibility they might have been lured into a trap, and you thought it would be a good idea for us to follow them?"

Snyder clasped his hands together. "Hence the combat drones and weapon upgrades."

Chen rolled her eyes and let her head fall back. "Oh, fucking *hell*."

CHAPTER TWO

FULL-THROTTLE ARMAGEDDON

HARUKI

Seventy-five years ago, the world came to an end. I was in my greenhouse at the time, talking to my personal assistant.

"They've launched nukes." We had been discussing the worsening political and global climates, but now Juliet's crisp and professional demeanour faltered.

Trowel in hand, I rose from the line of tomato plants I had been tending. "How many warheads?"

"At least two thousand." She was standing on the wooden duckboards between the vegetable beds, tablet computer in hand, and her face was pale. "Some aimed at military and infrastructure targets, but the majority targeting civilian population centres."

The air in the greenhouse was humid, and rich with the comforting scent of warm tomato plants. I shook my head and looked up at the rock ceiling overhead. I felt like crying. After years of escalating tension, the idiots had finally gone and done it. This wasn't going to be limited to a tactical exchange—they were going for full-throttle Armageddon. "What triggered it?"

"The British Prime Minister made a joke about pressing the button. He didn't realise his mike was hot."

I suppressed a groan. That clown. I should have expected it. "So, who launched first?"

"Does it matter?"

"Projected survivors?"

"Globally, less than thirty per cent in the short term, dropping considerably over the next few weeks."

Beneath the ceiling-mounted sunlamps, bumblebees drowsed along the orderly rows of flowering plants. In contrast to Juliet's exquisitely tailored grey business suit, I wore a simple white t-shirt and a pair of blue designer jeans. It was as close as I ever came to being dressed casually. I put down the trowel and peeled off a pair of five-hundred-dollar gardening gloves. "Well, I guess that settles it," I said. "It's time to see if this place is as safe as it's supposed to be."

"Full lockdown?"

Some of the other gardeners had paused in their work to listen. I rubbed the bridge of my nose. My knees and back ached from hunching over the soil. "It's our only option." For months, my team had been preparing this bunker in the Canadian Rockies, financed by my personal fortune. When it was complete, I'd intended to gather my friends and key employees in order to sit out Doomsday—whether that came from climate change, pandemic, or asteroid impact—in relative comfort. But now the birds were in the air, none of that mattered anymore. There wasn't time to get everyone here. My aged, leathery parents were in New York; my trophy popstar girlfriend at a charity gig in Boston; my management team still on their way from Los Angeles and not expected to touch down for another forty-five minutes, by which time it would probably all be over, one way or another. I'd have to cope with the skeleton staff already on site. Everything was screwed. All I could do now was make the best of what I had.

Thank god Juliet was here. She was my rock. What she didn't know about the running of this bunker wasn't worth knowing.

I was especially disappointed Frank Tucker wasn't here. The young physicist showed real promise, and I had been sponsoring him for some time. Now, just as the kid's research into wormholes reached an exciting point, everything was going to hell. I had hoped that in another five or ten years, I'd have been able to use Frank's research to create a network of portals that would allow instantaneous travel between the major cities of the world. Maybe between Earth and the moon. But right now, Frank was stuck in his lab in Oxford and there was nothing I could do to change that. And even if I could magically conjure a wormhole to escape the coming holocaust, where would it lead? Earth was fucked and there simply wasn't anywhere else to go.

I pulled out my own tablet and linked to Juliet's. "Show me missile tracking."

"This is what we have so far." She fed through a Mercator projection of the Earth based on data assembled from hacked military feeds and instruments concealed aboard my own fleet of digital communication satellites. High above the scrappy remnants of the North Polar ice cap, Chinese and Russian missiles were nearing the zenith of their trajectories. Only minutes remained. On the ground, the population would be panicking. Some would be engaged in a futile scramble for shelter, while others raged at their leaders. Newsreaders would be clutching their earpieces and turning pale, unable to believe what they were about to report. Panicked crowds would be fighting to get into subway stations and underground car parks. Families would be huddling together, helplessly trying to protect each other in the face of the impending holocaust.

I had lived through stock market crashes and flu pandemics. I'd grown up with the ever-present threat of a steadily deteriorating climate and had devoted much of my personal fortune to discovering ways to fight back and ensure I could keep my loved ones safe during the next emergency. My whole life, I'd been preparing for the end of the world, and now here it was.

I cleared my throat. "Okay, sound the alarm and get everyone inside."

"Yes, sir."

Could this really be *it*? My shoulders felt like weights. All that struggle, all that work. The modern world had instant access to all the great achievements in science, art, music and philosophy, but now the barbarians were torching the library. After today, most of it would be forever lost. In the bunker's archive, I had digital files of almost every book ever written and every song ever recorded—but they would only be of use to me, here, with my own private generator and electronics hardened against the effects of EMPs. I couldn't use them to rebuild civilisation.

"We should have done more," I said. If we'd had another couple of months, maybe we could have started to turn the tide of public opinion. Rigged an election or two. Deposed a few leaders or funded a few grassroots campaigns for peace. What was the point in being the richest man in the world if I couldn't save it? I'd spent years preparing this underground refuge for myself. What billionaire hadn't taken similar precautions? But now the hour was at hand, all I felt was a crushing sense of failure.

I should have done more.

"They pressed the button," Juliet said, seemingly reading my thoughts. "Not us."

"They caught us unprepared. I didn't expect things to escalate this quickly."

"I know." Juliet's voice was starting to lose its professional calm. "I've been hearing rumours. Something's been going on behind the scenes. Something nobody's been talking about."

"Any idea what it might be?"

"I don't know. Something to do with the outer solar system."

"How could anything out there possibly be relevant to this?"

"There's been some buzz about it over the past day or so."

"I don't understand."

"Neither do I. Not that it matters now." She broke off to check something. "Okay, outer doors sealed. Air filters operative. We're all zipped-up and as ready as we'll ever be." Her voice cracked into a nervous smile. "We did it, Haruki. We're going to live through this."

I pushed a hand back through my thinning grey hair. I knew she was right, but I still found it hard to reconcile the deaths of billions of people with any metric of objective success. Especially when I still had fresh dirt on the knees of my five-thousand-dollar jeans. I had intended today to be all about cultivating new life. About relaxing and taking a break from the infernal complexities of the planet's politics. A few hours with my fingertips submerged in the loamy mulch of the gardens, my awareness pared down from the wider global perspective to the basic needs of the plant before me. I hadn't been ready for *this*.

One of the missiles on the screen flashed red and my heart seemed to convulse in my chest. "Are *we* being targeted?"

"Fuck!" Juliet tapped her screen. "Yes, it's a Russian Topol-M with six one-kiloton warheads."

Indignation washed through me. "Why are they firing it at *us*?"

"Who knows? Maybe they think we're a military installation."

"Shit." I glanced around at the garden I'd created and knew with terrifying certainty that we were about to die. This bunker hadn't been designed to withstand a direct hit from a nuclear warhead. The idea anyone would waste a missile on this remote section of the Canadian Rockies had seemed laughable. But now, even if the lower levels survived the heat of the explosion, the upper levels would collapse like a concertina under the pressure wave, crushing everything within.

"How long?"

"Just under a minute."

I fell to my knees in the soft dirt. This far below the surface, I didn't think there was much chance of being instantly vapourised; but when the floor above gave way, we were likely to be flattened by megatons of semi-molten rock.

Oh gods, I thought, *I hope it's quick*. I couldn't bear the thought of being trapped in the rubble, injured and slowly dying of thirst and radiation poisoning.

"Thirty seconds," Juliet said.

All this work, all the money I'd spent. I'd wanted to preserve something for the future and protect my family, but now I was going to die along with everyone else. Somehow, it seemed unfair.

If I'd have known it was hopeless, I would have stopped worrying and spent more time surfing.

"Twenty.

"Fifteen." Juliet's cheeks were wet with tears, but she seemed determined to stay at her post until the end.

"Ten."

I thought of my parents in New York.

"Five."

I thought of my ex-wife.

"Four.

"Three."

My dog.

"Two."

I closed my eyes.

The lights flickered.

The world shook to a huge pulse of sound—a thrum so deep it was barely audible, yet I felt it vibrate through every cell of my being…

And then there was nothing, save the whisper of the ceiling fans and the hammering of my heart.

I was still alive!

Had the timings been wrong? I looked at my palm screen, but the map was blank.

"Juliet?"

She had fallen into the dirt. "I'm here. Goddammit, I'm here!"

"Juliet, what's happening? Was it a dud?"

She was silent.

"Juliet?"

"I'm reading zero impacts. No detonations."

"So, we survived?"

"No, you don't get it." She sounded dangerously close to hysteria. "I'm talking zero impacts *globally*."

"You're kidding?" The missiles had been falling like a hard rain. Nothing could have stopped them. "Is the data correct?"

She swiped frantically through her feeds. "It has to be! It's coming through on a live channel. All military bases and monitoring stations are still online. The satellite network detects no EMPs. No seismograph readings. No detonations at all."

I fought down a wild laugh. "But that makes no sense."

I climbed to my feet and brushed myself down. The other gardeners were standing around in puzzlement and shock. Two of them were hugging.

I'm alive. My fists clenched with a wild and unexpected fury. *They tried to kill me! They tried to kill the whole damn world, but we're still here.*

The anger burned away any trace of relief. *I don't know how we survived, but I'm going to find out.*

"Prepare a conference call," I snapped. "I want all the world leaders on the screen in my briefing room within the hour."

"They're probably rather busy right now."

I scowled. "I'm beyond caring. They'll have to talk to me; I've got dirt on all of them. After what they just tried to pull, they're lucky they're not being torn apart by angry mobs."

I stepped from the garden into the elevator that took me down to my private floor, almost half a kilometre below the surface. If I was going to confront the rulers of the world using my leverage as richest man and owner of the planet's largest global communications network, it would be better not to be dressed as a muddy peasant.

I was halfway down the shaft when Juliet came back online. "We've got something from the satellite network," she said. Her voice was shaky. She was probably in shock. "Some weird readings. Something big…"

"What is it?"

She choked back a strangled noise. "Holy shit," she breathed, "you are not going to fucking believe *this*."

And she was right, I didn't. At least, not at first. Because high above the atmosphere, something vaster and older than the Earth had reached down and snatched every ICBM from the sky, every torpedo from the ocean, and every tank shell, mortar round, and bullet from every battlefield on the planet.

And it was not at all amused.

CHAPTER THREE

BOILING MIASMA

ERYN

After the briefing, Chen brought me a cup of coffee. I was back up on the bridge. I couldn't be away from my duties for more than an hour or so, or the pathway I had intuited would collapse. This usually meant the ship had to drop out of the substrate when I needed to sleep. But right now, I didn't feel able to rest. The faster we reached our destination, the sooner I'd know whether Shay was alive.

Chen looked out at the unreal light surrounding the ship. "You must love it up here," she said.

"I guess." While grateful for the coffee, I wasn't in the mood for distraction. Chen seemed nice enough, but the ship couldn't find its way through the substrate without my help. No computer could.

She perched on the co-navigator's couch, and I felt a prickle of resentment at her casual invasion of my workspace.

"Have you been doing this a long time?" she asked, oblivious to my annoyance. "Navigating, I mean."

"About five years."

She looked out at the glittering, unreal light. "I can see the attraction."

The substrate underlay our universe the way a seabed underlies an ocean. But instead of being made up of sand and mud and dead whale carcasses, the substrate existed as a kind of plasma: a roiling hot soup of disassociated atoms freed from the normal laws of physics. As it underpinned our reality, we could use it to jump from one point in space to another, crossing in hours distances that would otherwise take years or even centuries to traverse using conventional means. Unfortunately, it couldn't be done without a conscious biological mind at the helm. I'd been told this was due to an unanticipated variation of what the physicists called the Observer Effect—the quantum physical theory that tells us the act of perceiving a phenomenon inevitably changes the phenomenon itself. Once observed, particles that have also been behaving as waves (and vice versa) collapse down into one state or the other. All the different possibilities resolve into one singular reality. The box opens and we find out whether the cat's dead or alive. That's how it was with the substrate. The act of looking for a pathway brought that pathway into being. At least, that's how it had been explained to me. There had been pages and pages of equations that I skipped.

Substrate navigation relied as much on intuition as calculation. And while ships such as the *Ocelot* could think considerably faster than the average human, they were still just glorified computers. When they looked at the substrate, all they saw was chaos. A place where the laws of physics were more like vague guidelines than hard and fast rules. The base reality of the universe only revealed itself to a living brain. So, to get around the problem, the ships of the Continuance were connected to a specific navigator via a two-way link to an implant buried deep in the navigator's subcortex, where it could interface with their subconscious mind—a process that had become known by the navigators and their ships as 'dream-linking'. So, while the ship handled all the tricky mathematics, all I had to do was sit here and look out of the window while my subconscious mind collapsed the wave function ahead of the ship, turning formlessness into flightpath.

Chen turned her head to face me. "So, Snyder's a bit of an asshole, huh? I mean, I don't dislike the guy, but he could have fucking told us what we were getting into."

I shrugged. It didn't matter. I'd have been here either way.

Chen lay back in her couch. "And what do you think of Torres?"

"I get the impression he doesn't much care for the confines of a Vanguard scout ship."

Chen smiled. Her eyes were still the same purple colour as her hair. "He doesn't like getting too close to people, if that's what you mean, but he can actually be almost polite when he makes the effort."

"I guess I'll have to take your word for that."

"I guess so."

I sipped my coffee and kept my attention on the swirling void.

"So, Eryn." Chen leant across the gangway separating our chairs. "Is there anyone waiting for you back in the fleet?"

"Like who?"

She gave a little shrug. "I don't know. A boyfriend, maybe…?"

I shook my head. "No."

Chen stuck out her bottom lip. The unnatural light of the substrate played across her cheek. "That's a shame."

"I guess it is."

"So, are you looking?" She gestured at the chaos outside. "Or does all this get in the way?"

"The only person I'm looking for is my sister."

Chen drew back. "I'm sorry. I've offended you."

She looked hurt, and I belatedly realised why she'd brought me the drink. The close confines and forced proximity of life on a scout ship seemed to have an aphrodisiac effect on some people. It was like time away from the real world—a limbo between existences where anything was permitted and nothing counted, and whatever happened in that netherworld stayed a secret known only to those involved. As far as I was concerned, since leaving the fleet our relationship had been nothing more than professionally cordial. We'd made small talk and shared the occasional coffee. But now, on our last night before facing who-knew-what, she'd apparently decided to take a chance.

"Ah." I felt my cheeks redden.

"I'm sorry." Chen wrapped a short strand of purple hair around an index finger. "I thought whatever happened in the substrate stayed in the substrate."

"This really isn't a good time."

"Damn it," she said. "I should have known you wouldn't be interested."

She looked so crestfallen, I felt kind of bad. "I didn't say that." My cheeks were absolutely burning now, but I felt I owed her an explanation. "I don't know. It's… just been a long time. And I don't usually… Not with—"

"Girls?"

"Passengers."

"Ah."

Flustered, she rose to leave.

I called after her, "Thanks for the coffee, though."

"You're welcome." She paused at the hatch. "And I'm sorry I dropped this on you out of nowhere. But you know where to find me if, you know, you change your mind."

"Let me think about it, okay?"

She smiled and turned away.

"Don't take too long."

•

The ship's cat claimed not to be able to remember his original name, so I just called him Sam. For some reason, it suited him.

Sam was a ginger tabby of indeterminate breed. He had an orange coat with black vertical stripes running down his sides and banded stripes on his legs and tail, like a miniature tiger. I'd acquired him a couple of years back, when he'd trotted up the cargo ramp and curled up on a pile of used packaging material. Like most of his kind, he sported a shiny white collar that translated his thoughts into sound, allowing him to communicate with humans.

"What do you think of Chen?" I asked. We were on the bridge, and he was curled up in front of one of the heating vents.

"The female?"

"Yes."

"She doesn't drop enough food on the floor."

On the couch beside mine, the ship's envoy sniffed. He'd never really approved of Sam's presence on board and had only learned to tolerate the animal since the cat had reluctantly agreed to use a litter tray rather than whatever random corner of the ship he happened to be in when he needed a pee.

I said, "I think she likes me."

Sam cocked his head to one side. "I think you're right."

"It's that obvious?"

"Pheromones everywhere." He scratched behind his ear. "If I had to guess, I'd say she was in heat."

The *Ocelot* cleared his throat. "I don't think humans work that way."

"You could have fooled me."

"What do you think I should do?"

The envoy rolled his eyes. "You're seriously going to ask dating advice from an unneutered tomcat?"

"Oh god, I am, aren't I?" I made a face. "What's wrong with me?"

The cat sniffed. "In my experience," he said haughtily, "humans really overthink sex."

The *Ocelot* interlaced his blue fingers across his ample midriff. "I guess compared to you, they do."

The cat scowled, but otherwise chose to ignore him. "I'm serious, Eryn. It's been months since you last got laid."

I flinched at the way he phrased it. "I can't think about that kind of stuff right now. I'm going out of my mind worrying about Shay. I don't have the spare emotional bandwidth."

"All the more reason." Sam stretched and slouched towards the door, tail high. "Blow off some steam. Relieve some stress."

"What are you, my shrink?"

The cat looked back at me. "I worry. I want you to be okay. You're one of the least intolerable humans I've ever met."

•

The following morning, Chen came to see me in the crew lounge while we were prepping equipment for landing. She wore a charcoal grey jumpsuit with the Vanguard's logo embroidered in large letters on the front and back.

"Reporting for duty," she said. She'd tied back her purple hair and ditched the matching contact lenses, revealing her eyes as a lustrous chestnut brown.

"Good morning," I said.

"I'm not too early, am I?"

"No, you're fine." I still wore my pyjama bottoms and a battered old t-shirt. I had only slept for a couple of hours, and now all I wanted was an IV-drip filled with coffee. Or maybe a mental jumpstart from the ship's batteries. Snyder, on the other hand, had been awake since six o'clock this morning, checking and rechecking our equipment, and testing himself on the shooting range the *Ocelot* had improvised in the cargo hold. According to the ship, he'd only paused once, to drink a litre of water and inhale a printed sandwich filled with pastrami, sauerkraut and pickles.

Despite my anger at him for keeping us in the dark about what we faced, I had to admire his hustle. He had a kind of driven toughness I could never match. A hardiness learned on the job, rescuing explorers marooned on the landscapes of strange and potentially dangerous worlds. According to his personnel file (which I'd surreptitiously downloaded when I finally admitted that I wouldn't be going back to sleep any time soon), the guy had faced all sorts of shit and always come through. When an aggressive alien pollen incapacitated the other members of his jungle team, he'd been the one to drag the survivors to safety. Caught in an avalanche, he alone managed to dig his way out and drag himself four kilometres to raise the alarm, despite a broken leg. I'm sure every mishap he'd handled and colleague he'd lost had left their share of scars on his soul—but perhaps the cruellest blow he'd suffered had been the loss of his wife in a shuttle accident while still in the fleet. Reading about it, the hairs had risen on the back of my neck. She had died in the same accident that had taken my parents, and I began to feel that maybe I understood him a little better. That maybe all his exterior toughness and apparent callousness masked a void he could never refill.

Or maybe Chen was right, and he was just an asshole.

Chen looked at me like she knew what I was thinking. "Hard night?"

"Bad dreams."

"About your sister?"

"It won't affect my work."

"So, what if it does?" She gave me a sympathetic smile. "Honey, it's okay to feel scared and upset now and again.

We're all the same on the inside. We're all just kids in adult bodies. Everybody feels frightened and alone most of the time, and nobody knows shit about anything; we're all just winging it the best we can."

My eyeballs bristled with unexpected tears. "Shut up."

Her smile broadened, and she covered my hand with her own. "You're going to be okay," she said. "And if you're not, well..." She squeezed my fingers. "Maybe you don't have to face it alone."

•

I dozed during the night, waking occasionally to make sure the *Ocelot* was still following the correct heading. When we eventually reached our destination, his envoy was on the bridge with me as we rose out of the substrate. Together, we watched the boiling miasma give way to the cool, star-speckled darkness of ordinary space.

Candidate-623 lay directly ahead, wreathed in yellow-tinged clouds that gave it the aspect of an ancient, rheumy eye.

"Out of the fire..." he murmured.

"What?"

"Oh, nothing." He settled intertwined blue fingers contentedly over his protruding stomach. "It's an old Earth saying that means, 'I'm sure we've thought of everything and there's nothing that can possibly go wrong.'"

In front of the heat vent, Sam the cat made a tutting noise, and curled himself into a tighter ball.

CHAPTER FOUR
SUBSTRATE FLUCTUATIONS
HARUKI

The angel entered our inner solar system aeons before the dinosaurs first walked on land. For millions of years, it lurked dormant in the sepulchral darkness of the Oort cloud—that tenuous halo of comets and ice far beyond Pluto's orbit—watching the inner planets for signs of a technological species on the rise.

During its long life, it had evaluated every potentially habitable world within a thousand light years. But while ninety per cent of those evaluations would record nothing more significant than the slow bubbling of bacteria around submerged hydrothermal vents, or the playful insouciance of marine creatures with no ambition beyond their simple sub-aquatic subsistence, this particular assessment picked up atmospheric changes on its target world that suggested the inhabitants were evolving along a dangerous path.

The angel had already seen a brief flowering of life on Venus, before the huge tectonic ructions that caused the planet to spiral into an unrecoverable, runaway greenhouse effect, boiling away all its liquid water and leaving it with a surface temperature sufficient to melt lead. It had also monitored promising hints of life on Mars. Some single-celled organisms; even some small, skittering crab-like creatures. But the little planet was just too small to hold onto its breathable air.

The middle planet—Earth—was the only one to remain capable of sustaining living beings. The angel watched ice ages come and go. The advance and retreat of glaciers. The slow dance of the continental plates. Dispassionately, it monitored a parade of extinctions, the last of which led to the demise of the dinosaurs. It could not prevent any of these disasters, nor did it wish to. Such events were part of the natural order of things. They encouraged evolutionary adaptation and experimentation and led to the rise of new species. The only time it would have interfered would have been if it detected a threat to the existence of all life on the planet—and that didn't happen until the eighteenth century, when it registered a sudden uptick in atmospheric carbon. Prior to that date, fluctuating levels of the element in the atmosphere could easily be explained by forest fires or other natural processes—but when an abrupt, continuing increase registered on the angel's passive senses, suggesting the mass burning of fossil fuels, it began to rouse itself from its millennial slumber. And then later, when it started to detect radio transmissions, it knew it had been right to return to full wakefulness. We had begun to develop and exploit a scientific understanding of our world. Over the next few decades, it paid close attention to our weak signals—first radio, and then television—archiving everything for future reference and study.

Finally, when electromagnetic pulses announced the development and testing of fission and fusion warheads in the atmosphere, the angel began to make preparations to intervene. By that time, the technological overspill from our factories and power stations had begun to heat our planet's atmosphere to levels that risked triggering irreversible and catastrophic climate change. Trajectories were calculated, dangers assessed and minimised. And then mighty wings flapped silently in the lonely darkness, nudging the angel on its way.

Drifting in undetected, it took up residence within the atmosphere of Jupiter. By the time we became aware of it, it resembled nothing more uncommon than a minor whorl of reddish storm clouds. Meanwhile, it had ruthlessly scanned our Earth, soaking up every TV and radio broadcast, every Wi-Fi signal and mobile phone transmission. Its senses traced the fine webs of information encircling the globe. They plundered the Internet more thoroughly than any hacker could ever dream. They traced electrical power grids and population densities; mapped out the routes of ships and trains and migrating herds in order to divine the complicated, interdependent nature of international trade; and gathered data on the savage reduction in biodiversity caused by pollution and other forms of climate disruption.

Then, when the angel had milked the electromagnetic spectrum for every possible scrap of information, it paused to cogitate.

Humanity threatened the existence of its own ecosystem. However, through a complex analysis of the data gleaned, the angel predicted that the problem would shortly solve itself. Global tensions had risen to a flashpoint. All it would take to trigger an international nuclear conflict would be one inciting incident.

The angel sat back to watch the coming conflagration. The destruction would be horrendous, but some species would survive, the same as with all of the previous extinction events. Once the humans had taken themselves out, new forms of life would evolve and crawl from the seas to take their turn on the Earth's stage.

But even as the war began and the first missiles launched, the angel perceived fluctuations in the local substrate. Down on the surface, in a place called Oxford, a wormhole had been opened.

If the angel had been capable of an emotion small enough to be understood by humans, it would have registered surprise, maybe even shock. Its assessment of our technological capabilities had suggested we would not have time to discover substrate travel before our global civilizational collapse. Nevertheless, there could be no mistaking the faint dimensional disruption. Somehow, it had been done.

New protocols clicked into place.

The angel reclassified the Earth as being of the highest possible priority. It revised the status of the human race from 'problematic' to 'worthy of further study'.

But the war was already in motion.

So, it intervened.

CHAPTER FIVE

INVISIBLE HOOKS

ERYN

We came in fast, accompanied by two combat drones.

Usually, I'd have performed a survey of the terrain from orbit, but Snyder didn't want to expose our presence until it was absolutely necessary. His reasoning being that it would be better to get in close, where the combat drones could provide us with a certain amount of cover, before revealing ourselves.

Candidate-623 was a cloud-swirled crescent. As warm, humid air spread north and south from the equatorial ocean, it clashed with cooler fronts from the planet's large polar caps, producing storms, hurricane force winds, and almost perpetual rain.

The *Ocelot* said, "According to my sensors, the ocean plays host to an ecosystem based around an abundant krill-like species, which absorbs enough CO2 and pumps out enough oxygen to keep the atmosphere almost breathable. I wouldn't go out there without a suit, though."

I looked at the waters circling the equator. "There's life down there?"

"Only in the sea. As far as I can detect, the land's bare and lifeless. If multicellular organisms ever crawled up out of the surf, they didn't stay long. Either they gave up the struggle, or something drove them back into the water."

We dropped through the upper layers of the thin atmosphere with the ship's leading edges glowing a dull crimson. Beside us, the two drones sliced cleanly through the air. They were designed to fall fast and cool, presenting as little in the way of a visual and thermal target as possible. With their wings swept back, they resembled diving hawks. When they reached the rainclouds, they tipped back and spread those wings, aerobraking savagely while simultaneously bringing their belly-mounted weaponry to bear on any potential dangers from the surface.

From the *Ocelot*'s bridge, I watched them disappear into the overcast, banking and weaving around in order to shed more velocity. Then we hit the cloud deck ourselves and visibility dropped to almost zero. Lightning flickered and thunder rolled. The ship could have pierced the murk with its active sensors, but I had them turned off in order to draw as little attention as possible. We were plunging into the unknown, and I was forced to agree with Snyder that the less we advertised our approach, the better.

The mists cleared at ten thousand feet. The *Ocelot* fired his thrusters and deployed all airbrakes and parachutes in order to make a harder-than-standard landing on a rock-strewn plain five kilometres from the source of the transmission.

For a moment, we bounced on the ship's shock absorbers as thick, thumb-sized raindrops drummed against the hull's upper surfaces and the wind lashed its sides. The drones were already establishing a perimeter. In the crew lounge, Snyder and his team were unstrapping and reviewing the data we'd collected during our descent.

"The signal's being broadcast from a ravine in these mountains," Snyder was saying as I climbed down the short ladder from the ship's bridge. "It's not very high-powered and because of the rock walls, difficult to detect unless you happen to be right overhead."

•

The mountains were too rugged for the crawler carried by the *Furious Ocelot*, so the only alternative was to suit-up and hike. While the others were down in the hold preparing their pressure suits and equipment, the *Ocelot*'s envoy pulled me aside.

"I have to tell you something," he said. He took me up to the bridge and activated one of the screens. "Snyder was telling the truth when he said your sister's team landed here. I picked up some footage from one of their helmet cams."

"They're still functioning?"

"The suits are running on battery power, and they're still trying to upload their last recordings to the *Couch Surfer*, which isn't here anymore."

"So, what have we got?"

"It's pretty bad." The envoy tipped his head to one side. "And by that, I mean horrendous. I don't think you should actually watch it."

My fists tightened in my lap. "I rather think that's for me to decide, don't you?"

The blue man let out a sigh. "I'm only trying to spare you."

"Then don't."

"Eryn, I'm serious. This footage is going to upset you. It depicts your sister's death in some detail."

"Just show me."

"As you wish."

The screen resolved into a picture. I sat forward. The scene was frozen. A young woman was caught in the act of turning away from the camera. It was Shay. Inside her helmet, strands of long, dark hair had come loose from her ponytail. Someone else's blood had splattered her suit and visor.

My stomach went light. The *Ocelot* was right; this was going to be *bad*...

"Are you ready?" he asked.

I took a steadying breath. Under the table, my hands gripped my knees.

"Just play it."

Hoarse, indignant screams are coming from somewhere off-screen. Shay flinches. She looks back at the camera with terrified eyes.

"… ripping him apart," she says.

The picture rocks.

"I don't know what it's—"

More screams. A different voice this time.

"Jesus, they're all dying!"

Static drowns the image. When it comes back, Shay has backed away from the camera. She has her hands out, trying to ward something away.

"No! No!"

"Look, I really think we should stop," the envoy said.

I didn't look up. I couldn't take my eyes from my sister's face. "Not yet."

More static.

She is running now. The picture jerks from side to side as whoever is holding the camera runs after her.

"Help," she says. "Help me!"

And then it happens.

Her body bursts from the inside. Layers of skin furl back. Her ribs snap open, and the contents of her torso spill out. Her entrails unwind as if being pulled by invisible hooks. Her pulsating heart tears from its mount. Fist-sized chunks of lung and spleen are ripped aside. And all the while, her voice—if you can call it that—keeps up a high-pitched wail.

The picture sputtered and died.

I fell back into my chair and covered my eyes with the palms of my hands. "Christ."

"I did warn you."

"Fucking hell." I was silent for some time. I couldn't seem to form words and my hands shook. And for some insane reason, I felt like laughing at the sheer horror of it all.

Finally, I said, "What could do that to a person? To a whole ship full of people?"

The envoy put a sympathetic hand on the back of my chair. "I have no idea."

"It's crazy."

"You're in shock."

"Of course I'm in fucking shock. Wouldn't you be?"

The blue man drew back. "Eryn, I'm a five-hundred-tonne starship. I don't think I'm capable."

"Have the others seen this?"

"Not yet."

"Then I think you should show them, don't you?"

•

I couldn't bring myself to watch the helmet footage for a second time. My stomach felt like a clenched fist and I couldn't stop trembling. As the others sat around the table, I stood to one side and gripped the handle of my china coffee mug. Even though I knew what was going to happen and what to expect, the cringing anticipation of the screams and bone cracks somehow made the experience worse.

When it was over, Sam the cat was the first one to speak.

"That," he said from the top of a storage locker, "is seriously fucked up."

Chen sat back in her chair. "The fleabag's right."

Snyder didn't say anything. He had his hand across his mouth. His cheeks were pale.

Finally, he said, "I had no idea it was this bad. You have to believe me."

Torres bristled. "You knew the *Couch Surfer* disappeared. That should have rung some alarms, shouldn't it?"

"They just told me it failed to re-establish contact. I didn't think for a minute..." He gestured at the blank screen.

"No," I said, fighting down bile. "I don't think you thought at all."

Snyder's expression clouded and he rose to his feet. He didn't like his leadership questioned. He said, "You came here looking for your sister. Don't you want to find out what killed her?"

"Of course I do."

"Then the mission's unchanged. We go out there and investigate."

"What about the danger?" Torres asked.

Snyder shrugged. He seemed more in possession of himself now. "We'll take precautions."

"But they're all dead," I whispered.

"Yes, and that's unfortunate." He squeezed my shoulder. "But you have to see the big picture here. Scientists are going to be examining that footage for years, just figuring out the mechanisms behind those injuries. And who knows what other discoveries are waiting for us out there." He smiled. "Can't you see how exciting that is?"

I stared at him open-mouthed. Then I stepped forward and punched him in the face. His head snapped sideways and blood burst from his lip. I brought my hand back the other way, in a backhand slap, and caught him across the cheek. The skin split. He cried out and sat heavily on the deck.

I stood over him, the breath rasping through my teeth. My heart thumped, and I wanted to kick his stupid head off.

But then the *Ocelot*'s envoy put a blue hand on my shoulder.

"Eryn," he said.

Blood dripped from my torn knuckles. I closed my eyes but all I could see were images from the helmet footage.

Shay screaming.

Shay screaming.

Shay screaming.

I turned and threw my arms around the envoy, burying my face in the little hollow where his fat shoulder met his thick neck. A sob wracked my body. Then another. And then I wept like I'd never wept before, great convulsions of grief seeming to boil up from the soles of my feet in order to explode through my throat.

I cried for the little girl I'd once been; for my sister and the horrific agonies she had endured; for my parents, who'd been taken from me; and even for Snyder, and the stupid, unnecessary violence I'd just inflicted on him. I cried for all that and more, and when I was finished, I straightened up and wiped my eyes on my sleeve. Nobody had moved or spoken. Snyder sat on the floor holding his cheek and dabbing at his lip. I wanted to run away and hide, but knew I had to maintain authority on my own ship. I took a step back, sucked in a deep, ragged breath and kicked the nearest of Snyder's boots.

"Somebody get this idiot some first aid," I said, then turned and walked back to my cabin with tears streaming down my face.

CHAPTER SIX

REALLY WILD THINGS

ERYN

I'd half expected Li Chen to come after me. I hadn't expected, when the door chimed, to find the skinny figure of Alvin Torres standing in the corridor.

"Can I come in?" he asked.

I stepped back, making room. "Sure, why not?"

I slumped on my bunk, still feeling sick to my stomach.

"What do you want?" I asked.

The man stood there for a moment. His overalls were clean and pressed, and a thin moustache haunted his upper lip like beads of sweat.

"Your outburst was understandable."

"Pardon?"

"Snyder led us into endangerment. He was insensitive about your loss. It was only natural for you to injure him." Torres drew himself up. "If I had been in your situation, I might have done the same."

I tried to imagine Torres punching somebody and if I hadn't already been fighting back tears, I might have laughed. His slight frame seemed almost entirely untroubled by musculature, and I was sure that if he ever tried to hit someone, his thin wrists would shatter on impact.

"We need you, Eryn."

"Why?"

"Because Snyder's determined to press on with the expedition, and you're our only navigator. Without you, the ship can't operate. Without you, we're under a shower of excrement without an umbrella."

"And so, he sent you here to apologise?"

Torres' cheeks flushed. "To broker a ceasefire."

"What kind of ceasefire?"

"One based on mutual profitability. After you left, Snyder revealed he has emergency Vanguard authority to take command of this mission."

"The hell he does."

"I'm afraid it is true. I have seen his credentials. If you refuse to follow his directives, your contract with the Vanguard may be revoked."

I swore under my breath. I didn't need this bullshit. All I wanted to do was crawl under a blanket and mourn my sister.

The Vanguard was the organisation responsible for the protection of the Continuance. Its ships scouted ahead of the main fleet, scouring the stars for potential threats or opportunities. Its research vessels gathered data on the planetary systems we passed, and any life that might be lurking around. Shay and I had always wanted to join the Vanguard. It had been our dream as kids. We'd craved the chance to get off the arks and explore the universe, to get up close and personal with star systems the Continuance would otherwise pass at a safe distance, and plant crisp boot prints in the virgin soil of unnamed alien worlds. We'd wanted adventure, excitement, and really wild things… and we'd received them in abundance.

Just not in the way we'd hoped.

There was an old Chinese saying about living in interesting times, and a later European one about being careful what you wished for. Both seemed to apply here. We'd been young and foolish, and it seemed the universe had given us exactly what we'd requested. I had been gifted the adventure and excitement of a hopeless rescue mission in a ruined alien city, and Shay had been torn apart by something wild.

I was just grateful my parents weren't alive to see what a clusterfuck I'd made of everything.

My cabin was small and functional. There was a shelf above the bed filled with heirlooms and talismans, including a book that had once belonged to my grandmother. The yellowed paper of its brittle pages had come from actual trees, on Earth. The cabin walls were currently set to show a wraparound archive view of the night sky across the rooftops of New York. Lots of softly lit windows, with the silhouettes of tall buildings, stilted water towers, and a pale silver coin moon. Recorded traffic noise adorned the air.

My mouth felt dry. Not knowing what else to say, I resorted to: "Would you like a cup of coffee?"

"That would be most agreeable." Torres held up a hand. "As long as you're not planning to hit me with it."

"I'm not."

"In that case, yes, thank you."

I ordered two cups of strong coffee from the printer. I was hungry but wasn't sure I was ready to eat. My stomach still felt as tight and bruised as a boxer's fist. But right now, I'd settle for caffeine. And as caffeine delivery systems went, coffee was by far my favourite weapon of choice.

When the drinks were ready, I handed one to my guest, and took the other for myself. I sniffed the steam coming off my cup, drawing a thin comfort from its warmth and familiarity.

I said, "So, how did he convince you this was a good idea?"

Torres cradled his cup in pianist's fingers. "Snyder's offering triple bonuses and joint credit on any discoveries to anyone who will accompany him to the site of the beacon."

"What?"

"I think your friend Chen may be tempted."

I shook my head. "No way, she's much too smart to fall for that."

"She is impulsive, and financially disadvantaged. And this could turn out to be a defining moment in her career."

"As a xeno-archaeologist?"

"If she discovers a new alien civilisation, she'll be a celebrity."

"Do you really think she'll side with Snyder?"

"Have you given her a reason not to?"

I frowned. "What's *that* supposed to mean?"

Torres held up a hand. "I thought maybe you and her..."

"There's nothing going on."

"Are you sure?"

I took a sip from my cup. Exhaled. "Fuck Snyder and his 'emergency powers'. He can't make us do anything."

"Ah, but he can." Torres rocked back on his heels. "As I said, he has the authority, and he's offering a fair deal."

I slammed my cup down on the bedside table. Coffee slopped across the tabletop and onto the deck. "Bullshit!"

"He makes a good case."

"For suicide?"

"For the acquisition of knowledge. I'm a paramedic, but even I can see and there's a whole dead alien civilisation out there. Whatever becomes of us, we can't turn away from this opportunity."

"The hell we can't."

Torres' lips compressed into a hard line. "I was hoping to persuade you to cooperate willingly, to join us and save further unpleasantness, but if necessary, I will remind you of the terms of your contract."

I felt the heat flush through me. "Fuck the contract."

"You are duty-bound to follow orders from a duly appointed representative of the Vanguard."

My hands threatened to shake, so I squeezed them into fists. "Only up to a point."

"What point?"

"Up until the point their bullshit threatens the ship itself."

We stared at each other and I wished I could understand what he was thinking. He had none of the facial cues that usually facilitated human communication. He might as well have been a waxwork.

I said, "Look, you've seen the footage."

"You know I have."

"Doesn't it scare you?"

He clicked his tongue. "Of course, it does. But the opportunities here are incalculable. If that beacon is coming from an alien ship, just think of the advances it might contain."

"But the danger—"

"An opportunity for profit."

"Or a fucking death trap."

Torres placed his untouched coffee on the bookshelf and stood over me.

"You are no longer in command," he said, "and we've confiscated your emergency gun. Snyder wants to offer you the chance to join us willingly, but we will compel you if we have to."

I sat back on the bed, refusing to show any hint of intimidation. "And how are you planning to do that?"

"If you refuse to assist in the investigation, we will insist on a court martial. You'll never get another scouting contract again as long as you live."

"You wouldn't."

Torres narrowed his eyes. I had to tip my head right back to look directly up at him. A pencil-thin finger caressed my throat.

"Don't test me."

•

I saw them to the airlock, but I wasn't going to accompany them. I wanted to know what had happened to my sister—of course I did—but that didn't mean I was going to walk straight into the jaws of whatever killed her. I may have been stricken by grief, but that didn't mean I was about to act like a fucking idiot. I wouldn't set a single boot on this cursed planet. If Snyder and his pals wanted to throw their lives away, that was their own fucking business. They might have legal control of this expedition, but that didn't mean I had to follow them into whatever hell awaited.

"Have fun out there." I glared at Torres. "And make sure you've all updated your wills."

Chen said, "I still think you should come. Maybe find some closure?"

"No." Snyder had his helmet visor open. The fabric of his suit was worn and scuffed from long and heavy use and had been patched in several places. "Eryn's our navigator. The ship won't fly without her, so we need her here, keeping the engines warm."

In the *Ocelot*'s cramped hold, between cargo pallets and equipment lockers, the team squirmed into their suits as they prepared to step through the outer door, onto the surface of a new world. Snyder's eyes were a deep, steady green with creases at the corners. His temples were flecked with strands of grey. "It's non-negotiable. Without her, we can't get home."

"For once, we're in agreement," I said. "I have no intention of leaving the ship until we're safely back with the fleet."

"But this could be big," Chen said. "Real history book stuff."

Snyder put a gloved hand on her shoulder. "That's even more reason to make sure we each do our part properly. You do understand that, don't you?"

She rolled her eyes. "Of course, I do. I'm not simple. I just thought it might do her good to find some answers. Might help her process her grief."

"I never said you were simple. But it's not as if Eryn wants to come, is it, Eryn?"

I shook my head. "Fuck, no."

Undeterred, Chen said, "But you should be part of this. Your sister—"

"No." Snyder met my eye. "Eryn's more important to this team than anyone."

I said, "Hah!"

"I'm serious. If something goes wrong out there, you're our lifeline. We're relying on you."

I huffed and shoved my hands into the pockets of my coveralls. "Says the man who just overrode my authority on my own fucking ship."

He winced. "I'm sorry."

"No, you're not. You don't give a shit about any of us; all you care about is that stupid beacon."

Snyder put his fingers to the dressing on his cheek, where my knuckles had split the skin. "I am sorry. I could see you were in shock and I should have been more sensitive."

"You were an asshole."

"Again, I'm sorry. But in this case, I'm willing to let bygones be bygones. We could be on the verge of something really important." He drew himself up slightly. "The discovery of a whole new intelligent species."

"Yeah, I bet the other team thought that too, and we all saw what happened to them."

"That's why we're taking the combat drones and the ship's envoy."

"The hell you are."

I turned to the *Ocelot* for support, but the envoy spread his chubby blue palms. "I do have a duty to protect my clients."

"Even if they're doing something stupid?"

"*Especially* if they're doing something stupid."

"But what happens if you get injured or killed out there?"

He enfolded my hand in his. "Oh, Eryn. You know this is just a shell. My mind stays on the ship. If this body gets lost, I'll simply make another one."

I wasn't happy, but Snyder chose that moment to reassert his authority.

"Okay," he said, rubbing his gauntlets briskly. "This is it. It's going to take a while to hike into that ravine. But when we get there, I don't want anyone touching or disturbing anything without my explicit permission. Do you understand?"

Li Chen and Alvin Torres voiced their assent. They knew this was their chance to hit the big time. The next few hours would provide them with the material for academic papers, memoirs, and talk show appearances. The discoveries they were about to make would ensure long and successful careers.

"Okay, then. Get your helmets on and get your asses outside." He turned back to me. "We won't be long."

"You'd better not be." I helped Chen close and seal her visor, then patted her chest to let her know she was good to go. "Otherwise, I might get pissed off and leave you all here."

CHAPTER SEVEN

ROGUE GROWTH

HARUKI

Now, seventy-five years after our salvation, most humans lived their entire lives aboard the Thousand Arks of the Continuance. They were born, raised and found useful employment within those protective hulls. Their world consisted of corridors, arenas, artificial beaches and parks. Only those who had ventured a little further afield saw the fleet as it truly was—as a thousand islands in an ink black sea. A whole species uprooted from its home planet and set to wander the void in starships the size of nations. Whatever our ancestors had once been on Earth, we were all refugees now—and these arks, while large on a human scale, were almost insignificantly small compared to the infinities of darkness around them. A handful of jewels lost in the night. With no particular destination in mind, they moved slowly, at a few per cent of the speed of light. Just fast enough to maintain a sense of purpose without blurring the stars or having to worry about the effects of relativity. If they needed to be anywhere in a hurry, they simply dropped into the substrate.

Things had been this way for three quarters of a century, since the first Angel of the Benevolence had been drawn by the experiments of the physicist, Frank Tucker, who had created his own flick terminal linking one side of his laboratory to the other.

At the time, I had been too busy reacting to the threat of imminent nuclear destruction. It was only later, in the confused aftermath of our deliverance, that I reviewed the footage he'd sent me.

•

"Is that camera running?" Frank pulls an old tissue from his lab coat pocket and uses it to clean his glasses. "We're only going to get one shot at this."

Victoria Quinn speaks from off-screen. "For the fourth time, yes."

Frank Tucker's laboratory resembles the aftermath of an explosion in an electronics store. A tangled mess of power cables trails across all the flat surfaces, linking components and instruments that have been scattered seemingly at random across the workbenches. Some are new and expensive-looking, but many others have been cannibalised from old televisions, laptops, toasters, and other obsolete consumer junk. A fading spider plant stands in a pot on the windowsill. Software manuals and dog-eared old paperbacks fill the bookshelves beside the desk. Scientific journals and gaming magazines lie stacked on the carpet beside the door in gently subsiding piles.

Frank scratches his pigeon chest through the Hawaiian shirt he habitually wears beneath his lab coat. His hair and beard look particularly wild and unkempt. "If this works," he says, "Haruki's going to have to renew my funding." Behind him, through the window, beyond the anonymous units of a rainswept industrial campus, you can just make out the uppermost tips of Oxford's distant spires.

"And if he doesn't?" Victoria is Frank's link to me. They are supposed to be firm friends, but something in her tone suggests she sometimes wishes he'd just get on a plane and fuck off back to Minnesota.

"Then I've nothing to lose," he says, oblivious to her irritation. "I might as well go out with a bang."

The camera twitches as Victoria winces. "Speaking on behalf of the owners of this facility, it's the bang part that concerns me."

Frank ignores this. He leans over and places his fingers on the spacebar of his laptop. "Have you got the camera rolling?"

"Yes, I've got the bloody camera rolling."

"Thank you." He grimaces awkwardly into the lens. "Well then, here goes nothing. Experiment forty-three." He taps the keyboard and the equipment hums into life. All the readouts swing into the red. The air crackles with static electricity, and two tiny silver spheres swim into existence on opposite sides of the room, hanging in the air about a metre above the floor. Frank grunts and makes a few adjustments to his equipment. The power circuits whine ominously, and the spheres grow in response, until each reaches the size of a football.

"Yes!" Frank punches the air.

The camera trembles in Victoria's hands. Later, she'll say that even though he'd been working on the final equations for months, she hadn't really expected his experiment to bear tangible fruit. It was too early. There were still too many aspects of the theory he didn't understand. Too many variables. And yet…

And yet…

"Bloody hell," she says now.

Frank is ecstatic. He's doing some sort of victory dance. "We did it!"

"You need to check they're stable," Victoria says, propelling his scrawny frame back towards his instruments. "Have you got the probe ready?"

The 'probe' is nothing more than a wooden broom handle Frank has appropriated from the cleaner's cupboard down the hall.

"Nah." Frank leaves the handle where it is, leaning up against the workbench. He slips off his white coat. "I've got a much better idea. Keep filming."

"What are you going to do?"

Frank's shirt has a garish blue and yellow pattern. Its short sleeves expose his bony forearms. "I'm going to try something."

"Frank…"

"It's fine." He steps over to the nearest sphere and pushes his hand into it until it has swallowed his arm up to the elbow.

Suddenly, Frank's and Victoria's phones both chime with alerts. The camera wavers as Victoria glances at hers. Somewhere far away, a siren wail. The war has started. Victoria mutters, "Oh, shit; Oh, shit," but for some reason, doesn't drop the camera.

"Frank!"

"It's okay." Still caught up in his experiment, Frank remains oblivious to the onrushing apocalypse. "Look."

Ten metres away, on the other side of the lab, Frank's disembodied hand protrudes from the other sphere. He waggles his fingers.

•

Nobody on Earth was aware of Frank's discovery. They were more preoccupied with the looming holocaust. But across the gulf of space, his clumsy manipulation of space-time drew the attention of an alien intellect vast, cool and sympathetic, and it regarded our world with its pitying eyes.

Through humanity's telescopes, the creature resembled a vast red storm cloud. Lightning crackled in its whorled depths as it reached down and casually averted our apocalypse. Then, the angel shattered Mimas, stripped Saturn of its majestic rings, and used the collected raw material to forge a thousand arks.

Intrigued by Frank's experiments, it had decided to spare us.

As the world held its breath, the angel used small wormholes to redirect each and every warhead into the sun, where their fury left a small but ugly scar on its roiling surface.

That done, it placed flick terminals in every city, town and village; in parks and football stadia; at airports, bus stations and ferry terminals. Blue-skinned envoys politely escorted every person from Earth. No one was forgotten, and no one was left behind—not even those who wished to stay.

Of course, it was never really about saving us. The Benevolence excised humanity like a cancer, for the good of the world we were destroying. Already, millions of species had perished, and we had almost irrevocably altered the composition of the atmosphere. From their point of view, we were a rogue growth that threatened to kill its host. We had to be stopped, and balance had to be restored.

Luckily for us, the Benevolence were not monsters. Nor were they cold, calculating machine intellects. Instead, they acted with compassion, allowing us to survive the procedure. We were a nuisance on our own world, but the universe was a big place, and Tucker's initial experiments with the substrate convinced them we were intelligent as well as destructive, and therefore worth preserving—or at least being given a second chance. As long as we agreed to be bound by certain strictures—including a promise never to return to the Earth or compromise another established biosphere—we could be permitted to roam the stars.

Some of us resisted, of course, and wars were fought—but the Angel of the Benevolence was patient. Our deadliest weapons were of no consequence to it. We were like children wielding plastic swords.

The truth was, we had always been closer to ants and bees than we ever suspected. We just couldn't see our nests and hives for what they were. We called them nations, armies, political parties, universities, corporations... Non-biological, incorporeal entities able to endure across generations, outliving their original members and accomplishing goals taking more than a single human span to achieve. Goals that, as we saw towards the end of our collective life on Earth, weren't always in the best interests of the humans themselves.

But when the adults arrived, it was time for us to grow up and shed those parasitic structures. We swept aside the established politics, economic systems, and traditions that had locked us into a self-destructive spiral. In many cases, this transition was painful. But it was also necessary, and those who suffered most were those who had most benefitted from the destruction of our climate and the subjugation of the poor.

John Lennon once asked us to imagine a world without countries, religion, greed or hunger. Now, that world had come to pass, and we were living in an imposed utopia in which everyone had shelter, food and clothing, and access to education and self-betterment.

However, as wonderful as this all was, I couldn't help feeling we'd been let off the hook a little too easily. Instead of reaching this state by ourselves, we had it foisted upon us. We hadn't had to take responsibility for our behaviour or clean up our own mess, and maybe that meant we'd missed learning an important lesson.

CHAPTER EIGHT

COMPREHENSIVELY TRASHED

ERYN

From the *Ocelot*'s bridge, I watched them pick their way across the rocky surface of C-623. Snyder went first, of course, striding ahead as best he could in the old and cumbersome suit, only pausing occasionally to wipe the rain from his visor. Behind him, huddled against the strength of the wind, came Torres. Chen brought up the rear, in a heavy, armoured suit designed more for rescue than exploration.

The envoy, of course, needed no suit. He ambled along in their wake with his bald head bare to the sky, and his blue tie straggling out to one side, whipped by the wind.

I watched until they faded into the downpour. Then I switched my attention to the bridge screens, which relayed pictures from the envoy's point of view, and the cameras on each of the others' helmets. Rain and grit blew like static through their headlight beams. They kept their heads down, concentrating on keeping their footing. Chatter was at a minimum. No one wanted to stumble and fall in a pressure suit.

"I'm picking up indications of ruined buildings in the soil," the *Ocelot* said. "There were walls here once."

Chen's voice broke into the feed. "This was a settlement?"

"If these geophysical readings are right, we're walking over the site of an ancient metropolis."

I tapped into the feed from one of the combat drones. Through its cameras, all I could see was uneven ground, but the geophysical results from the envoy's sensors showed ghostly traces of collapsed circular structures and buried roads. Once upon a time, this place had been heavily populated.

"What do you think killed them?" I asked over Chen's channel. "Plague?"

"That would have left more buildings intact," she said between breaths. "The remains of these look pretty comprehensively trashed."

"Singularity?"

"Same."

"Unless the artificial intelligence launched nukes?"

Chen waggled a gloved hand. "That kind of thing only happens in movies. Honestly, if you're a civilisation stupid enough to wire your nuclear arsenal to an emergent neural net, you deserve everything you get. And besides, I'm not picking up any trace of residual radiation in the soil."

"Then what was it?"

"That's what we're here to find out."

Ahead, the wind and rain blew around the solid bulk of the mountains framing the ravine. Even on the screen, the split in the rock looked huge and imposing.

Chen swore.

Snyder turned to her. "What is it?"

The archaeologist stood with her headlight beam looking off to the side. She pointed. "Bones."

I switched to her camera-view. Along the base of the mountain, in the shelter of a low wall, stood an orderly pile of dirty white sticks that could have been something analogous to a thigh bone. They had been stacked in an interlocking pattern to form a rectangular mound at least two metres in height and maybe ten or fifteen in length. Beyond them, I could see another pile, only this one seemed to be comprised of misshapen three-eyed skulls. And beyond that, another pile of different bones—but this one too far away to resolve properly through the incessant rain.

Snyder looked the other way. On his screen, similar piles receded in the opposite direction. Some seemed almost to have been arranged in order to mimic the layout of the vanished buildings.

Torres said, "Who would do this? And, why?"

"We don't know," Snyder told him. "Maybe after whatever flattened the city, the survivors got together and—"

"There weren't any survivors," Chen said. "Remember our initial scans? There's life in the sea but the land's barren. All the animals and plants must have been wiped out at the same time. Anyone not killed in the initial event would have died shortly afterwards from lack of food. They wouldn't have had the time or energy to undertake a project of this magnitude."

Torres made a noise that was somewhere between a laugh and a snort. "So, you're saying something wiped out the entire planet, and then stopped to *tidy up*?"

Chen shrugged. "We'll need samples from each pile," she said. "At least enough to try and reconstruct a complete skeleton."

I felt a chill. These weren't just mass graves. Each carcass had been rendered into its component parts, and those parts arranged in groups according to some pattern I couldn't intuit. It seemed an inexplicably disrespectful way to treat the remains of intelligent beings.

Snyder's camera swept away from the ossuary and back to the mouth of the gorge. "We can pick through the bones later," he said decisively. "Right now, we need to find what's transmitting that signal."

I felt my heart thumping in my chest. This was the point where the last expedition had been attacked—although so far, there had been no sign of their remains. I shivered, struck by the sudden mental picture of my sister's bones lying stacked on top of a nearby pile, her empty eye sockets turned to the sky, collecting rain.

I fought down a surge of panic.

"Be careful," I said.

The cat hopped up onto the arm of my couch and started purring and nuzzling my shoulder. "Is it food time yet, darling?"

"Not right now."

"But I'm hungry."

I jabbed a hand at the screens. "Our passengers are in danger."

The purring stopped. Sam's little furry face pulled back in surprise. "So?"

"So, I'm going to monitor their status and provide help where I can."

He cocked his head to one side. "But I am hungry. Surely that's more important right now?"

"Go catch a rat."

"Charming."

He hopped down and stalked from the bridge, nose and tail held high, feigning injured outrage—but I knew he would be back as soon as the crisis abated, winding around my legs and thoroughly prostituting his dignity in return for food and attention.

On the screens, the crew were ascending the rocky slope that led to the mouth of the ravine. It was hard going, and their cameras bumped around a lot. I could see Snyder's heels caught by Chen's camera. He was plodding ahead, the back of his legs illuminated by her helmet lamp. The wind buffeted against them, adding to the camera shake, and the rain falling through their lights turned everything to a static-like blur.

It looked disturbingly similar to the footage recovered from Shay's helmet.

CHAPTER NINE

EARTH WAS OVER

HARUKI

The first weeks and months of the evacuation were particularly traumatic. People passed through the portals the angel had erected in groups but arrived separately. They were shunted to whichever ark had spare capacity, irrespective of familial or cultural bonds. Earth was over and with it everything we had taken for granted. Cast into the stars, the only thing we could do was search the flick network that linked the Thousand Arks of the Continuance for our friends and loved ones. They were all we had to cling to. And having survived the end of the world, those relationships had acquired a new and poignant urgency.

At the same time, we were coming to terms with our new situation and our new surroundings. The arks had been constructed as ideal habitats for human beings. Inside they contained wide open spaces designed to resemble various environments on Earth. But even so, to those of us who were there at the time, they resembled nothing more than giant hotels with roof gardens. I was reminded of my bunker. The trees and grass inside were real but depended on artificial lighting to grow and thrive, and therefore seemed somehow fake.

We were also having to adjust to the idea that we were no longer the centre of creation. The universe was not there for our personal enjoyment and exploitation. Rather there were beings out there who policed the galaxy and who owed no allegiance to any set of laws or morals devised by a human being. And that human life was not particularly prized by these creatures. They had seen the damage we had wrought upon our planet and had decided to cast us out upon the interstellar winds, exiled and bound by oath never to return to a living biosphere.

To those of us used to the idea of humanity as the pinnacle of evolution, this was something of a blow. Indeed, to those of us who somehow figured we were the centre of the universe, somehow made and chosen in the image of God, this out-casting proved to be a humbling and traumatic experience. As a species, we were cut down to size. We were given a wakeup call that redefined our entire view of ourselves, and not all of us survived that transition. Certainly, our previous social structures could not adapt. Cast into an environment in which all had access to food, clean water, healthcare and clothing, many of the traditional political models were no longer applicable. With everybody fed and sheltered, and all of us now refugees, the old divisions and exploitations of the past ceased to have any meaning. That doesn't mean there weren't prejudices and tensions as the fleet struggled to achieve an equilibrium, but only that for the first time in human history we realised we were literally all in the same boat.

•

I remember visiting London in the last days of the evacuation. Frank, Victoria and I had been given permission to return to the surface while the fleet made preparations for departure. We flicked down to one of the evac portals in Trafalgar Square. Around us, London baked beneath a hot yellow sun, its streets silent and depopulated for the first time in two thousand years.

All over the city, everything remained exactly as it had been left. Underground trains slumbered in their sidings, doomed to wait forever for the return of their drivers; theatre posters advertised West End shows nobody would see; and neat rows of clean pint glasses stood stacked behind pub counters, ready to slake the thirsts of punters who were even now adjusting to a new life in space. In time, I knew the weather, rising floodwaters and fire would reduce most of the capital's buildings to empty, burned-out husks. The trees would spread across the streets; weeds would push their way up through the concrete; and wildlife would return to the city. In a thousand years, only a few surviving towers would remain standing above the canopy, their blackened, broken windows like hollow eye sockets, while the rest of the surrounding buildings would have sagged and crumbled, as their metal structures rusted and they gradually sank into either the forest floor or the invasive mud of the swollen river.

"It's the end of the world," Victoria said. A cloud of pigeons clapped skyward. I put a hand on her shoulder.

"It's the start of a new chapter." As usual, I wore a tailored business suit. Victoria had opted for an ankle-length white cotton dress with big wooden buttons up the front, and Frank wore his ridiculous Hawaiian shirt.

"But seeing it all like this," he said. "Seeing everything so empty..."

"It's amazing."

"And sad."

A glittering Benevolence drone cruised soundlessly over the Thames on some incomprehensible errand. Its dangling limbs gave it the appearance of a crab pulled from the waters and held between a child's finger and thumb. Just looking at it made my stomach flip with excitement. My heart leapt at the reality of something that clearly didn't belong in this world. It was like finding a triceratops in my back garden—

something so incongruous that its sheer preposterousness filled me with childish delight. "I think it's exciting," I said.

The flick terminal behind us—like all the millions of flick terminals that had been placed at strategic points around the globe in order to efficiently evacuate the entire human population—led back to the brand-new arks currently in orbit around Saturn. Frank's experiment had managed to link two sides of my laboratory; these terminals allowed us to cross 1.2 billion kilometres in a single stride. I felt giddy just thinking about it.

The three of us stood there listening to the silence that had now fallen over this ancient capital. No traffic noise, no aeroplanes overhead, and no human voices at all. The only sound was the wind sighing between the buildings and the occasional flapping as a phalanx of pigeons clattered skywards. Behind us the National Portrait Gallery was being emptied of its wares by blue-skinned envoys from the fleet. Across the world, museums, galleries and ancient sites were being similarly looted. As far as the Benevolence was concerned, we were scum—but we were scum with a certain kind of promise, and so they were very keen for us to maintain and remember our culture, because as a species with access to the substrate, we had blundered our way into a small and selective club. Ninety per cent of intelligent species found some way to wipe themselves out before they ever discovered substrate travel. They lived and died confined to a single star system. But a species that had discovered the substrate was something to cherish. Even if we were a menace to our own world, there was something about us worth saving. We might be destructive children, but our discovery of wormholes hinted at the potential for a useful adulthood somewhere down the line.

We just had to grow up first.

CHAPTER TEN

ABRASIONS OF SAND AND TIME

ERYN

When Shay and I were children, we used to play hide-and-seek in the air ducts on deck eighteen of our ark. My mother hated it. She thought we would get into trouble or fall into one of the giant circulation fans, but for reasons of its own, the *Damask Rose* tolerated our presence in the ducts. Its blue fox envoy accompanied us on many adventures. It even let us build a little den in an alcove where three ducts met. That was our private space, and we filled it with the treasures of childhood. I remembered an old doll, a collection of broken electrical components, a wrench, a handful of dried and pressed flowers from the gardens on deck twelve, and pictures of stars and galaxies printed from books and news reports and taped to the metal walls. We used to pretend we were navigators in the Vanguard, and our little nook the bridge of an intrepid scout ship out on the ragged edge of explored space, chasing the massive storm-like forms of the angels as they moved through the void on their own incomprehensible errands.

We were playing there the day the *Rose*'s envoy came to find us, to tell us our parents had been killed in a shuttle accident—the same one, I would later find out, that killed Snyder's wife—and that while we'd been absorbed in our imaginary lives, our parents had vanished from our real ones, and nothing would ever be the same again. We sat there for hours, hugging each other and crying into the fox's blue fur, until we fell asleep and the envoy used cargo pallets to transfer us to our beds. After that, we depended on the ship. Although we attended school as normal, and had attention lavished on us by our teachers and the parents of our friends, it was the ark that was there for us at the end of the day; the ark that made sure we ate right and did our homework; and the ark that tucked us in at night.

Now we were grown, and Shay had a daughter of her own. Madison was fifteen years old, and about to go through the same shock of losing a parent. Whatever happened, I had to be there for her. I had to look after her. I was sure it was what Shay would have wanted and expected me to do. Madison and I were the only family each of us had left, and we had to stick together.

•

Snyder, Chen and the *Ocelot*'s envoy reached the mouth of the ravine. Torres was a few metres behind. When Chen looked back the way they'd come, her helmet cameras revealed only the faintest glimmers of the ship's lights through the rain and cloud.

Ahead of her, the ravine was a deep, almost vertically sided split in the mountain's flank, where an ancient quake had sundered the cliff face.

"Three hundred metres deep, give or take a few centimetres," the ship's envoy said as they entered, looking up at the walls towering to either side. "And made of some kind of volcanic rock. Very old, by the looks of it."

The humans' helmet lamps could only penetrate a dozen or so metres into the darkness before them. The combat drones' IR sensors mapped a V-shaped gulley extending half a kilometre into the cliff. Secondary splits radiated out from its walls, further dividing the rock.

"It's good to be out of that wind," Chen said.

Snyder stopped to perform a comms check. "Eryn, can you still hear us?"

"The ship's lined up with the entrance, so you're coming through loud and clear right now, but if you turn a corner in there, I might lose you."

"Roger, we'll try to maintain line-of-sight."

They began to tramp into the darkness. I sat back in my couch. My heart was thumping.

"Ship," I said on a private channel, "I'd feel a lot better if your envoy was back here."

"I have a duty of care to our guests," he replied. "But rest assured, if you're in any sort of danger, I will abandon them and make my way back to you with all haste."

"Thank you."

"Now, if you'll excuse me, I think I detect something up ahead..."

•

Seen through the envoy's eyes, the floor of the chasm was uneven and covered with loose rocks that slid and skittered unpredictably when one of the crew put weight on them. Every step they took risked an ankle injury and maybe a serious fall. They had to watch where they were putting their feet, which meant I didn't get a clear look at the object they were approaching until they were already quite close to it.

It was a ship.

At least, I couldn't think of anything else it might be.

"Well, fuck me." The image showed the 'ship' as an elongated rock, dusty black against the darkness of the chasm, with asymmetrical bumps and knobs protruding at random from its surface. It didn't look like something that could have been conceived and built by humans. The nose was a particularly thick protuberance, skewed like the petrified remains of an elephant's trunk. One of the bumps on the side appeared to have been sheared off, leaving an uneven, shiny stump. As a whole, the ship looked like a deep-sea creature—a dolphin or humpback whale possibly, although it didn't really look like either. Its appendages had been worn to nubs by wind and rain. Only the rear was flat, as if the ship's builders had hacked the tail from the animal and installed engines in its place. And somehow, possibly hundreds or thousands of years ago, it had fallen into this ravine and become wedged. Stalactites dangled from its lower surfaces, and in places, it was difficult to tell where the rock surface ended, and the ship began.

"How big is it?" Snyder asked, sweeping his headlight upwards along its flank.

"The ship measures a hundred metres from bow to stern," the *Ocelot* replied. "At the stern, it's thirty metres across the beam, narrowing to two metres at the bow. The large protrusion at the front measures five metres across at its widest point."

"Eryn?" Snyder said. "What do you make of this?"

I let out the breath I hadn't realised I'd been holding. Had Shay seen this? What would she have thought?

"No fucking idea, sorry."

"Chen? Do you recognise the design?"

"Holy cow," the archaeologist said. She sounded breathless with exertion and excitement. The surface of the ship seemed to flinch where her light touched it. In the flickering shadows, it appeared viscous, like oil or tar. "It's old," she murmured.

"What makes you say that?"

"The cliff walls above it. It must have scraped the sides on its way down, but the scratches it left are almost as weathered as the rest of the rock. They're almost invisible. And the stalactites, of course."

Snyder made a thoughtful noise. I watched him play his lamp up and down the rockface.

"Noted," he said after a minute or so. "Thank you. Torres, do you have anything to add?"

"Nothing that wouldn't be pure speculation at this point."

I watched through Snyder's camera as he reached out. In the light of his helmet lamp, the black surface of the structure's frame became almost translucent, with little pinpricks of light shining in its depths like stars embedded in a nebula. I felt a chill as I realised what it reminded me of. The whole hull of the ship looked like the surface of a flick terminal! Maybe whatever killed Shay had come through that skein? What if her team had somehow activated something in its depths and now Snyder was about to do the same?

"Wait!" I shouted into the mike. "Don't do it. Get out of there now!"

But my warning came too late. Snyder's questing fingers brushed the surface of the alien ship, and he exploded.

Torres staggered back, swearing and wiping at the blood coating the outside of his visor. But even as he smeared it with his gloves, Snyder's body began to reassemble itself. The skull appeared first, hanging in the air at head height. Then shoulders and a partially muscled arm.

Chen screamed as Snyder's liver and spleen accreted in the air to one side of his skeleton, his circulatory and nervous systems to the other, laid out like the results of a clinical dissection.

The *Ocelot*'s envoy burst into action. He grabbed Chen, who seemed rooted to the spot. "Run," he said. "Get back to the ship."

She began to back away and the envoy tried to take a step towards Torres. The skeleton's hand stabbed out, catching the envoy in the back. I heard him grunt in surprise as the bony fingers passed through fabric and skin and muscle, to emerge glistening from his cobalt chest. Torres was watching him. Through his camera, I saw the envoy's three-piece suit bulge from within. Fist-sized tumours erupted from his face and neck, obliterating his features. Seams split along his arms and legs as similar growths forced their way out like obscene new musculature.

I recoiled from the image. "Oh shit," I said. "Oh shit, shit, shit."

I stabbed the control to activate the combat drones' defensive protocols, and scrambled off my couch. As I hurried to the airlock, the combat drones opened fire, energy pulses from their weapons shattering what was left of Snyder and the envoy. Chen and Torres were making their way back towards the ship, slipping and stumbling on the wet, uneven ground.

"Eryn," Chen cried. "Eryn, help us!"

It had taken them fifteen minutes to carefully pick their way to the canyon. Now, they were running.

Torres' voice burst over the emergency channel: "Damn it, Eryn, seal the ship. Get out of here. Don't let the contamination on board!"

I felt cold.

He was *right*.

"Eryn?" Chen had heard it too.

"Li, I'm so sorry." I pressed the control that closed and locked the external hatch, sealing both of them out of the ship.

"What are you doing?" She was almost back, Torres trailing behind.

My heart seemed to be thudding at the base of my throat. "I don't have a choice!"

"You can't leave me here!"

She gave a cry, followed by a curse.

"Li?"

"I fell. I think I've broken my ankle. You're going to have to help me."

"I'm sorry." My duty was clear. The ground team had been compromised. I couldn't risk contaminating the ship. Someone had to report back to the fleet. Someone had to warn the arks to stay away from this haunted shit-pile.

"For god's sake, Eryn! Open the fucking hatch."

I swallowed back nausea. Eyes blurred and watering, I leant my head forward to rest on the cold metal of the inner door.

"I'm sorry," I said.

"Eryn, please!"

She was almost back at the ship now, scrambling and slithering, more terrified of what was behind her than the pain from her leg.

I waited until she reached the hatch. Her gauntlets hammered on the metal.

"I'm sorry."

"Eryn, *please*!"

Her voice stabbed my heart, and I swore. That could have been Shay out there. I had seen what this thing could do. Would I have left *her*? Would I have ever been able to forgive anyone who did?

With a shout of frustration, I turned back and punched the button to open the lock. Chen tried to climb inside, but Torres grabbed her shoulder, hauling her back. Mud and rainwater splashed across the deck. I got hold of Li's glove, but Torres was still holding on.

"Let go!"

"No. You can't let her in!"

"You'll both die."

"It doesn't matter."

"It does to me!" Still holding Li's arm, I twisted my body and kicked Torres in the faceplate. The blow wasn't enough to do any damage, but it jarred him and I heard him swear.

"Let go of her."

"Fuck you, Eryn."

I didn't have time for this. I let fly with a second kick, harder than the first. Torres' head snapped back inside his helmet and he fell over into the mud. I yanked Li through the internal door and closed it, sealing us both in.

Torres gave a strangled, indignant cry. "It's got me!" Then I heard his faceplate shatter. Something wet slammed against the mike, and his channel went dead.

Leaving Li where she lay, I scrambled for the bridge and, with shaking hands, initiated the emergency take-off sequence. Alarms rang through the ship. The engines whined into life, and I barely had time to strap into the navigator's couch before the *Furious Ocelot* leapt up through the glowering clouds. It flashed momentarily in the dazzling white glare of the sun, and then hurled itself into the substrate.

CHAPTER ELEVEN

CACTUS SHADOWS

HARUKI

Of course, some people resisted. In a few cases, entire armies fought against the Benevolence. Not everybody trusted a sentient thunderstorm to have our best interests at heart. I remember one evening in particular: Frank and I had been allowed to flick back down to the planet to witness one of the final enclaves being brought into the Continuance.

We were standing in the New Mexico desert on the edge of a ranch. Three families had holed up inside the main building and were refusing to come out. They had guns but—thanks to the angel—no bullets. Not that it mattered. The Benevolence had not stumbled upon their name accidentally. We were a 'significant species' now, which meant no harmful action would be visited upon us. Rather than storming the compound, a small group of blue envoys stood in the front yard, patiently enduring the curses and household objects being hurled from the ranch house windows.

Frank stood with his hands in his pockets, watching.

"Did you ever see the Blue Man Group?" he asked.

I shook my head, but I knew what he meant. In those days, before the arks had fully developed their current personalities, their envoys were all identical. There had been no time for individual idiosyncrasies to creep into their design, so they resembled a congregation of crash test dummies: bald, blue and naked, genderless and of average height and build. Judging from the shouts and threats issuing from inside the house, the terrified residents regarded them as alien body snatchers here to pressgang us all into a communist dystopia.

As I watched, an iron skillet struck one of the envoys in the head. Instead of flinching, it smiled and said, "Aboard the arks, cooking will be an optional activity. Any meal you desire can be synthesised almost instantly and delivered to your quarters."

I glanced at Frank, but his attention had wandered to the cactus shadows cast by the lowering, orange sun.

"You know," he said, scuffing his shoe in the dust, "this might be the last real sunset we ever see."

"And we might be the last humans to see one."

"A pivotal moment for our species." He shrugged. "We started in a desert, and now we're ending in one."

"But it's not the end, is it?" I nodded to our blue friends. "It's just the start of a new chapter. That's why we've named the fleet the Continuance. Our life on Earth might have run its course, but humanity will endure. We've adapted and evolved so many times in our history, this is just the latest step."

Frank didn't look convinced. "We've been cast out of Eden again," he said. "We've sinned and been exiled. We almost destroyed ourselves and our planet, and I worry how that knowledge will affect us in the long term, psychologically speaking."

I put a hand on his shoulder. "You saved us from annihilation."

"Yeah, and isn't that just a massive head-fuck?"

He walked a few steps out into the desert, then stopped and turned. "I guess I don't know where I fit in anymore."

"What do you mean? Everybody knows you."

"Yeah, but what do I *do*. I can't spend the rest of my life dining out as the saviour of humanity. I'm a scientist. I had my research. I spent my entire career studying the substrate, but now Big Red's given us all the answers. We have the flick terminals and ships that can actually travel through the substrate itself. There's nothing left for me to *do*."

I sympathised. Throughout the Continuance, people were coming to terms with similar realisations. We no longer had need for telemarketers, fire fighters, fishermen, soldiers, stockbrokers, cleaners, bus drivers, traffic cops, bankers, car salesmen, estate agents, farmers or shop assistants. Our new circumstances had rendered obsolete the whole web of international trade and logistics associated with global capitalism. There were very few jobs anymore, and those who performed them would not be doing so in order to gain the means to survive and put food on the table. Now everyone had shelter, clothing and enough to eat, many of the old worries had fallen away. The question was, how would we use this new-found freedom?

My own feelings were mixed. I had been the richest man in the world. I had been used to having everything I needed. I had worried about the end of the world, but not about where my next meal was coming from. I had possessed a lot of money in a world where money was power, and I had employed other people to do the actual labour that kept me fed and clothed. But now, all that money meant nothing. Now, I was no different to anyone else. The only reason I was even here in this desert was because Frank had invited me along. Raijin, the angel, had selected Frank as the spokesperson for our species. This gangling, socially awkward young man had become everything I'd once aspired to be. In our new order of equality, he held the closest thing there was to actual power. He communed with the angel. People listened to him. His name had even been put forward as a candidate for

President of the newly formed Council of Ships. And yet, he wanted none of that. He wasn't a politician or a saviour; he was a scientist with a restless mind and nothing on which to focus it.

An evening breeze quivered the desert scrub. Behind us, the siege had come to an end and the dispirited families were allowing themselves to be reluctantly led towards a flick terminal resting on the sand of their front yard—a terminal that would instantly transport them to one of the arks. A few of the children, and even a couple of the adults, were crying, as if they were being led to their deaths.

As a species with a history as turbulent as ours, it amazed me to realise that as individuals, we were still so afraid of change.

CHAPTER TWELVE

ACCRETION DISC

ERYN

Li was unconscious, so I left her where she was. Her suit would have to take care of her until I could figure out how to find out whether or not she was infected. If necessary, I'd get the ship to move her when it had grown a new envoy.

"Get us home," I said.

We were already powering through the roiling furnace of the substrate.

"I can't do that, Eryn."

"*Why the hell not?*"

"Emergency protocol. You know as well as I do that in cases of hard contact with a hostile force, our duty is to evade capture and broadcast a warning to the fleet."

"But Li could be dying!"

"And by rescuing her, you may have allowed some form of contagion to board this vessel. Until we hear otherwise, we have to consider this ship and all its personnel to be under the strictest of quarantines."

"Hell, and damnation!" I kicked the nearest console. But he was right. Of course, he was right. I hadn't been thinking straight. The shocks had come too hard and fast, raining down like body blows: Snyder and the envoy both ripped apart; Torres' curses and final scream; and before that, the footage of Shay's final agonies.

Following procedure, we performed four more or less random jumps through the substrate, emerging into the real universe for only a few seconds between each one. Just long enough to spin-up the engines, choose a heading, and leap again. The process took seven hours, and by the end of it my eyes felt like boiled onions. I'd been running on caffeine and adrenalin for so long, all I wanted was to collapse and sleep for a month. But even as we were preparing to squirt through the first signal, the hull shuddered. I heard metal scrape against metal.

"What was that?"

The ship said, "I don't know, but I've lost some hull plating on the port side."

"Shit."

"What?"

"It's the thing. Whatever took our people. We're not free of it."

"That doesn't seem possible."

"Oh, really? What do you think happened to the *Couch Surfer*? What would it have done when its crew died?"

"Jumped away and—"

"Exactly."

Another rending moan shook the bridge. The *Ocelot* said, "That was my main comms dish."

I said, "Forget it. Jump! Now!"

The ship quivered and leapt. The stars vanished, to be replaced by the reassuring chaos of the substrate.

"I still feel something tugging at me."

"Can you hold it together?"

"I'm diverting all available resources to damage control."

We were diving through a heaving sea of white-hot plasma. So far, we'd been travelling at random, but that didn't seem to have thrown off our attacker.

I said, "How can it track us through the substrate?"

"I don't know."

"Fuck." I gripped the arms of my couch. The substrate churned before me. So far, we'd taken five jumps, and the entity (for want of a better word) from Candidate-623 had kept pace. We hadn't shaken it. And so, maybe it was time to get a bit crazy.

I put my hand on the main console.

"Do you trust me?"

The ship's voice came from hidden speakers. "With my life."

"Then, let's set a new course."

I felt the thrust build behind me. The ship said, "What did you have in mind?"

"Something suicidal and insane."

"Let's do it."

I took a deep breath, and leant forward, one hand on my knee. "Follow my lead."

In the substrate, the ship mostly used my subconscious mind to navigate. But if I really concentrated, I could help determine the course we set. If I screwed up my eyes and clenched my fingers and toes, I could sometimes project enough desire into the equation that our destination would be correspondingly altered. And so, with the ship threatening to be torn apart around me, I closed my eyes and thought of Cygnus X-1.

I'd only glimpsed it once.

Cygnus X-1 was a black hole approximately four times the mass of the sun. It was three hundred kilometres wide but had enough mass to enslave a blue supergiant star and rip gas from the star's atmosphere to form an accretion disc whose temperature could only be measured in millions of degrees. If I could plot a course through that maelstrom of x-rays and insane gravitational gradients, we might stand a chance. With luck, whatever was hounding us would be unable to follow us through a fire thousands of times hotter than the substrate—and, if we survived, we might be able to lose it.

I focused on my memory of the black hole.

"Go," I said.

The ship didn't stop to ask questions. The engines fired again, and I braced myself.

It took six hours to reach the Cygnus system. By the time we got there, our invisible tormentor had ripped away aerials, a whole sensor blister, and one of the ship's landing legs.

"Tell me the heat shield's still intact?"

"I can't guarantee it. I'm fixing things as fast as I can, but it's hard to keep pace."

I bit my lip. Ahead, the black hole's ferocious gravity pulled streamers of tortured star stuff from its giant companion. The accretion disc roared across the sky, its brightness overloading our remaining forward sensors.

The *Ocelot* fired its main fusion drive and we leapt towards it. This was going to work, I told myself, because if it didn't, we were going to die—either flashed to vapour by the tremendous heat or torn to shreds by an invisible alien entity.

"Aim for this bit," I told the ship, pointing to the place where the infalling plasma hit the black hole's event horizon. Compared to the titanic whorl of fire surrounding it, the actual hole appeared vanishingly small, only a few hundred kilometres across and almost completely lost in the heart of the conflagration.

Many years ago, the *Ocelot* had been equipped to investigate the outer layers of a star's photosphere. The molecules of its hull could be electronically reinforced to withstand temperatures far in advance of anything it would normally encounter. I just hoped that system remained in place and functional, and that it would be up to the job. There was a world of difference between diving into a relatively stable G-Class star and threading a path through the violent death throes of a blue supergiant.

The cat jumped up on my console.

"Are we going to die?" he asked, eyeing the churning destruction ahead.

"Probably."

"Oh." He licked a paw and wiped behind his ear. "Well, I'm not going to lie, I'm a little disappointed."

I heard a grinding crash to aft and a red light told me we'd just lost one of our stabilisers.

"I suppose you could do better?"

The cat looked up. "Of course I could."

"But…?"

"I *can* see a way out of this."

"Really?"

The animal stretched. "Trust me, I'm a cat. I climb things. I catch birds and fish. I'm all about spatial awareness."

"Then, what do you suggest?"

"Get the *Ocelot* to dream-link to me."

"You'd need an implant."

"I've got an implant. How do you think this collar works?"

We were getting close to the maelstrom now. X-rays bombarded the hull, and the very fabric of space and time were being warped by the singularity at the black hole's heart.

The *Ocelot* said, "It might be possible."

The bridge lights dimmed as the ship diverted all available power to strengthening the molecular bonds in the hull.

I said, "But, can't you figure a way through?"

The *Ocelot* was silent for a moment. Then he said, "I can compute a trajectory likely to bring us out the other side. But we are talking about taking a close pass around a mathematical singularity dense enough that its gravity interacts with the substrate. I would prefer to have a navigator hooked-in should we hit any unpredictable quantum fluctuations."

"And you think the cat can do it?"

"Much as it pains me to admit, I believe he can."

The cat regarded me with his yellow eyes. "Well?"

I sat back in my couch. "I must be going crazy."

"Is that a yes?"

"Yes, do it. What have we got to lose?"

We were about to hit the outer layer of the infalling disc. Something tugged at my insides. I could feel the entity's incorporeal fingers pulling at my ribs, threatening to rip me apart as it had ripped apart my sister.

Then, in the depths of my mind, I sensed a new presence, as lean and hungry as a coiled spring. Sam's mind had joined our consensus.

Lateral thrusters fired, throwing the *Ocelot* into a spin. At the same time, our nose dipped towards the event horizon itself. We were going to strike the black hole a glancing blow, right where the star's burning material hit the point of no return.

That's it, I thought. *We're dead.* Nothing could pass through an event horizon and emerge from the other side. The gravity within that boundary was so fierce not even light could escape.

That's the last time I trust a fucking cat.

Sam stretched, seemingly unconcerned by the doubt leaking through the link from my mind to his. "Have the jump engines ready to go." The little prick was actually purring.

The *Ocelot* said, "Ready on your mark."

"Okay, standby."

Tail flicking, Sam crouched, as if about to spring. His eyes were like saucers. His ears were tipped forward, and his paws were kneading the deck. I'd never seen a cat concentrate on anything so keenly. A blinding curtain of death rushed towards us. The forward screen had dimmed so much to protect our eyes, it was practically black.

"Full thrust," the cat said, and the room lurched so hard I found myself thrown onto my back. The claws of the alien were digging into my lungs. I could feel my ribs starting to flex. I was going to be burned and eviscerated all at once. We reached the point where the molten cascade impacted the event horizon. All the alarms on the ship went off. The *Ocelot*'s prow stretched out like drawn taffy. My fingers streamed out like spaghetti. We were stretched until I thought we were about to snap apart.

And then…

And then, we were whole again, but everything moved in slow motion, as if we were underwater. The light outside looked strange. I don't think it even was light, not in the way we understand it, and yet somehow, I could still see. The sound of my breathing roared in my ears. My skin itched and prickled in unfamiliar ways as my nerves fired off in random sequences. Time and space pressed in against me like air, and I realised we were inside the event horizon.

Oh, shit.

I… I could feel the dead around me. Shay and Snyder, my parents, my grandparents. Everyone I'd ever lost. The past, the future. They were all there in that moment, inseparable in the liminality between the real and the unreal. I felt the heat of their love. My ears rang with their half-heard pleas and warnings. My arms ached at my inability to hold them. Somewhere, a child cried. A dog barked. Footsteps echoed along the length of an aluminium air vent. I thought I heard a choir singing and caught a whiff of vinegar and burned toast. Angels of the Benevolence whorled before me, mirroring the larger spiral of the galaxy, which in its turn formed part of the greater revolution of the Local Group. My perspective broadened to eternity. The universe shrank to an echoing nutshell containing infinite space and bad dreams, and I realised my lungs weren't working. I hadn't taken a breath since we crossed the threshold. I hadn't moved so much as an eyelid.

I knew little about the physics of black holes, but I'd once read how the ferocious gravity would cause time to slow as you approached the singularity at its centre—until finally you'd be trapped like ghosts in an eternal, unending moment, as trapped as flies in amber.

But then the jump engines fired.

The *Ocelot* dropped into the substrate and skipped out of the black hole like a fork bouncing from a spinning garbage disposal.

The clawing sensation evaporated from my chest. The damage to the ship ceased.

We were free.

For now.

CHAPTER THIRTEEN

PERIPATETIC MEGACITY

ERYN

I sat at the table in the crew lounge, nursing a scotch. Sam lay sprawled on a fleece jacket someone had left draped over an equipment crate. It seemed only a few hours since this space had been crowded with bodies; now, it seemed almost pathetically empty.

I swirled the amber liquid in the bottom of my tumbler. "I can't believe we're alive."

"And I can't believe I dream-linked to a *cat*." The *Ocelot* was still growing a replacement envoy. For now, his voice came via the internal comms system. "If any of the other ships find out, I'll be a laughing stock."

"It worked," I pointed out. "We survived."

"I know," he replied. "But it's so humiliating. No one can ever find out that I linked to that refugee from a petting zoo."

"I heard that," Sam muttered sleepily.

"You were supposed to."

"Ouch." The cat pretended to flinch. "And I thought I was the one with claws!"

We lapsed into companionable silence. I contemplated the burn of the whisky on my tongue and thought of Tomas.

I met him at an official reception, back when I'd just

joined the Vanguard and was waiting to be assigned a ship. He was a graduate student majoring in substrate physics. He had collar-length brown hair and soulful green eyes.

"Excuse me," he said. "Would you like to dance?"

I'd been backed into a corner by one of my instructors for the past twenty minutes, unable to politely extricate myself, and so eagerly grasped this unexpected lifeline.

The ballroom occupied the topmost floor of one of the grander skyscrapers rising from the *Damask Rose*'s skin. It was housed beneath a transparent crystal dome. Chairs and tables occupied the rim of the room, while the dance floor took up its centre. Artificial fireflies swarmed above the heads of the guests, providing a shifting, liminal light in counterpoint to the unchanging stars. I let Tomas lead me to the middle of the crowd.

"Thank you," I said.

He smiled and took my hand, wrapping his other arm around my waist. "You looked as if you needed a way out."

We began to sway in time with the music, and I was conscious my classmates were watching and whispering among themselves.

"What's your name?" I asked.

"Tomas. What's yours?"

My breath seemed to stick in my throat. I couldn't speak.

He gave an understanding smile. "I think I've seen you around," he explained. "You must be this new recruit everyone's talking about."

I felt the tips of my ears burn. "What are they saying?"

He laughed. "Oh, nothing bad. But all night, I've heard stories of this promising recruit with a tough attitude and an exceptional potential for dream-linking."

Around us, other couples moved in the gloaming light. Sequins glittered. Perfumes tickled the nose. Tomas moved like he knew what he was doing, and I shuffled along gamely, trying to not stand on his feet or break the rhythm.

After a while, I realised I was enjoying myself.

I asked, "So, what brings you here tonight?"

"I was ordered to come."

"Ordered?"

"My supervisor thinks I spend too much time working."

I glanced over to where my instructor had entrapped another unfortunate cadet and was regaling them with some diatribe that involved a lot of hand gestures. "Mine thinks the opposite of me."

"Are you not studious?"

"I do my best."

"But you're heart's not in it?"

I looked up at the stars beyond the dome. I longed to be out among them, away from all this nonsense. I said, "But with the amount of training required, it'll be five to ten years before I get my first mission."

Tomas raised an eyebrow. "I see."

"You think I'm being impatient?"

"Not at all. I spend all my time studying the substrate, and I admire anyone with the confidence to think they can guide a ship through it." He sounded sincere, so I squeezed his hand. In response, he gathered me closer, and I could feel the warmth of his skin through his shirt.

He said, "Ark life's hard for us introverts. I can totally understand why you'd want to take off in a scout ship."

"I hadn't thought about it like that."

"You're in it for the adventure?"

"Call it a childhood dream."

The music stopped, and we found a table. An envoy brought us wine and tapas, and we talked long into the night.

I said, "You're not like most of the physics students I know."

He grinned. "I'm just pretending to be confident in the hope the feeling will eventually catch up with the behaviour."

"Fake it 'til you make it?"

"Something like that."

I raised my glass to my lips. "Well, you had me fooled."

"Now, if I can only fool myself…"

I laughed and put a hand to his cheek. "Let me help you with that."

•

I woke in his bed.

"Urgh. What time is it?"

He had just stepped out of the shower. "Mid-morning, I'm afraid."

I watched him root through a pile of clothes, trying to select his look for the day, and asked, "Do you have somewhere you need to be?"

He bit his lip. "Yeah, I kind of do. I'm sorry."

I saw him frown as he tried to remember my name, and then relax as he realised I hadn't given it to him. The sheet was twisted around my feet. I wriggled loose and sat up, drawing my knees up to my chest. "Don't worry about it. I've got a lunch date myself."

"A guy?"

"My sister."

"Ah." He scratched his cheek. "Well, help yourself to a shower. And feel free to print yourself some fresh clothes and some breakfast."

He pulled on a pair of jeans and a loose tunic and tousled his wet hair in the mirror.

"Am I going to see you again later?" I asked.

"Sure, I guess. Just maybe not tonight." He seemed flustered.

I climbed out of the bed and stood before him with my arms crossed. "What's the matter? You got a hot date?"

The guilty start he gave told me everything I needed to know.

"Look," he said, and cleared his throat. "Look, this has been fun. You're brilliant and sexy and I've had a really great time."

"But you're seeing someone else?"

"Kind of, yeah. There's this other recruit. We've got this thing going…"

I rolled my eyes. "You could have just told me that last night."

"Would it have put you off?"

"Maybe, maybe not."

"I'm sorry."

I shrugged. "Don't worry about it. It's not like I'm in love with you or anything."

Cheeks burning, I walked past him, into the bathroom. When I came out, he was gone. I got dressed, swilled my mouth with mouthwash, and left with a smile on my face. He might have been an asshole, but there was something special about Tomas, some mysterious chemistry that caused my stomach to flutter when he kissed me, and my skin to shiver at his touch. The brush of his breath against my collarbone had raised the hairs on the back of my neck. And those eyes. When he'd looked at me through the throes of passion, I'd felt he could see right into me, and I into him. Like we really understood each other.

No one had ever made me feel like that.

"Damn it," I muttered. If he hadn't already been in a relationship, I might have considered falling for him. But how could I ever trust someone so willing to cheat on their partner?

I flicked over to the other side of the Vanguard training facility, where Shay was waiting for me in our favourite restaurant—the one with a series of waterfalls that ran down the centre of the dining area, linking small pools filled with orange and white carp.

She looked good. Her hair looked thicker and fuller of life than usual, and her cadet uniform was freshly printed.

"I have some news," she said. The air smelled of blossom and fried chilli oil.

"You've been given a mission?"

She laughed. "No. In fact, I may have to put that idea on hold for a while."

"How come?"

Her eyes sparkled, and she took my hands. "Eryn, you're going to be an aunt."

"You're *pregnant*?"

"Yes."

"How far along are you?"

"Four weeks. You're the first person I've told. Not even the father knows."

"And when am I going to meet this mystery man?"

Shay's eyes looked past my shoulder, and she smiled. "Here he comes now."

I turned in my chair.

And of course, it was Tomas.

Somehow, he hadn't connected us. He'd been more interested in the game than the backstory of the players involved. I doubt he could even remember our surname. But now, seeing us together, the penny finally dropped. His eyes widened and he put a hand to his chest.

And that was when I punched him in the face.

•

Sam nudged my leg with his head.

"Hey," he said. "You're not paying me attention. What are you thinking about?"

"Past mistakes."

I reached down to stroke him.

I could hardly believe all that had happened fifteen years ago. It seemed more recent. The pain certainly still felt fresh. Shay said she didn't blame me; she said she forgave me; but I don't think she ever did, not really. And now she was dead, Tomas lived on another ark somewhere, and Madison had grown up into the spitting image of her mother.

•

Two days after our encounter with the black hole, we emerged from the substrate a safe distance from the bulk of the fleet, which currently lay spread out over half a light year of interstellar space. Each of the thousand arks measured twenty-five kilometres from bow to stern, and five across the beam. Between them, they carried all that remained of the human race.

"Hold here," I instructed the *Ocelot*. "We're not getting any closer until we're certain we're in the clear."

"Roger that."

We came to a halt relative to the stretched cloud of giant vessels. Even to someone like me who had been born and raised during the diaspora, with no memory of any other way of life, it was an impressive sight. While some of the more distant arks were either invisible to the naked eye or tiny bright points against the stars, the nearer ones shone with constellations of light. It spilled in sunlit tones from windows and open hangar bays. Navigation lights flashed red and green, and revolving orange beacons marked exhaust ports and other hazards. Some of the more agriculturally minded vessels shone emerald and jade where their internal lights were filtered through various types of vegetation. Although the arks had all started out looking the same, most of them had adapted their appearance in the years since. Where once they'd all been uniform blocks, some now sported outriggers or forests of skyscrapers. Others had slimmed down into needle-nosed cylinders, or bulked up into asymmetrical collections of inflatable modules. No two remained alike.

I recognised a few by sight. The skyscraper-covered *Damask Rose*, of course—everybody knows what their home ark looks like—but also the dumbbell-shaped *Dawn Shore*, where I'd spent three years at college; the chaotic sprawl of the *Nuevo Los Angeles*, where I'd once spent a summer living in a shack on an artificial beach; and the sleek, demure lines of the *Northern Sky*, where I'd learned how to be a navigator. The *Ocelot*'s HUD also identified other nearby vessels such as the *Standing Rock*, the *Dar Pormoza* and the *Croatian Princess*.

In the first days of the evacuation, the population of the Earth had been scattered randomly between the arks, but over the weeks and months that followed, people naturally sought out their families and friends. They rebuilt their communities, seeking comfort in each other's company. Different neighbourhoods developed along different cultural lines, but as they were all linked by the fleet's network of flick terminals, they were all part of the same peripatetic megacity.

On a human scale, the arks were massive, but even they seemed minute in comparison to the angel that created them.

As school kids, Shay and I had been shown the footage and been taught the history. When it first appeared in the outer solar system, the angel resembled a gargantuan, red-tinged hurricane. A storm to end all storms. And yet, despite its apocalyptic appearance, it only had the best interests of Earth's biosphere at heart. Vast and terrible as it was, it *cared*.

The humans of the time named it 'Raijin', after the Japanese god of storms. Since then, our telescopes had detected half a dozen others. After Raijin, had come the diffuse, almost imperceptible Forfax, who'd spread itself across multiple systems and light years. Then we found tight, angry Ba'al, whose swirls sparked with constant lightning, and Big Bertha, whose billowing clouds enveloped a cluster of suns in the space between our spiral arm and the next.

We were shown the testimony of Frank Tucker. During his communion with Raijin, he had learned that the Benevolence were a migratory species. They spent their lives spiralling out from the galactic centre, studying all the Milky Way had to offer. Then, when they reached the Rim, they spent aeons sharing and cataloguing their observations before setting course back to the seething core in order to spawn and die.

Raijin, and the others currently passing through our region of space, were all billions of years old, and would endure many billions more before they finally reproduced. To them, our entire species represented a transitory phenomenon, no more significant than the lifespan of a gnat. And yet, Raijin treated us with kindness. It saw we were destroying our planet and rather than stomp on us, it used a metaphorical glass and sheet of paper to put us outside, so we could continue to live without continuing to cause a problem.

I listened as the *Ocelot* contacted the *Damask Rose* and explained our situation. The ark requested all files and recordings pertaining to Candidate-623 and asked us to hold position while it consulted the Vanguard and the Council of Ships.

I lay back in my couch. "Well, I guess we'd better make ourselves comfortable. We could be in for a long wait." Although the artificial brains of the arks were able to think a million times faster than their human charges, the bureaucracy and associated protocols they'd negotiated between them were at least a million times more complex than even the most pedantic human had ever been able to dream.

The deck lurched and I gripped the arms of my couch, shaken from my reverie. "What was that?"

"Some idiot dropped out of the substrate almost on top of us."

"The hell they did!" There were safeguards. Everything with mass cast a shadow in the substrate. You could detect—and therefore avoid materialising too close to—suns, planets and asteroids of all shapes and sizes. Even individual ships. Dropping out so close to another vessel had to be considered dangerous, reckless and... downright rude. "Who was it? Was it one of the Vanguard? I'll rip them a new—"

"Uh-oh."

"—breathing hole. *What?*"

"The other ship."

"What about it?"

The main viewscreen crash-zoomed onto the offender. It was a Vanguard craft, but it looked wrong. There were huge gaps in its structure. Whole sections were missing, and those that were present seemed to have been fused together with little regard to logic or functionality—almost as if it had been taken apart and then reassembled by someone who'd never seen such a craft before…

"Jeez." I couldn't believe that thing was flying. "What happened to it?"

Behind me, I heard the creak of the bridge hatch. I turned to see the *Ocelot*'s replacement envoy step into the room. He was as blue, bald and portly as his predecessor, and his expression was grim.

"It's the *Couch Surfer*," he said. "Or what's left of it." He slid into the couch next to mine and interlaced his fingers across his belly. Together, we watched the patched-up wreck of a ship fall towards the *Damask Rose*.

I said, "By the looks of it, it's been through eight kinds of hell."

"I have no idea how it's still functional."

"Is the *Rose* putting it in quarantine?"

The envoy waved me to silence. "I'm trying to monitor their conversation."

"Can you put it on speaker?"

"Okay, hold on—"

There was a crackle of static.

Requesting emergency docking clearance. We have casualties.

Negative, Couch Surfer. *You will maintain a safe distance.*

They need immediate medical treatment.

You have your orders.

I felt my skin prickle. "That voice."

The *Ocelot*'s chins rippled as he turned his head towards me. "It's your sister."

"But she's dead." I blinked away the recollection of her screaming face.

"Indeed." The envoy frowned. "And the *Surfer* was lost. But here they both are."

"This isn't good."

In the corner, Sam the cat stretched. "We're fucked."

"That's not very helpful," the *Ocelot* told him.

"I just say it as I see it." The cat sniffed. "When you have ghostly ships piloted by dead navigators, I think the word, 'fucked' pretty much covers it."

I told them both to shut up. On the link, Shay was arguing that she needed priority clearance to unload injured personnel. I'd seen her eviscerated with my own eyes. Had it all been some kind of terrifying illusion? Was she still whole and breathing, despite everything? I didn't know what to think.

Control, this is Couch Surfer. *We're coming in anyway. Have a medical team standing by.*

The screen went white as the *Couch Surfer* fired its engines and began moving towards the ark. I opened a channel. "Shay, this is Eryn."

The radio crackled.

"Shay!"

More static. The *Couch Surfer* had its nose pointed at the open doors of one of the *Damask Rose*'s hangars. Its exhaust flared as it ramped up its acceleration.

"Shay, what the fuck? You can't do that. They're going to think you're trying to ram them. You need to reduce your thrust!"

No reply.

"What is she doing?"

The *Ocelot* shrugged. "It seems she's trying to force her way aboard."

"But that won't work. The defence protocols—"

The *Damask Rose* fired a plasma cannon. The bolt hit the *Couch Surfer* on its pointed snout, scoured its way through the scout ship's innards, and exploded from its rear in a cloud of glowing debris.

"No!" I put my hands to my mouth, but it was too late. The *Couch Surfer* had been cored like an apple. "Shay!"

Against all expectations, the brightness of the little craft's engines increased. It powered forward, even as subsequent bursts tore livid chunks from its patchwork hull. Too late, the *Damask Rose* tried to close its bay doors. Orange warning lights revolved in the vacuum. But the *Couch Surfer*—or rather, the molten remnant of what had once been the ship—was now moving too fast to be deflected. It hit the narrowing gap between the doors and burst like an exploding meteor, scattering white-hot fragments across the hangar deck.

•

In the aftermath of the crash, we waited, helpless, while emergency crews battled to contain the damage. The hangar bay was in vacuum, so the risk of fire was minimal, but radioactive shrapnel from the *Couch Surfer*'s ruptured reactor had peppered the back wall like buckshot, knocking out minor systems and causing electrical fires in several ducts.

Dazed, I listened to the radio chatter of the repair teams. Nothing made sense anymore. I felt hollow inside. For the briefest of moments, I had dared to hope my sister might be alive. To have that hope so brutally dashed felt like losing her all over again. Sensing my distress, Sam hopped onto my lap and began to purr. It was his way of comforting me, and I found myself absently scratching his ears as I re-watched footage from the moments leading up to the *Couch Surfer*'s demise.

I listened again to Shay's voice coming over the channel, demanding access to the hangar bay.

Shay, whom I'd seen die.

The invisible entity on C-623 had torn her apart. It had also reached across light years to attack us as we fled. Who knew of what else it might be capable? "It must have rebuilt the ship," I said. "The same way it reconstructed Snyder."

The *Ocelot*'s current envoy raised an eyebrow. "That would certainly explain the look of it."

"But why would it do that?"

"I have no idea."

"And does that mean it also rebuilt Shay?"

"Again, I have insufficient data to speculate."

I rubbed my forehead in frustration. "And then, why the hell did she ignore the ark's instructions? She would know what would happen if she tried something that stupid."

"So would the ship," the *Ocelot* agreed.

Of course, the ship's navigator would have had to be alive. The *Couch Surfer* couldn't have found its way back here without being dream-linked to a human mind. And Shay had been its navigator.

"Eryn," the envoy said.

"Yes?"

"You may want to turn off the feed now. They've found a body."

The screen showed live pictures from the emergency crew in the hangar. One of the women was relaying pictures from a handset. Among the wreckage, they'd come across a charred and mangled corpse.

"Oh."

The heat had blackened the skin and stretched it tightly across the skull. The hair had gone, and the facial features melted. It could have been anyone…

But not Shay. The proportions were wrong. This had been a man. DNA testing and dental records would reveal his identity in due course, but right now, all that mattered was that this wasn't my sister.

"It kind of looks like Snyder," Sam said, blinking up from my lap. "It's got the same big, clumsy feet."

"Are you sure?"

He yawned, exposing his needle-sharp teeth. "You *never* forget a foot that's stepped on your tail. Especially if it wore hiking boots at the time."

"But how could it be him? He wasn't aboard the *Couch Surfer* when it left. Not unless…"

Sam's ears twitched. He said, "What is it?"

"We have to warn them."

"Warn who?" the *Ocelot* asked.

I waved my hand at the screen. "Them, get them out of there."

"What's wrong?"

"Snyder was put back together to kill your envoy and Torres, and he would probably have gone on to kill Li too, if I hadn't let her back into the ship. So, what if that's still the plan? If it can control matter over light years, it could rebuild Snyder wherever it wanted. What if it put him and the ship back together in order to infiltrate and corrupt the fleet? What if it's using them as a *delivery system*?"

The envoy's face froze for a split second as the ship digested the idea. Then he said, "I have sent an emergency signal to the *Damask Rose*. It will remove the humans and seal that section of the hangar deck."

"Too late."

On the screen, Snyder's body had started to deliquesce. It seemed to be melting into the floor. The emergency crew were panicking. One of them had touched a fragment of the *Couch Surfer* and now found himself unable to break free as it too turned to oozing slime and began to engulf his arm. Around them, the rest of the wreck had also begun to liquify. It seeped into the deck and walls like water soaking into cardboard. The guy with the trapped arm let out a bubbling scream as the thick black gunge forced its way in through his skin and out again through his mouth and nose. At this, the footage became chaotic as the woman with the handset tried to run for the exit.

She made it to the door, only to find the ark had secured it. We watched her gloved fingers scrabble at the keypad, trying to override the lock. Her breaths came in little sobs. She sounded like a frightened animal.

I don't know why she turned around. Maybe she'd felt a vibration through the deck, or maybe someone watching via another camera had warned her. She stopped stabbing the panel and turned slowly back into the hangar.

There, in the centre of the room, the slime had reconstructed the hapless crewman with the stuck hand into a skinless creature from the depths of a nightmare. Compact and powerful like a hyena, it stood crouched and dripping in the overhead lights. Four short, muscled legs that each ended in a single large claw. Vertebrae that stood proud on its back like thick, blunt spines. And worst of all, a head like a flayed human face with empty eye sockets and wire-like sinews stringing its jaw.

The woman screamed. The creature leapt. Inhuman teeth flashed, and the picture died.

•

The next few minutes were a confusion of people talking over one another. Comms discipline was forgotten as everybody shouted at once. The slime that had soaked into the walls and floor had now seeped through onto other decks. Reports were coming in of horrific creatures loose in the corridors and air ducts, and of people infected by the black goo being torn apart and reassembled into more monsters.

Sam had gone very still on my lap, his little body bristling with tension. "What the fuck was that?" he demanded, glaring at the screen where the woman had died.

The envoy frowned. For once, he gave the animal a serious answer. "It seemed to be a creature assembled from a variety of sources. The head was clearly an adaptation of the human skull. The legs and teeth were from a predator species. And whatever else it was, it clearly had no use for skin in the sense we understand it."

I felt numb and hardly able to believe what I'd just witnessed.

"Tell the *Rose* to shut down the flick network," I said. "We need to stop this spreading through the fleet."

"Already on it," the *Ocelot* replied, and I felt a stab of embarrassment. The ship could think many times faster than I could, and the arks many times faster than that. They would have assessed the situation in microseconds, while my shocked mammalian synapses clicked through their laborious calculations like an antique difference engine.

"Yeah, okay. Sorry."

"The *Rose* is fighting back. It's lost several envoys already, but those dog-like things aren't indestructible. It's trying to contain their spread, but that black slime appears to be some form of molecular technology. When one of the monsters is destroyed, it just dissolves into the deck and gets recreated elsewhere."

"Fuck."

"And every living thing that comes into contact with the black goo gets broken down and turned into more black goo. All except—"

"Except what?"

He called up some security feeds from the *Damask Rose*. "Recognise these?"

The pictures were of corridors and common spaces. "What am I looking at?"

"Those rectangular structures."

"No, my god." I put a hand to my mouth. "Those are stacks of bones, the same as we saw on C-623."

"Except, these are made from human bones."

I turned away.

Sam hopped down off my lap. "Well," he said, "I guess we now know what happened to all the inhabitants and animals on that miserable planet."

I hugged myself. *And what happened to Shay...*

Shay...

"Oh no."

The envoy glanced up from his feeds. "What is it?"

"Madison. My niece. She's still on the *Rose*!" I scrambled up from the couch, threw myself through the hatch and took the ladder in a single slide. Five seconds later, I was standing in Li Chen's cabin. I'd kept her sedated during the flight home. She'd experienced so much trauma, it seemed kinder to keep her woozy and half-asleep. Now, I asked the *Ocelot* to rouse her.

She blinked up at me, shading her eyes with her arm. "Are we home?"

"I don't have time for explanations," I said. "But I'm about to do something really fucking stupid, and I thought you should be awake for it. Plus, I need to know where my gun is."

Li pushed herself up onto her elbows. "What?"

"My gun, the one Snyder took from me. Do you know where it is?"

"It's in his cabin, in a bag of digging tools. What's going on?"

"The ship will fill you in."

Leaving the envoy to get her upright and on her feet, I marched down to Snyder's cabin. Sam trotted along behind me, with his tail held at a quizzical angle.

"Human," he said, "are you *really* going to do this?"

"I don't think I have a choice."

"You could ask the *Damask Rose* to find Madison for you and keep her safe."

"The *Rose* has a fifteen million other people to worry about right now." I reached the equipment locker adjacent to the main airlock and dug inside for a box of ammunition. I found four extra clips and tucked them into the thigh pockets of my ship suit. "Shay's dead; I'm not abandoning Maddie now."

At the back of the locker, I found a hi-threat pressure suit, designed to withstand hazardous environments. The outer suit had metal plates at the chest, stomach, upper and lower back, and on each shoulder. It was heavy as hell and scuffed and dinged from wear, but it was better than nothing. I wormed into the upper section, leaving the armoured trousers and heavy boots where they were; they would only slow me down.

The *Ocelot*'s envoy appeared at the door. "What are you doing?"

"Getting tooled up."

"You want to go after her?"

I rolled my eyes. "What's so hard to understand? Of course, I'm going after her. She's fifteen years old, for fuck's sake. She needs me."

"You don't know what you'll be walking into."

"And I don't care. This is a family thing. You can come in here and tell me whatever you like, but that kid is my flesh and blood. She's my only living relative, and I'm not going to leave her to those… things. So, if you want to help, grab something you can use as a weapon; otherwise, get the hell out of my way."

The envoy's head jerked back, and his eyes widened. For an instant, he looked utterly shocked. Then he reached out and gripped my shoulder. "I'm with you," he said. "I've always been with you. We're dream-linked and we depend on each other." He reached down and picked up a fire axe designed to break the hinges on the airlock hatch in case of power failure and slapped it into his palm. "We're a team, and if you think I'm going to let you walk in there alone, you're even crazier than you look."

CHAPTER FOURTEEN

AIRTIGHT SEAL

ERYN

We didn't make the same mistake as the *Couch Surfer*. We told the *Damask Rose* what we were doing, and it cleared us to land. At that moment, it had bigger things to worry about. We were monitoring the internal newsfeeds. Civilians were trying to flee the black slime and twisted hyena-things. Rumours crackled like electricity. The *Rose*'s envoys attempted to keep everything calm, but people in the infected areas kept broadcasting footage of the monsters via their handsets. The appalling savagery of the attacks coupled with the apparently intelligent spread of the infection was enough to spread panic through the population—and when all connections between the ark and the inter-ship flick network cut off for the first time in living memory, that panic boiled over into outright terror.

I turned off the images as the *Ocelot* set down in a small hangar on the ship's port side. "This is as close as we can get to your sister's apartment," he said.

Li and I were standing at the top of the cargo ramp as it lowered. She leant on a crutch; the ship had set and plastered her ankle and injected her with bone regrowth. As it was a load-bearing joint, she'd have to use the crutch for about a week, but after that she'd be fine.

"Stay here," I told her. "Keep the doors shut and the engines warm. If anything goes wrong, the ship will get you to one of the other arks." I turned to squint at the envoy, who waited behind us. "Won't you?"

He spread his blue hands. "Of course, I will."

I started down the ramp with the pistol held out before me. The envoy followed, the fire axe gripped in his fat hands.

We passed through the hangar door and emerged in one of the *Rose*'s foyers. People were shouting and screaming and trying to push past us. It was chaos, but all I could think about was Madison. She was in danger, and I had to get her out of there. I'd failed to rescue her mother, and I'd be damned if I was going to fail her in turn.

We fought our way to the edge of the room.

"That gun you're carrying?" The *Ocelot* looked worried. "What's it packing?"

"Hollow points and armour piercing."

"Nice." He scrunched up his face. "But promise me you'll try to only point it at things you want to kill."

"I'll do my best."

"No important bulkheads. Try not to puncture the hull."

I gave him a look. "I'm not an idiot."

"I know, but I have to run through the standard disclaimers. With great firepower comes great responsibility."

"Tell that to Snyder." I checked the readout on the side of the pistol. Twenty rounds of each. If I needed any more, they were in my pockets.

I led the *Ocelot* up a side corridor, away from the crowd. "Across three blocks and up two levels," I said, even though I knew the envoy would have the location pinpointed on his internal map.

"Will she still be there?"

"She'd better fucking be."

The ark groaned as its lateral thrusters pushed it in an unaccustomed direction. People staggered. The *Rose* was a vessel designed to travel forward—ever forward—and not sideways. Components that had settled under constant acceleration were now complaining as they adjusted to this change in orientation. Whatever Candidate-623 might be up to, it was straining the old ship in ways it hadn't had to endure in decades.

Usually on an ark, all you had to do to find someone was ask the ark's consciousness where they were. Like it or not, there was little privacy in the fleet. But with the *Rose* compromised, we were on our own now. It didn't have the spare capacity to keep track of all fifteen million inhabitants while simultaneously fighting an incursion on so many fronts.

"We check the cabin first," I said, "and then if she's not there, we try to work out where she went next. And we keep looking until we find her."

We were moving through one of the leisure decks, between squash courts, swimming pools and saunas. The air smelled of sweat and chlorine. A few confused people hurried past us in bathing suits and workout clothes. Somewhere, a man screamed.

"Here," I said. "We can take a shortcut through the basketball court." I pushed open the door and actually took two steps into the room before I registered what I was seeing. "Oh, holy shit."

Dismembered corpses filled the room. There must have been at least fifty of them scattered across the playing surface. Some had been players, others possibly spectators. They lay at awkward angles, necks broken, arms snapped and twisted, legs wrenched from their sockets, eyes staring. A few had been completely disembowelled, their bones tugged loose and arranged in small piles. Exposed, open-mouthed skulls gleamed obscenely clean and white through ropes of blackening gore. Lungs and entrails lay heaped in greasy, slowly liquefying mounds. Blood and other fluids pooled around them on the shiny wooden floor. I covered my mouth and nose against the smell. It was like C-623, only much worse. This time, I couldn't slam the airlock and bolt for orbit.

"Our tactical situation has changed," the *Ocelot* said.

"How so?"

"We have no way of knowing how many killings are taking place. The spread through the population may be accelerating at an exponential rate."

I'd lived the majority of my life on this ark. Although I didn't have a lot of friends now, I had plenty of acquaintances. My fellow navigators. The neighbours in the cabins and apartments to either side of mine. The old guy down the hall. Hundreds of faces I saw every day without consciously registering. I'd spent a lot of time finding ways to escape this place, but it was still my home. Gripping the gun and holding my breath, I picked my way across the gore-strewn court, trying not to recognise any of the mutilated bodies. I didn't breathe again until we'd made it through the doors on the far side, and into the stairwell beyond.

We had to go up a couple of decks. Usually, I would have flicked up there, but now I didn't want to entrust my safety to the ark's internal network, even if it was still working. Something might go wrong at any moment, or the ark might shut the network to slow the spread of the infection. I had no idea what would happen if the miniature wormholes collapsed as we stepped through them—and I was pretty sure I never wanted to find out. The idea of either being trapped in a collapsing bubble of reality or ejected into the boiling airless chaos of the substrate held no attraction.

Two decks. Fifty steps. By the time we reached the right level, my heart was clattering in my chest. I paused for a breath, trying to calm down. I couldn't go in jittery; I didn't want to shoot Madison by mistake. So, doing my best to control my shaking hands and thighs, I crept forward, inching along the side of the corridor from the top of the stairwell towards Shay's cabin door.

As we moved, I wrinkled my nose. "What's that stink?"

Against the corridor's other wall, the *Ocelot* sniffed. "Burning plastech. There's most likely an electrical fire somewhere close."

"Jeez." All my life, I'd taken the internal fire suppression systems entirely for granted. Smelling actual, uncontrolled smoke was a disturbingly novel experience. My hackles rose with the prehistoric, hardwired dread of a forest creature facing a bushfire, and I prayed the gravity and life support were going to hold out until we were done.

The deck trembled beneath our feet and the bulkheads groaned.

A figure rounded the far end of the corridor. His face had been flayed, his lower jaw was missing, and his skeletal arms ended in machete-like claws. I tightened my grip on the pistol. "Shit."

"You should get behind me."

"Maybe you should get behind me?"

The *Ocelot* gave me a look. "I'm expendable, you're not." He brought up his forearms, revealing the clustered gun barrels that now poked through the blue flesh around his wrists. "And besides, I'm packing enough here to take down an army."

I glanced at the cabin door. "If I run, can I make the apartment before that thing reaches it?"

"Risky."

"Can you cover me?"

The envoy grinned. His fingernails morphed into scalpel blades, his canines expanded with an audible creak, and targeting reticules appeared in his eyes.

"It would be my genuine pleasure."

I didn't stop to thank him. As he spoke, I turned on my heel and pushed off with my left foot, hurling myself down the length of the corridor. As I did, two of the bastardised hyena-like creatures rounded the corner behind the flayed man, but I didn't falter. Madison might be alone and unprotected in her cabin, and I had to reach her before these fuckers. I couldn't leave her to face them on her own; she would be defenceless against such an onslaught. Projectiles zipped through the air around me as the *Ocelot* opened fire. The skinless man staggered, blown backwards by a withering fusillade of explosive bullets. But even as he fell, more of his kind appeared from around the corner. Some carried guns, others held improvised clubs made from table legs, lengths of pipe, or (in a couple of particularly grisly cases) bloody human thigh bones. A few more of the hyena-beasts were with them, too. Their jaws chomped and slavered.

I reached the door a few steps ahead of the nearest horror and grabbed the handle to stop myself skidding past. I heard gunshots from both sides but didn't have time to flinch. I mashed my fingers against the lock. The half second it took to recognise my print felt like a subjective eternity. The creatures were reaching for me when blue light flashed beneath my hand. The door clicked open, and I tumbled inside.

•

Madison was in her mother's bedroom. She looked up at me with panicked eyes, and for a moment resembled her mother so strongly, I almost called her by the wrong name.

"Maddie, it's me. We have to go."

"Aunt Eryn?" She frowned as if she couldn't be sure I was really there. "What's happening? What's going on?"

"There's no time to explain."

I heard gunshots in the hallway. Something heavy crashed against the apartment door.

The kid backed away. "I want my mom."

Her words were like a cold knife to my heart. I turned away and tapped my earbud. "How's it looking out there?"

The *Ocelot*'s voice answered, "There are too many of them. I'm being forced back."

Although the apartment door had locked behind me, it was only an internal door and wouldn't be capable of withstanding a determined assault. Already, black ooze had begun to seep underneath it from the corridor outside—the remnants of the creatures taken down by the *Ocelot* looking to reassemble themselves on this side of the obstruction.

"Maddie, we have to go."

I cast around for an alternate exit, already knowing I wouldn't find one. These cabins were all the same. The only way in or out was via the door that led onto the corridor, and that was no longer an option. I pictured one of those hyena-things coming for Madison, and suddenly, the pistol in my hand seemed woefully inadequate.

"*Rose!*"

"What?" The ark's voice came through the entertainment speakers in the main living area.

"We need help."

"I'm a bit busy here, Eryn."

"Danger close."

"I'm sorry. I'm fighting running battles on all decks. I only have so many envoys. I have to prioritise."

"But we're cornered."

"There's only two of you, and I have a hundred and eight people trapped in a restaurant a deck above you. Who should I help?"

I pinched my forehead between finger and thumb. There had to be a way out. As kids, Shay and I had always found somewhere to hide when we needed it. We'd always had our den in the vents...

"Can you download a schematic of the ventilation system onto this cabin's entertainment screen?"

"I am a bit busy right now..."

"Please?"

"Already done." The audio channel went dead. I waved my hand to activate the wall-mounted screen and, trying to ignore the thumps at the door and the slowly growing slick of black goo on the floor, I scrutinised the intricate web of ducts, pipes and cabling that lay behind the walls and under the floor of each cabin, bringing in water and power and hauling away waste to be recycled.

Madison came out of the bedroom behind me. Her eyes were wide, but her jaw was tight, and she had an aluminium hockey stick gripped in her hands. "I'm ready."

"Good, because we need to move." I finished tracing a duct on the screen, then turned and faced the wall. "Stand back."

"What are you going to do?"

"Find a way out."

I fired half a dozen armour-piercing rounds into the wall. It was only an internal divider and not that thick. The shots punched a series of fist-sized holes.

"Got an axe or something?"

"I have this." Madison handed me the hockey stick.

"That'll have to do." I stepped onto the sofa, inserted the stick into the hole closest to a seam, and used it to lever open a section of the thin metal partition. Beyond, the pipes and ducts lay exposed. I found a place where two sections of air duct were joined and started kicking it. Behind me, the hammering on the cabin door grew louder.

"Come on," I muttered, swinging my foot. "Come on, you bastard."

And then, on the fifth or sixth kick, the joint gave. I pushed the two pieces of duct apart and turned to Madison.

"Get in."

For a second, it looked like she might object. Maybe it was just a residual teenage default response. But shapes were already bubbling up from the black slick on the floor. Without further protest, she bent low and slithered into the tube. I clambered in after her and did what I could to bring the damaged sections back together, but I was working with my feet in the confined space and it wasn't very easy. I just hoped whatever those monsters were, they weren't very bright.

Inside, the ducts seemed smaller than I remembered, and I found moving more awkward than I had as a child. Shay's cabin had once belonged to our parents and had been the one in which we'd grown up. As kids, we used to access the ducts from a vent in the corridor and slither up to our den, but now I had to discard my chest armour as there simply wasn't room for it. My elbows kept banging against the metal sides and I couldn't lift my head to see properly. I just followed Madison's feet as she squirmed along ahead. As I moved, I relayed our position to the *Ocelot* so he could keep track of us.

"Just keep on your current heading," he said. "I'll let you know when I can reach you."

Occasionally, we heard screams and cries from outside. At one point, gunshots snapped loudly below us, and I cringed, half expecting bullets to come ripping up through the thin floor of the duct into our helpless bodies.

"There's a wider space ahead," Madison reported after what seemed like an eternity of painful crawling.

"We'll rest there."

"Oh."

"What's the matter?"

"It's full of stuff."

I caught my breath, picturing the black goo filling the vent and drowning us in an obscene, inescapable ooze. "What kind of stuff?"

She moved out of the way and I pushed my head and shoulders into the dimly lit alcove.

"Dolls' heads," she said. "Old food wrappers..."

My mouth fell open. I could scarcely believe it. After all

these years, our old den was still intact. The *Damask Rose* hadn't tidied any of it away. I'd always suspected the old ship possessed a strong sentimental streak, and now here was the proof. The pictures of stars and planets were still taped to the walls. The old cushions we'd pretended were our navigator's couches still sat side by side beneath a layer of dust. Each movement disturbed another pile of memories. In the gloom of this familiar place, Madison's resemblance to her mother almost overwhelmed me. And yet, I couldn't allow myself to be distracted. I could hear the echoing booms and clanks of something heavy flailing through the ventilation system in our wake. I hauled myself fully into the alcove and looked around for some way to block the duct behind us.

"*Rose*, are you there?"

"Yes, Eryn."

"You can close the air ducts in case of fire, is that right?"

"Of course."

"Can you close them individually?"

"Every duct has an airtight seal every hundred metres."

I felt a rush of relief. "Then, please close every seal between Shay's apartment and our current location."

I could hear claws scrabbling against metal. One of those hyenas was on our trail, thrashing and slavering its way towards us.

"Closing them now. Stand clear of the duct."

A metal plate snicked guillotine-like into place, sealing the opening. Two seconds later, the hyena impacted it from the other side, leaving a sizeable dent in the metal. I fired twice at point-blank range. The gunshots were punishingly loud in the confined space, but both bullets penetrated the warped barrier and were met with satisfying yelps and squeals as they found their target.

"Okay," I yelled over the ringing in my ears. "Let's get the fuck out of here. That won't hold it for long."

CHAPTER FIFTEEN

ONE OF THE GOOD GUYS

VICTORIA

I remember the day after the war-that-never-happened. Even now, those moments remain etched with crystal clarity.

Dressed in pyjamas and thick slippers, I stood in the kitchen area of my tiny upstairs flat on Woodstock Road and listened to the rain hammering on the skylight. The street outside was empty. People were hunkered down. They didn't know what to do. We had almost all just died, and now a rust-coloured light permeated the clouds. Winds whipped leaves and papers between the parked cars. But this was no ordinary storm. The umber vortices above were the body of an angel lowering itself into our atmosphere.

I showered and changed into a fresh t-shirt and jeans. Then I made coffee and roused Frank, who was still snoring on the beaten-up old sofa.

The buses weren't running, so together, we walked the two miles to the building that housed his laboratory. The rain beat down mercilessly as we passed the remains of last night's unrest. Glass lay smashed in the gutter by the bus stop. People had looted a convenience store and the tins of food they had dropped lay on the pavement like missed opportunities.

"So, yesterday's experiment was pretty awesome, huh?" Frank's reddened eyes peered quizzically at me from beneath his damp, windblown fringe.

"Yes." My words were hollow. "Amazing."

He grinned, drawing strength from my approval. An alien intelligence had stepped in to avoid a nuclear holocaust, but all Frank cared about was his work.

After passing under the station—no trains either, by the look of things—we walked a short distance along Botley Road, and then turned off onto the tow path that led along the banks of the Isis to the industrial estate where his lab was located. Narrowboats sheltered beneath the overhanging boughs of sparse autumn trees. Moorhens came and went in the sallow reeds.

Christ, I thought. *Is this how the world ends?*

Beside me, Frank still appeared oblivious to everything. He seemed to be enraptured by the rain speckling the floating yellow leaves on the river's surface. His bony hands were deep in his pockets and his faded red baseball boots scuffed the beige dirt of the path.

When we reached the estate of single storey buildings that formed the industrial campus, we were greeted by the sight of vehicles clustered outside the block that housed Frank's lab. Land Rovers with darkened windows. Military lorries. Police cars.

"What the hell…?"

Yellow tape screened-off the front door. Confused employees from firms that shared the same premises milled around in the car park sharing cigarettes and speculation. Figures in protective suits were removing equipment and piling it in the trucks.

"Hey!" Frank pointed an accusing finger at what they were carrying. "That's my stuff!"

He barged forward, only to find himself facing the gun barrels of half a dozen soldiers in full camouflage.

A man stepped forward. He was packing a wrestler's build beneath his Armani suit. "You're Frank Tucker?"

"Yeah, pal. And you'd better have some kind of warrant for this."

The man smiled as if at some private joke. He glanced at me, and then raised the tape, beckoning us both through.

"Come on in," he said, and we followed him through the cordon, into the laboratory, which had been stripped of everything except the workbenches and built-in cupboards. A pair of technicians in hazmat suits were taking Geiger counter readings at the far end, where the second of the spheres had appeared last night.

"Bloody hell," I said. "What is this?"

The man spread his hands. "I was hoping you were going to tell me."

"You've taken everything."

"Yes, we have. Do you want to know why?"

I looked him up and down. "And you are?"

"My name's Conrad."

"Conrad what?"

"Just Conrad."

Frank cleared his throat. "And who do you work for, Conrad?" It was the first time he'd spoken since entering the building.

Conrad inclined his head in acknowledgement. "Let's just say it's a government agency."

"Which one?"

"You wouldn't have heard of it."

"I meant, which government?"

Another smile. "Hey, I'm one of the good guys."

"Really?" Frank raised himself to his full gangly height. "Because from here, you look like you're stealing my work."

Conrad looked Frank in the eye, taking in his reddened face and clenched fists.

"Easy, fella."

"Don't tell me to calm down."

Conrad reached into his jacket and produced a pair of plastic zip ties. "I'm not telling, I'm insisting. Because I'm afraid your equipment isn't the only thing we'll be impounding."

I took a step back. "You're *arresting* us?"

"We just want to ask you a few questions."

"Then why the restraints?"

Conrad's smile had grown tight. He was obviously under stress and losing patience. "Just let me put them on, okay?"

Frank shook his head. "No way."

Conrad sucked his teeth. He placed the zip ties on the empty workbench and pulled a small, black pistol from his belt. "I'm afraid I'm going to have to insist."

Frank gave a snort. "What? You're going to shoot me if I don't come quietly."

Conrad's expression didn't change. "I'm under instruction to bring you in alive, but nobody said anything about keeping your kneecaps intact."

"Christ."

"Now," Conrad said. "Are you going to cooperate, or are we going to have to carry you out of here?"

I was about to open my mouth to protest when a tiny silver sphere appeared in the air between us. Almost too quickly for the eye to register, it expanded to a width of roughly two metres, its growth sending a blast of air in all directions, rattling the windows and disturbing stray sheets of paper.

A tall, bald man stepped through. He was naked, with skin the colour of a summer sky.

"Frank Tucker?"

Beside me, Frank gaped like a bony fish. The blue man reached out a hand in greeting.

"I am so pleased to meet you," he said.

CHAPTER SIXTEEN

SERIOUS FUCKERY

TESSA

I was in the middle of preparing my daily video blog when the feeds went apeshit.

"The fuck?" I had sixteen million regular subscribers waiting to hear about last night's party on the *Sea of Okhotsk*, but I also had a hangover the size of a galactic supercluster and was definitely *not* in the mood for interruptions. I had content to make and gossip to impart.

My apartment was located on the forty-second deck of the *North Pacific*. I said, "Hey, *N-Pac.* What's happening?"

The ark's bass rumble of a voice resonated through my entertainment centre's speakers. "There seems to be a situation developing on board the *Damask Rose*."

"What sort of situation?"

"The exact nature of the threat is unclear, although it appears to be under attack."

"Shitting hell." I glanced down at my notes from the party and saw them for the tawdry innuendos and speculations they were. An attack on an ark, though? That sounded *newsworthy*. "Can I get aboard?"

"I would advise against it."

"But you wouldn't stop me?"

"Tessa Scott. When have I *ever* been able to stop you doing anything?"

"Fair point."

I threw my notes aside and picked up my handset. Its inbuilt camera would be good enough to capture anything interesting that might be going on. Then, I slipped my feet into a pair of soft-soled deck shoes and left the apartment.

Gossip be fucked. I'd been waiting my whole life for a real story, and something told me this could be it.

Outside, the corridor was wide and high-ceilinged. Small birds darted between potted trees. Maintenance bots cleaned overnight graffiti from the walls and swept up litter. Some apartments had their doors open. Children watched me as I passed.

Although the corridor stretched several kilometres ahead like an exercise in perspective, small flick terminals had been placed at every intersection, meaning I only had to walk for a couple of minutes before being able to flick down eight decks to the main hub, from where I hoped to be able to use one of the larger terminals to reach the *Damask Rose*.

My heart pumped and my head pounded. Why had I consumed so much champagne last night? That stuff was too easy to drink; it went down like an eager lover but left me feeling brittle and second-hand the next morning. And I must have chugged at least eight or nine glasses over the course of the evening, maybe more.

Fuck you, Past Tessa, and all your stupid life choices.

The Inter-Ark Hub wasn't especially crowded at this time of the morning. It consisted of a long room with benches and information terminals, and a row of ten silver spheres. I joined the people queuing for the nearest and used my wrist terminal to select the *Damask Rose* as my destination.

One by one, the folks in front of me stepped into the sphere's silver surface and vanished, their bodies instantly routed to their chosen ark via miniature substrate wormholes. I caught a couple of them staring at me and smiled. Everyone in the fleet had access to the ArkNet, but only a handful of us achieved genuine celebrity status. I'd started a few years ago, posting daily updates on lifestyle and fashion. Every time I found a stylish new template for the clothing printers, I put up pictures and links. I mixed new designs with old-school Earth fashion to create a distinctive look. I paired silver smart fabric tops with faded blue jeans and chunky pressure-suit boots. Short floral-pattern halter tops with standard issue cargo work pants. Delicate Chinese silks with tough canvas jackets and chunky steel bracelets.

Soon, people were wearing my combinations in the corridors and parks, and I started to accrue a sizeable following. Shortly after that, I started getting invites to theatre openings and art shows. Other tastemakers and influencers sought me out. News services and gossip sites started asking me for comments. And then I met Glen, and everything changed.

Glen was Frank Tucker's son. Unlike his father, he was sociable and possessed of a quiet charisma that gradually drew all the attention in any room he happened to be in. We dated for a year, but I'm not going to go into all that now. If you want to search out the details, the public record documented the whole fabulous flop. Suffice to say, by the time we parted on amicable terms, my total number of subscribers had soared over ten million and was continuing to climb.

Since then, my most popular updates had been reports on the various parties I'd attended, and the prurient activities of the other guests. But deep down, I wanted to do more. I had a public platform and I wanted to use it for something more significant than the infidelities of artists and comedians.

And now here was a disaster unfolding in real time, and I was perfectly placed to cover it. I could flick across to the *Damask Rose* and live stream the unfolding events to the rest of the Continuance. I could make myself a part of the story and cement a reputation for serious reportage. After that, maybe start my own news channel, and use it to promote my ideas for how the fleet should be run. Then, politics. Maybe even a seat on the Council…

But I was getting ahead of myself. Pictures were already leaking from the *Damask Rose*, but they were difficult to interpret. Lots of shaky footage of people running and screaming. Some sort of black mould on the walls. Fox-shaped envoys encouraging people to stay calm. I needed to get in there and make sense of it all, so I could frame a narrative the rest of the fleet might understand.

The elderly woman in front of me shuffled forward and disappeared into the sphere. I straightened my back and braced myself. My handset camera was recording; from here on, I had to act like a professional. I drew in a deep breath and stepped forward—only to collide with a surface as cool and unyielding as thick glass. I stepped back in confusion. The sphere had turned from silver to black. Behind me, voices were raised in indignation and alarm.

I caught sight of a *North Pacific* envoy pushing through the crowd and collared him. "What the fuck is going on?"

He wore a hand-stitched suit worth several days of a tailor's time. "The flick network to the *Damask Rose* has been suspended."

"Suspended?" I'd never heard of such a thing. I didn't even know individual flick links could be turned on and off; I thought they were permanent things.

"Quarantine measures are in effect," the envoy said. "Please remain calm."

"Calm?"

I glanced back at the impassive black sphere. The next person in line tapped their bracelet to set a destination, and it turned back into a mirror. They went through without a problem, which meant they had been going elsewhere in the fleet. According to my bracelet, the *Damask Rose* was still off-limits. If the Council had decided to isolate one of the arks, there must have been some serious fuckery unfolding on the other side of that link.

CHAPTER SEVENTEEN

INTERNAL BIOLOGICAL PROCESSES

ERYN

In the vents, the only illumination came from ambient light spilling in through the grilles set at irregular intervals in the floor or sides, wherever a room or corridor needed a supply of circulating air. As I crawled, I tried to keep watch behind, often levering myself up on my elbows and toes so I could look back through my spread feet to check if we were still being pursued, but the gloom and awkward angle made it difficult to see properly and left me feeling exposed and vulnerable. Several times, scalp crawling at the sensation of being hunted, I flinched at threats that weren't there, ready to unload my remaining ammunition at shadows. When Madison finally said she could see some real light ahead, I almost sobbed with relief.

"It's me." The *Ocelot*'s voice came booming down the aluminium duct. "I've opened a hole here big enough for you to get out."

We emerged into an empty service corridor. The duct ran along the ceiling, and the envoy helped us both down to the floor.

As he lowered me to the deck, Madison brushed at the

dust and grime on the front of her clothes and said, "What the fuck was that all about?"

The *Ocelot* looked at me. "Have you explained?"

"There wasn't time."

Maddie scowled. "If she'd explained, I wouldn't be asking, would I? I'm not an idiot."

"I never implied—"

"Shut up."

I put a hand on the *Ocelot*'s shoulder. "You haven't spent a lot of time with teenage girls, have you?"

The blue man spread his hands. "Alas, I am but a humble scoutcraft, living out my days in the darkness of unexplored space, far from the simple human joys of hearth and family."

Madison glared at us as if we were mad. "Would one of you please tell me what the hell is going on?"

I checked the ammo readout on the side of my pistol. "We're being invaded."

"By aliens?"

"Who knows what the fuck they are. Point is, they seem to want to tear us to bits in order to make piles of our bones."

"Gross."

"The *Damask Rose* has been compromised," the *Ocelot* said. "Your aunt insisted we come aboard to find you."

Madison's eyes narrowed. "You did?"

"Of course, I did. But we're not out of this yet. We need to get back to the ship." I looked to the envoy. "Which way?"

Madison looked confused. "There's a flick point a block from here. Can't we use that?"

The *Ocelot* shook his head. "Most emphatically not, I'm afraid. The rest of the fleet have already acted to seal the *Rose* off from the main network, and we've no way of knowing whether the internal routers are in danger of damage or compromise. It's too much of a risk. Our best option is to proceed on foot and cut across the main park."

I pursed my lips. "Won't that make us more visible to the enemy?"

"There is some danger we will be more easily spotted, but tactically it gives us more escape options than we currently have in this corridor, where only two directions are available to us."

I gripped the gun firmly with both hands. "That makes sense. Okay, lead on."

We started moving. The envoy went first, Madison followed, and I brought up the rear. Around us, the huge ship groaned as its propulsion system continued to fire randomly.

Every ark had a different internal layout, shaped to the preferences of its inhabitants or the quirks of its personality. The main park on the *Damask Rose* was a cavern six kilometres in length and three in width. The floor had been landscaped with a series of rolling hills; a half-kilometre-wide river wound sluggishly down the middle, criss-crossed by elegant footbridges, dotted with sailboats, and flanked by broad, sandy banks. Shay and I had come here many times as kids, to play on those long beaches beneath the glare of the artificial sun at the top of the chamber or ride the small land-trains that bumbled around the hills and valleys on their large, springy tyres, providing transport for those too young or infirm to walk the paths and climb the peaks.

Today, the trains weren't running. One of the sailboats was on fire, another had sunk, and the brightly coloured dirigibles that had once wafted through the skies were mostly on the ground—although one still hovered near the ceiling, turning slow, ponderous circles as its one remaining engine tried to move it forward.

"The exit we want lies on the other side," the *Ocelot* said. "Three kilometres across and one kilometre sternward."

I pointed to a shallow gap in the nearest hills. "I think we're probably best following that valley. It's going in the right direction and will give us some concealment. At least as far as the river."

"Agreed," the *Ocelot* said. "We should avoid the skyline as much as possible. There's no sense in making our presence any more obvious than it needs to be."

I glanced at Madison's thin deck shoes. "Are you going to be all right in those?"

"I'm going to have to be, aren't I?"

The *Ocelot* raised his eyebrows. "Sarcasm?"

Madison shrugged. "Pragmatism."

We stepped out onto the grass. Immediately, the air seemed fresher. The light from the artificial sun felt warm and nourishing on my face.

God, I've missed this place.

I remembered so many days spent running barefoot on the soft grass or wading in the river's shallows; picnics on the hillsides; games of hide-and-seek in the little groves of beech and olive trees that lay dotted around the place like oversized houseplants; chasing the goats that grazed wild in the park, with their heavy bells that made a hollow *clonk*, *clonk*, *clonk* noise as they ran. Once, this place had been my idea of heaven. How utterly strange it was now to realise grief and threat could so easily and quickly transform a beloved venue into something eerily unfamiliar and terrifying. The *Damask Rose*, which had provided life and sustenance to roughly fifteen million people, had now transfigured into an unpredictable alien environment filled with violence and death.

The thought was horrific. Nothing like this had happened before. The arks were solid and dependable. They had rescued our ancestors from the environmental shitstorm the Earth had become and nurtured us ever since. They weren't supposed to *fail*. They'd been designed by angels for heaven's sake!

I felt the cold hand of fear close around my stomach. Despite their largely inscrutable motives and sometimes impenetrable behaviour, the Angels of the Benevolence were widely considered to be as close to infallible as it was possible to get. Humanity had accepted their judgement based on this assumption. So, if an entity existed that could so swiftly usurp and sabotage their works, how powerful must that entity be? Or conversely, how actually fallible were Raijin and its brethren?

A stream ran along the base of the valley. The water bubbled up from the ground and babbled its way downhill to the central river. We followed its stern-most shore. My boots splashed through the shallows, occasionally slipping on wet pebbles as our eyes remained fixed on the crests of the surrounding hills.

What do you do when your world falls apart? Me, I kept walking. If we could just get back to the comparative safety of the *Ocelot*, I hoped we'd be all right—although as we were dealing with a force that could reach invisibly across light years of space to take apart a ship in flight, that hope seemed almost vanishingly forlorn.

Around us, bracken and gorse decorated the rock-strewn slopes of the stream's banks. Clumps of tough, wiry grass burst from between the stones like cellulose fireworks. Tiny, almost impossibly delicate blue and white flowers wavered in the earthy, artificial breeze.

What if this thing couldn't be stopped? If it infiltrated the other arks of the Continuance with the same apparent ease and rapidity with which it had spread through the *Damask Rose*, all would be lost. These big, old ships were our salvation; without them, we couldn't survive. Humanity would be lost as surely as the original inhabitants of Candidate-623, leaving only our piled bones to mark where once we'd stood.

After around twenty minutes of hiking, my legs had begun to feel shaky. The hills smoothed out, dropping down towards the central river. We paused to survey our options.

From here, I could see that many of the boats were adrift and being slowly drawn by the current to the far end of the park, where they were piling up against the wall. One of the land-trains had driven onto the sand and the first few carriages were partially submerged. We spotted a few groups of people further along the shore, but from this range, it was impossible to tell if they were infected.

Madison said, "Should we try and contact them?"

I shook my head. "It's too dangerous. I'm just trying to get you out of here in one piece."

The *Ocelot* agreed. "You two are my responsibility, and your continued survival remains my sole objective. Contact with other people can only increase the danger we face."

"Aw." I gave him a nudge with my elbow. "I bet you say that to all the girls."

He ignored me.

"We need to get across the river, but we'll be vulnerable if we try to cross a bridge." He indicated the nearest, which consisted of a delicate arch made of intertwined bronze ribbons. "At five hundred metres in length, they will take some minutes to negotiate, during which time we will be highly visible and easily trapped if a hostile force blocks both ends."

"Is there any other way across?"

"We could take possession of one of the boats, but none appear to be within easy range."

"Could we swim?" Madison asked.

I said, "We'd have to leave our equipment behind."

"But we'd be swimming with the current. It would be carrying us in the right direction, and we wouldn't be as noticeable."

"True."

"There is one drawback." The *Ocelot*'s envoy gave his protruding stomach a pat. "I am not as buoyant as I may appear."

"You can't swim?"

"I have too much internal equipment. I tend to sink."

I glanced at the river. The water didn't look particularly inviting, but it had to be a better option than the bridges. There had to be some way we could take advantage of it.

I had a sudden mental image of the *Ocelot*'s previous envoy walking unprotected on the surface of Candidate-623, his bald head and blue three-piece suit looking incongruous next to Snyder and Li Chen in their helmets and pressure suits. "You don't breathe," I realised, "do you?"

The envoy frowned. "I can choose not to, but I do require oxygen to power some of my internal biological processes."

"How long can you go without breathing?"

"Six to eight hours, depending on the expected level of exertion. Why?"

I smiled. "You don't need to swim. Just let yourself sink and walk along the bottom."

"That's rather an unusual and... elegant solution."

"Is that a yes?"

"It is."

"Let's go, then."

•

Keeping low and utilising every piece of cover we could find, we made it down to a small grove of olive trees near the waterline, where Madison and I stripped down to t-shirts and underwear. I handed my gun to the envoy, and he placed it in a hollow in his left thigh, where he said it would remain dry during the crossing.

We watched him wade out into the river, getting lower with each step, until his hairless head slipped beneath the water.

"It's been a long time since I swam," I said.

Madison hugged herself, not so much for warmth, I think, as for reassurance. It felt wrong to be getting half-naked while surrounded by potential threats. It went against every protective instinct to cover up and place as much material as possible between yourself and the danger.

"It's not something you forget," she said, and made a dash for the water. I sighed, trying to remember what it had felt like to be so young.

"I know *how* to swim," I muttered. "It's the physical side of it that I'm worried about."

Far away, an alarm sounded. I heard a distant scream and the crash of breaking glass.

"Ah, the hell with it."

I strode into the river until its chilly waters came up to my thighs, and then leant into its brisk embrace.

•

We were in the water a long time. At least a couple of hours. The lazy current bore us beneath several footbridges, but we saw no sign of anyone—or anything—on them. I tried to float when tired but didn't seem to be able to stop my feet from sinking. I guess I'd never learned how to do it properly. By the time we were getting near the opposite shore, my arms and shoulders burned with the indignation of muscles forced to exert themselves in unaccustomed ways, my fingers were wrinkled, and my extremities were numb with the cold.

We dragged ourselves out onto the bank and lay shivering and gasping until the *Ocelot* surfaced and came to help us onto our feet. Between the ducts and the river, my energy reserves were more or less gone, and I felt used up and done.

Somehow, we stumbled the remaining kilometres to the other side of the park, where an elevator took us down to the hangar decks. By the time we reached our intended level, my arms had stopped shaking and I could feel some sensation returning to my hands and feet.

We made our way along to the correct bay, but someone was waiting for us.

Snyder leant against the wall with his arms crossed.

"Hey," he said.

I looked him up and down. He seemed exactly as he had before C-623. The same dark skin and grey beard. No sign of injury or trauma.

I said, "Why aren't you dead?"

Snyder smiled. "Nobody's dead, Eryn. Not really."

"How did you get here?"

He waved a hand. "Oh, it's a long story."

Although he was talking to me, his eyes didn't seem to be focusing properly and his tone was a little too disconnected. Whatever this was, it wasn't the man I remembered.

The *Ocelot* had noticed too. He said, "What happened to you?"

Snyder shrugged. "I got better."

"What does that even mean?"

His hands spread wide. "Why not join us and find out? If you come willingly, it will be almost painless."

I pulled Madison behind me. "I saw you get taken apart. That looked pretty bloody painful to me."

Beyond Snyder, two of the hyenas-with-human-faces slouched around the curve of the corridor and advanced towards us. Another two blocked our retreat.

Snyder reached out a hand. He said, "It only hurts for a short time."

The tips of his fingers started dissolving into black dust.

Beside me, the *Ocelot* pulled my pistol from its concealed housing and fired twice, both shots catching Snyder square in the face. He staggered backwards and collapsed. Madison screamed and the hyenas howled with rage. The envoy shoved Madison and I through the hatch into the hangar. He sent a couple of shots in each direction, to slow down the beasts, and then dragged Snyder's body through and sealed the door.

Madison stared aghast at the half-dissolved corpse.

I said, "I thought you were forbidden from harming a human?"

"He isn't human."

"He used to be."

"Be grateful for fine distinctions."

The *Ocelot* stamped down, and the bones in Snyder's neck cracked. As the envoy took out a knife and lowered it to the corpse's throat, I led Madison to the ship. Li was waiting at the top of the cargo ramp where we'd left her.

"We're leaving!" I called. At the same time, the ship's engines came online, and its navigation lights started revolving, throwing red and green shapes on the hangar walls.

I pushed Madison towards Li. "Get her strapped in, and strap in yourself."

Then, without waiting for a reply, I forced my aching limbs to haul me up the ladder to the bridge and buckled in, even as the ship rose into the air, thrusters roaring.

The *Ocelot*'s envoy carried Snyder's head, his blue fingers wrapped in the man's hair. Blood dripped. He opened a sample container and dropped the grisly trophy inside.

I didn't have time to ask why. I requested departure clearance from the *Rose* but received only deranged howling in response.

"We can't wait," I said.

"I wasn't going to," the *Ocelot* replied.

The ship's main thrusters fired, filling the bay behind us with glaring fusion exhaust at near-stellar temperatures, and, surrounded by an incandescent cloud of superheated air, we punched out through the hangar's overburdened pressure curtain, into the cool, sharp vacuum of space.

CHAPTER EIGHTEEN

FRUIT ROTTING

ERYN

The *Ocelot* took station a few thousand klicks from the outermost edge of the scattered Continuance fleet. None of the other arks wanted to grant us asylum until they were sure we weren't the source of the infection that had overwhelmed the *Damask Rose*. So, we trundled along beside them and shared everything we'd experienced, including footage recorded by the *Ocelot*'s envoy.

We were all deeply shaken, but Maddie was still just a kid. On the *Ocelot*'s advice, I gave her a strong sedative and settled her into a bunk.

"Tell me when she wakes up."

"Of course."

Sealed in the cargo hold, the ship's envoy was examining Snyder's head, which appeared dormant. In my opinion, it had been stupid and dangerous to bring it aboard, but the *Ocelot* said the fleet needed a sample of what we were up against in order to formulate some sort of defence—and anyway, who was I to talk after letting Li back on board after her first exposure to the contagion? However, in deference to my concerns, when he was finished, he placed the container holding the head outside the hull, tethered to the ship but surrounded by vacuum.

While the Council of Ships chewed over the results of this brief autopsy, I swallowed some painkillers, dumped my clothes in the recycler, and took a shower. Hot water was always in plentiful supply, thanks to the ship's fusion reactor, and so I stayed in there for a long time, with my forehead resting against the wall and the revivifying stream cascading down over my head and shoulders. When I finally emerged, I felt much better. The tablets had drained the ache from my arms and legs, although they still felt weak and tired.

I patched up the worst of my cuts and grazes, lay down on my bunk, and slept for four hours.

When I woke, dry-mouthed and temporally disoriented, I donned a freshly printed set of fatigues and wandered out into the crew lounge in search of caffeine and food.

"Hey!" the cat said from the top of one of the storage lockers. "You look like shit."

"Good to see you, too."

"No, I mean it." The animal stretched his front paws and arched his back. "You look like you've used up at least six of your nine lives."

I glanced at my reflection in the little mirror above the sink and had to admit he had a point. I had several scratches on my face and red patches that indicated bruises in the process of coalescing. My hands were raw and scraped from clawing my way through the ducts, and I moved with stiffness and caution, trying not to aggravate my other aches and pains.

"It's been a rough week."

"You can say that again. I'm seriously tempted to search for a much quieter ship. No offence."

"Little ingrate."

"I'm a cat." Sam flicked an ear. "I may be fond of you, but there are limits."

I ordered a cup of coffee and a cheese toastie from the printer and took them over to the table. "Have you seen Madison?"

"She's still sedated, and Chen's down in the cargo hold."

I inhaled steam from my cup. "What's she doing down there?"

"Expending *far* too much energy." The cat rolled on his side and let his chin hang over the edge of the locker. "She found an old pair of boxing gloves at the back of the cupboard, and now she's sat on a stool, smacking hell out of a bag of sand."

"Why?"

"Ask her yourself." The cat's ears twitched. "She's on her way up."

Sure enough, Li appeared a moment later, still leaning on her crutch. Her plastered foot clomped on the deck. In her free hand, she carried a pair of scuffed and patched gloves. She'd tied back her purple hair, and had a towel slung round her neck. "Ah," she said, "sleeping beauty has arisen!"

She got herself a bottle of water and flopped down in the chair next to mine. "How are you feeling?" she asked.

"Like I got run over by a cargo loader."

"Well, I think you look great, considering what you've been through."

"Thanks." I could smell her sweat. It wasn't unpleasant. "How's the *Damask Rose*?"

Li frowned. "Still holding out, although reliable information seems hard to come by. There are pockets of fighting all over the ark."

My stomach felt hollow. That was my *home*. "Did anybody else get out?"

"A few hundred small ships. Some freighters, a few Vanguard scouts. A couple of dozen shuttles and pleasure craft. They're all being kept in quarantine, same as us."

"That doesn't sound like a lot."

Li shook her head sadly. "Maybe a couple of thousand people."

"Out of fifteen million."

"I know..." Her lips pressed together and for a second, I thought she was going to cry—and if she did, I would probably join her.

I said, "Is that why you were down in the hold?"

She examined her knuckles, which were reddened and visibly swollen. "I had to do something. If I'd kept listening to the news reports, I'd have lost my mind."

"How's the ankle?"

"Sore as fuck."

I made a sympathetic face and sipped my coffee. The human scale of the disaster had yet to fully sink in. I'd seen the horror first-hand, but it was hard to picture that much terror and carnage magnified a fifteen million times. The sheer immensity of the numbers involved made the whole thing seem a bit unreal and abstract.

Or perhaps I was still half-asleep.

I took another sip.

"Ship?" I said.

"I'll be right down," he answered.

I waited for the envoy to clamber down from the bridge and settle his ample posterior on one of the other free seats. He wore a clean suit and tie. He clasped his hands on the tabletop and said, "How can I help?"

"I want to know if there's any sign of infection on this ship."

"None whatsoever."

"You're sure?"

"I used those new beefed-up scanners and turned them inwards. There isn't a speck of dust on this ship that I don't have catalogued."

The tension inside seemed to unclench and I let out a breath. "Well, that's something."

The envoy held up a finger. "However, while the scan showed no evidence of current infection, it did indicate the outer hull had been infected in the past. Specifically, after our encounter on C-623."

"Something infested the hull?"

He interlocked his fingers, giving himself the aspect of a serene blue Buddha. "As alarming as that information seems, it's actually rather good news."

"How so?"

"Because it appears the attack we experienced immediately following our departure from that planet was not the result of some mysterious and impossibly powerful force reaching out across light years. Rather, it was due to the efforts of millions of molecule-sized replicators situated on the hull itself."

"The black goo?"

"Precisely. It must have infected the outer hull while we were on the planet, and then activated as we tried to flee. If we hadn't found a way to neutralise it by flying into that singularity, it would have disassembled the entire ship, much as it apparently did with the *Couch Surfer*."

Perched on his storage locker, Sam yawned. "Don't everybody thank me at once, or anything."

I ignored him. "That's really good news."

Li looked puzzled. "It is?"

"It means we're dealing with a physical entity rather than some omnipotent force of nature," I explained. "And so, if we avoid physical contact with it, we should be relatively safe."

The *Ocelot* looked sombre. "Regrettably, it seems the *Rose* won't be so fortunate. Further analysis of the damage to my hull suggests that as well as being able to take apart and reconstruct objects and people, these nanomachines are also adept at converting matter into further copies of themselves, which means they're able to reproduce and spread exponentially. If they keep multiplying at their current rate, they will have consumed the entire ark in a matter of hours."

I turned my gaze to the small tabletop screen that Snyder had used to brief us before we landed on Candidate-623, and which now displayed a view of the infected vessel. Although the tops of its skyscrapers looked untouched, there were already dark, discoloured patches on the skin of the main section and gaps in the hull where parts of the ship had been eaten away. The *Damask Rose* was a fruit rotting from the inside.

"You asked me to tell you when Madison woke," the envoy said.

I swallowed the last of the coffee and we went to see her. Her eyes were red and puffy, and she looked like she hadn't slept.

"Are you okay?"

She glared. She was sitting up in bed. Her arms were tightly crossed, and she hunched over them. "Of course, I'm not fucking okay. I want my mom."

The light glittered in her eyes. The poor kid had lost everything—her friends, her home, all her possessions. I was all she had left, but right at that moment, I think she blamed me for everything.

"I'm sorry," I said.

"Sorry about what?"

"Your mom."

Maddie paled. "She's—?"

"I'm so sorry, Maddie." I tried to reach for her but she pulled back.

The kid swallowed. For a moment, she sat there trying to absorb the news. Then she lay down and pulled the blanket over her head. I heard her breath catch. I made to step closer, but the *Ocelot* put a hand on my arm. "Let me talk to her," he said.

•

Li followed me back to my room.

"Are you all right?" she asked.

I sat heavily on the edge of my bunk. "I don't know what

I am. So much has happened, my emotions haven't had a chance to catch up."

"I know that feeling."

She lowered herself down beside me and took my hand. "The kid will be okay," she said. "At the moment, she's in shock. She just needs some time. The *Ocelot*'s looking after her."

"She hates me."

"Why would she do that?"

"Because it's all my fault."

Li squeezed my hand. With her hair tied back, her eyes their natural colour and her face scrubbed of make-up, she really was quite pretty.

"Nonsense," she said.

"I encouraged Shay to join the Vanguard."

"Shay made her own choices." Her other hand came up to touch my cheek. "None of this is down to you. You've done your best." Her palm was warm against my face. "And you saved my life."

"Fifteen million are dying."

"Not your fault."

"But—"

She leant forward and kissed me.

"But—"

She kissed me again.

"I—"

And again. Her lips were warm and soft. She leant back with a serious look. "I'm going to keep doing that until you stop beating yourself up. This isn't your fault, and it never was."

Gently, I pushed her away. "I know you're right. I just can't help what I'm feeling."

Without letting go of my hand, she lowered her head until it was resting on my shoulder. "Let me tell you a story," she said. "It's about a little girl called Li."

"You?"

"Obviously." She wriggled into a more comfortable position. "Okay, once upon a time, little Li had this friend called Jasmine."

"Jasmine?"

"Yes, now shush. Stop interrupting," she said. "Jasmine was the kind of girl who couldn't handle being told off. So, when kids in her class messed around and the teacher yelled at them, Jasmine would feel as if she was the one being punished. If her friends misbehaved, she felt guilty about it. Although she was only young, she assumed responsibility for her year group and came to blame herself whenever anything went wrong.

"This went on for years, until the bright, studious little girl grew up into a perpetually nervous, guilt-ridden teenager, always worrying that she was going to get into trouble because of the antics of those around her. She couldn't sleep, couldn't eat. She lost so much weight, we all thought she was anorexic. And then one day, right before our final exams, when the pressure got too much..."

"She killed herself?"

"No, she shaved her head and joined a convent, but it made you smile."

I laughed. I couldn't help it.

"That's better," Li said. "Now, let's see if there's some other way I can help you relax..."

She leant in for a kiss, but I pulled away. "I can't, not now. Not with Maddie in such a state."

Li winced. "I was just trying to help."

"The kid needs me."

"I'm sorry." She reached for her crutch. "You should go see if the *Ocelot*'s managed to calm her down."

"Do you think she'll talk to me?"

"There's only one way to find out."

CHAPTER NINETEEN

GREASY AND UNRELIABLE

ERYN

Madison's cabin door was open. I knocked anyway. She was in there on the bunk with the *Ocelot*'s envoy watching over her. Sam the cat was clasped in her arms like a rag doll, and the poor animal didn't look at all comfortable. She had her arm around his middle and his forelegs stuck out one way and his back legs the other. His head rested on her collarbone.

"How are you doing, kid?"

Madison said nothing. Her eyes were concealed behind mirrored aviator shades, her expression sullen.

The cat said, "We've been like this for a while."

When the first Angel of the Benevolence built the arks, it understood how much humans needed the companionship of other animals. Most species were left on the Earth to recover and thrive without us endangering them, but we'd been selectively breeding dogs and cats for thousands of years, until they were no longer strictly part of the natural order. They didn't have an ecological niche. So, the angel gave us dogs and cats for company, and goats, birds and insects to enhance the internal biospheres of the arks. But to make sure we never forgot to treat our fellow creatures with respect, Raijin imbued the cats and dogs with speech, via the collars they all wore, and were now somehow born with.

"Isn't she talking to me?"

The mirrored lenses moved fractionally in my direction, but Madison remained silent. The cat rolled his eyes.

"She's pissed off with you," he said.

I put my hands on my hips. "I can understand that."

"She thinks you should be dead, and her mother should be alive."

I struggled to keep my expression neutral. "I see."

Madison looked away. "Do you?"

"Of course, I do. Don't you think I've had the same thought? Don't you think I'd change places with her like a shot, if I could?"

"You would?"

"Of course, I would. It's kind of my fault she was flying that mission. I encouraged her, and so it's my fault she died. You've every right to hate me, and I won't blame you if you do; I pretty much hate myself right now." I took a deep breath. "But as I'm the only family you have left, we're stuck with each other. I don't have the first clue about how to be a parent. I never thought I'd get to have kids. But for your mother's sake, I'm going to do my damnedest to keep you safe, whether you hate me or not. Do you understand?"

Madison opened and shut her mouth a few times. "I guess so."

"Then how about letting that poor animal go, and coming to get something to eat?"

"I'm not hungry."

"Neither am I, but let's pretend, shall we?"

The printers were fairly reliable, but they just couldn't synthesise decent scrambled eggs. They always came out rubbery. So, the best way to get Madison and I a late-night snack was to print out four raw ones and scramble them myself on the hotplate in what passed for my cabin's kitchen, while heating freshly extruded bread in the toaster.

As I stirred the eggs, I wondered what Tomas was doing now. Had he been informed of Shay's death, and would he come looking for Madison? A small, traitorous part of me hoped he would.

Motherhood had never been on my agenda. I'd never felt grown-up enough to contemplate taking responsibility for a helpless new life. I certainly didn't feel ready to take on a teenager. But maybe if Tomas came back, I wouldn't have to do it alone…

No.

No, that wasn't going to happen. I'd accidentally betrayed Shay once while she was alive; I wasn't going to repeat the mistake now she was dead. Tomas was an asshole who'd cheated on his pregnant girlfriend, and then walked out on his little family fifteen years ago. He didn't deserve a second chance with Madison or with me. And even if he did, I didn't deserve a second chance with him. I had no right to even contemplate building any sort of desperate happiness in the ashes of my sister's life.

And besides, I had Li now.

Maybe.

Perhaps.

I buttered the toast and spooned on the eggs. They were done just right: not too runny and not too congealed. All they needed was a light dusting of pepper, and they were perfect. I took them into the main crew area and set them down on the table, only to find that Madison didn't need to eat; she needed to cry. I held her as she wept, and I held her as she raged and swore, and as she punched and kicked. I sat beside her and kept my arm around her shoulders until her anger was spent and her grief settled over her like a heavy blanket. Then, I held her as she slept. I listened to the gentle tides of her breath and vowed to do everything in my power to keep her from harm.

Later, I carried her to her cabin and left her dreaming on her bunk. Then, I went out to sit alone on the *Ocelot*'s bridge. Beyond the artificial diamond windshield, the stars burned like distant beacons, casting forth their light without worrying if anyone was there to see it. If all life in the universe vanished tomorrow—from the smallest single-celled organism to the vast, raging weather systems of the Benevolence—they would just keep on shining, indifferent to their lack of audience.

That was the hardest lesson humanity had been forced to learn: that the universe hadn't been created for our convenience. When Raijin came swirling into orbit, drawn by Frank Tucker's experiments with the substrate, we'd had to face the fact we weren't all that special. The universe didn't belong to us, we were just passing through.

My grandparents had been among the generation confronted by that bleak truth. My father had been a babe in their arms when he was first brought aboard the *Damask Rose*. His family came from a small town in Tennessee, near Nashville. They went from unemployment, discrimination and hardship to a life of relative comfort, with a suite of rooms bigger than their old clapboard house, and food that simply appeared out of the kitchen printer when they ordered it.

My mother's family came from the flooded ruins of London, and she was born two years after the Continuance left Earth. Without the intermixing of the Great Eviction, it's doubtful the daughter of white, affluent middle-class parents from Chelsea would have met and fallen in love with the son of a poor black family from the American South—but meet they did, and Shay and I were the result.

It was a story repeated with variations across the whole fleet. How ironic that it took the intervention of an alien creature to bring so many disparate strands of humanity together. You could argue that I literally owed my existence to the angel, or maybe even Frank Tucker, who drew it to save us in the first place.

I closed my eyes and listened to the familiar sounds of the *Ocelot*. Sometimes, in an ark, it was possible to forget you lived inside a giant machine. In the parks or VR suites, you could almost imagine yourself on the surface of an Earth-like planet. But on a scout ship, you could never forget. There were always the persistent hums of the air-cycling system, the occasional pings or groans from the hull as parts of it warmed or cooled, and the intermittent bleeps of the control consoles as they monitored essential functions. The main engines weren't firing now, but the manoeuvring thrusters blipped occasionally, keeping us stationary relative to the rest of the fleet.

When I opened my eyes, I dimmed the bridge lights to get a better view outside. From here, most of the arks were almost invisible to the naked eye. We were far from the nearest sun, so there was nothing to illuminate them except their red and green navigation lamps and the sepia overspill of light from their residential windows. They were like distant ships on a wine-dark sea, the serenity of their appearance giving no indication of the frantic communications going on between them as they tried to decide how to rescue their stricken sibling. And between those scattered ships stretched the intricate grid of wormholes that formed the flick network—each a tunnel through the substrate, with one end anchored on one ark, and the other on another. Altogether, there were several million of these imperceptible conduits, connecting each of the Thousand Arks to every one of its siblings, as well as to some of the larger ancillary craft. With time and planning, you could theoretically walk the length of the Continuance, setting foot on every ark from *Anatolian*

Sunrise to *Zodiac Dancer*. I had known some people who'd attempted it, but none that had completed the journey. They always got distracted along the way, because that was the thing about the Continuance: its arks contained all the verve and creativity of the entire human race, as well as influences drawn from every known religion and culture. Wherever you went, you found people doing new and interesting things, as well as upholding ancient traditions and preserving the arts and crafts of the past.

My grandparents' generation had considered all of these customs a vital link to their past lives and heritage on Earth; to Madison's age group, they were curiosities from the ancient past—beautiful and intriguing but not alive in the way they had been to those that had known them in their original context.

The hatch opened and the envoy said, "May I join you?"

"Of course."

"I thought you might be lost in contemplation." He sat on the other couch and sighed contentedly as he took the weight off his feet. The sigh was, of course, purely theatrical—just one of a hundred little mannerisms the envoy employed to appear more human in the eyes of his crew.

"I was just admiring the fleet," I admitted.

"I hope I'm not intruding."

I gave him a smile. "I'm always glad of your company."

We sat together in comfortable silence, appreciating the view. After a while, he said, "Can I tell you something in confidence?"

"Anything."

He sighed. "I spend all my life monitoring the stars through my scanners. At any given moment, I can tell you their distance, age, relative positions, temperature and composition—but it's only when I look at them through these organic eyes that I feel I've really *seen* them."

"Really?" I watched the lights of a cargo shuttle crawl between two arks, which the windshield told me were the *Portmeirion* and *Dreamy Lady*, hauling something that was too large or ungainly for the flick terminals.

"I don't know why."

"Does it matter?"

He shrugged his massive shoulders. "Other ships would think me peculiar if they knew. They prefer to put their faith in high-tech instrumentation rather than greasy and unreliable human biology."

"They have no poetry in their souls."

"That, they do not." He smiled sadly. "Also, no souls."

CHAPTER TWENTY

A BOUNDLESS UNIVERSE

FURIOUS OCELOT

I was ashamed. Although I had done well to warn the fleet of potential danger, I had failed in my primary objective, which was to keep my crew alive and return them safely to the Continuance. In five years of active operation, this had never happened before. People had suffered medical emergencies and random accidents while aboard, but Eryn and I had always returned to the fleet with a full complement.

Poor Eryn. She had been through so much, and still had so much left to process. Yet, without her, I'd be indefinitely grounded. Suitable navigators were rare beasts. Only one in a thousand humans could successfully dream-link with a ship, and once that bond was established, neither could work with anyone else, save in the rarest of cases.

Like all the other smaller ships of the Continuance, I had been manufactured by one of the arks—in my case, the *Damask Rose*—to fulfil a specific role. While my hull plates were being welded and my engines installed, the *Rose* had used a pared-down copy of its own consciousness to create my mind. Having stripped away the idiosyncrasies of its own personality, it imbued me with the curiosity and self-reliance it deemed necessary in a scout ship and used virtual simulations and accelerated learning programs in order to train me to the point where my mind was ready to be integrated with the finished ship. The whole process took around six weeks.

Even though I accrued thousands of subjective hours of simulated flight *in utero*, that first launch represented the defining moment of my life. My true birth. At last, my mind and body were one. I now weighed several hundred tonnes, and yet I could turn and pivot in the vacuum with all the grace of a dancer. I had become a discreet physical being in a boundless universe, and I exulted in my existence.

I think Eryn felt much the same. She had also been working in simulators, training her consciousness to dream-link with mine, and by all reports she had been as impatient and eager to get underway as I.

Those early missions we flew were routine by most standards, but nevertheless thrilling for us. We mapped asteroid belts; transferred personnel and equipment to outposts and monitoring stations in distant solar systems; and ran all sorts of errands in the volume of space surrounding the Continuance as it moved ever onwards. It was only later that the Vanguard entrusted us with genuine exploration, and we used the substrate to travel far ahead of the fleet, breaking new ground and scoping out resources and dangers as we went.

We saw a dying star being pulled into a black hole. Watched icy comets graze the atmospheres of super-Jovian gas giants. Discovered a matching pair of Earth-like planets locked in an orbital dance around a hot, young star, their oceans seething with the potential for life. I watched Eryn's confidence increase in step with mine. Her chaotic mind was particularly suited to navigating the counter-intuitive vagaries of the substrate, and we were able to travel faster and more accurately than anyone else.

And then Shay died.

When Eryn saw the helmet camera footage, something changed in her head. Through our link, I felt part of her harden. Her grief raged inside her, but she kept it confined, refusing to let it overwhelm her for Maddie's sake. Instead, I guess she treated it the same way I treated my fusion reactor: as a dangerous, bottled-up fire she could tap for the energy she needed to keep moving forward.

She would never be entirely the same.

And consequently, neither would I.

CHAPTER TWENTY-ONE

SKULL DAMAGE

VIC SHEPPARD

Genet wrinkled his nose. "Jesus, that stinks."

I looked up from the corpse and glared at him. "What the fuck do you expect? They always shit themselves."

We were in a residential apartment on the thirty-seventh deck of the *Tchaikovsky*, one of the forwardmost arks in the Continuance fleet, having been called to investigate an apparent homicide. Genet was wearing his cream-coloured suit with white leather Cuban heels and a selection of gold rings that made him look like a pimp.

"Any idea how he died?"

I stood up and wiped my hands. In contrast, I wore a plain business suit with my police ID clipped to the jacket pocket. "It looks like blunt force trauma to the head," I said. "My guess is the assailant hit him with something heavy, and then left him here, on the floor. Cranial bleeding would have done the rest. If the neighbour hadn't come around to invite him for dinner, he might have lain here for days before anyone found him."

Genet looked unimpressed. "What do you suppose the time of death was?"

"That's for the coroner to determine." I pursed my lips.

"But judging from skin temperature and lividity, my guess is he hasn't been dead very long. An hour or so, at the most."

"That recent?"

"At a guess." I frowned. "The only thing that puzzles me is the lack of any wounds on his hands or forearms. He was hit from the front, but there's no sign he tried to defend himself."

Genet raised an eyebrow. "He just stood there and let someone slug him?"

"Seems that way." I peeled off my gloves and pushed them into my jacket pocket.

"And there's nothing on the security sensors?"

"The sensors in the corridor show only our man here."

"And the neighbour?"

"Yes, but she wasn't in here long enough to whack this guy and hide the murder weapon. She walked in, saw him and screamed. Twenty seconds, maximum."

"So, we've no suspect?"

I looked down at the dead body and popped a tab of nicotine gum into my mouth. "Why the fuck," I asked, chewing irritably, "do we always get the difficult cases?"

Genet grinned. "Because we're the best."

"You know it."

•

We left the scene to the uniformed officers and took an elevator down to the nearest flick point. The dead guy's apartment was on the sixth floor of a tower block, and the corridor overlooked a wide atrium. I eyed some graffiti on the elevator walls. The maintenance bots hadn't cleaned it off yet, which meant it was recent. Perhaps whoever did it had witnessed something unusual that might shed some light on the murder? I made a mental note to get one of the junior detectives to track them down and question them.

I had grown up on board the *Tchaikovsky*, in these same corridors, the only son of parents from New York—both professors in their respective fields—who had always encouraged me to enjoy mysteries and puzzles. They'd been hoping I might become a physicist or astronomer and had been mildly perturbed and a little offended when, at the end of my education, I'd turned my back on a career in science in favour of one in law enforcement.

Yes, we still needed cops. There were no cameras inside private cabins. The arks left the formulation and enforcement of law to the humans aboard each individual ark. Different arks had different laws and restrictions, and it was up to humanity to police itself. The arks weren't here to make us behave; they were only interested in keeping us safe as a species—and keeping the rest of the universe safe from *us*.

The flick point was a two-metre silver sphere hanging a few millimetres above the goat-cropped grass in the centre of the atrium. I marched into it and reappeared an instant later from an identical sphere eight decks up and fourteen kilometres sternward, directly outside the front entrance of the Serious Crimes Division. Genet came through an instant later. Neither of us had broken stride.

He might dress like a peacock, but Genet and I made a good team. We'd been working together for a couple of years now, and I reckoned I understood him better than I ever understood either of my ex-wives. We gave each other a hard time. That was just our thing. But he was the closest thing I had to a best friend, maybe even a brother.

Not that I'd ever admit that to him, of course.

Once we were back in our office, I fetched a coffee, loosened my tie, and went through the security footage again. Genet jotted down the times of the main events. But as before, the only person who came or went from the apartment was the victim.

"09:30 hours," Genet said, making a note, "our victim leaves for his shift in the hydroponic farm."

I sped the recording forward. "17:30 hours, he returns home." I pressed the forward button again. "And then at 18:43 hours, he leaves the apartment again."

"Shit." Genet put down his stylus. "The next person we see is the neighbour, and she arrives at 19:00."

"Interesting," I said.

"What, that we have literally no suspects?"

"No." I popped a fresh tablet of gum and rewound the recording again. "I mean it's interesting we have footage of our man leaving the apartment a quarter of an hour before the neighbour finds his dead body, but none of him returning in time to be murdered."

"Holy shit!" Genet sat forward, suddenly alert. The diamond stud in his left ear caught the light. "Why didn't I notice that? Could the recording have been tampered with?"

"No, this came straight from the *Tchaikovsky*. It's the real deal."

"Then, what the fuck is going on?"

"I don't know." I leant close to the screen. "But he's carrying a heavy wrench consistent with the skull damage we found on his body. It could be the murder weapon."

"So, he leaves the apartment with the murder weapon at 18:43, gets hit over the head with it, and somehow magically teleports back to his room in order to be discovered by his neighbour at 19:00?"

"That's about the size of it."

Genet rubbed his chin. He hadn't shaved for several days, and the bristles were dark and wiry. "So," he said, "what are we looking at?"

"I don't know." I spat the gum into a used coffee cup. It had lost its flavour. "The only way he could have got back without being spotted would be if he used some kind of illegal flick technology."

"But if that happened, the ship would have detected the space-time disturbance."

"I know."

"Could that be his twin brother?"

"He didn't have any siblings. And anyway, it's never twins."

"Then, I guess we're left with two possibilities," Genet said unhappily. "Either we're dealing with a murderer and victim who can magically transport themselves into an apartment without registering on the cameras, or this footage has been deliberately edited."

I rubbed my forehead. "If it's edited, the ship would have to have done it. And that makes no sense. Why the fuck would the ship cover up a murder?"

An alert icon appeared on my screen. I opened the note and read its contents.

"Ah, hell."

"What is it?"

"Seems we've got another one."

CHAPTER TWENTY-TWO

MARILYN FUCKING MONROE

ERYN

Although we remained in quarantine, the *Ocelot* and I were invited to virtually attend a session of the Council of Ships. I settled down in the navigator's couch and let the dream-link implant connect to the ArkNet via the *Ocelot*'s main processors. One moment, I was gazing at the stars; the next, I appeared to be seated in a circular amphitheatre ringed with stepped rows of stone seats. The *Ocelot* and I were in the lowest row, closest to the Three Elders, who occupied a podium at the exact centre of the room.

The Elders had been chosen by the assembly for their sagacity and experience. If the Council failed to come to a decision on a matter of importance, the Elders would have the final say—often unanimously, but sometimes with a split of two-to-one.

I recognised them from the newsfeeds. The Elder closest to us was Victoria Quinn, who had been present when Frank Tucker conducted his famous experiment. She was over a century old now, but still healthy and alert. Beside her sat the thin, grey-bearded figure of Akin Adebayo. When he had been a child, his parents had been killed in a brutal genocide sparked by water scarcity, but he had spent the past seventy-five years working as a tireless champion of forgiveness and unity. And to his right, Tamara Kovacs occupied the final chair on the podium—the one that had once been taken by Frank Tucker himself. Her ancestors hailed from somewhere in Eastern Europe, but she had been conceived a couple of years after the Great Eviction—the only Elder to have been born as a citizen of the Continuance rather than Earth.

The rest of the seats in the amphitheatre were occupied by the blue-skinned envoys of each ark, and elected human representatives drawn from their populations. Hanging in the air above the Elders, a large brass clock counted the time elapsed since the fleet's departure from Earth, with hands to represent not only hours, minutes and seconds, but also days, weeks, months, years and centuries. So far, the total stood at seventy-five years, eight months, two weeks, four days, nine hours, forty-six minutes and twenty-eight seconds. Its slow, stately ticking had become the basis for our common calendar, replacing the confusing and antiquated calendars of our home world with a year divided into twelve months, and each month consisting of thirty days. As we no longer had to take account of the Earth's rotation, this system was a lot simpler, and saved all that tedious mucking around with leap years to make it work.

Tamara Kovacs had been born in Year 3, and I had popped into the world in Year 40, with Shay following a year later, in 41.

Looking around at the human representatives in the amphitheatre, I could see printed outfits assembled from a whole range of influences. Saris with faux leather jackets and hiking shoes; blazers with t-shirts and kilts; little black dresses with bolero sleeves and snow boots. When the availability of clothes was limited only by your imagination and the capacity of your local printer to recycle garbage into fabric, the results were an endless technicolour parade in which anyone could participate, regardless of age, body type or gender. I preferred to keep things simple—as a solitary scout craft navigator, I rarely made the effort to dress up, preferring the practical fatigues worn by most Vanguard spacers while on assignment. Shay had been the one with a flair for fashion. She'd designed her own outfits, often opting for neon bright colours and wide, frilly skirts. And perhaps that was why Maddie dressed so conservatively: from what I'd observed, teenagers tended to react against their parents' trends and styles.

The envoys in the assembly were as varied as the humans' outfits. The arks and lesser ships represented had each customised their envoy in some way. From where I sat, I could see examples that were lanky and attenuated, elaborately tattooed, fantastically costumed, and stark naked. Some had long hair, others sported dreadlocks, Mohicans, and every conceivable arrangement of facial hair. Some even had feathers. Every vessel had its own signature style, but with a thousand arks and several thousand lesser vessels employing envoys, you'd need to have an ark's memory in order to remember all the subtle differences that distinguished one from another. Luckily for me, this version of virtual reality came with a nametag feature that told me to which ship each envoy belonged. The information hovered in the air above their left shoulder. I glanced at the *Ocelot* and found he was similarly labelled. Name, designation and class. An exploratory vessel of the Vanguard, Scout Class, Commissioned in Year 70.

"What?" he asked, forehead crinkling in a questioning frown.

I shrugged. "Nothing."

Could he see a similar readout above my shoulder? None of the other human delegates seemed to have one, but that didn't mean they weren't there for the amusement of the machines. This was virtual reality, after all. Who knew what stupid skin mods the other representatives were employing?

For all I knew, some of them could be looking at me and seeing a blank, humanoid-shaped space; an animated CV; a talking panda; or maybe even Marilyn fucking Monroe.

Not that I really knew who she was. My father had talked about her a lot, but I'd never really seen the appeal of the old two-dimensional entertainments the first generation had brought with them from Earth. Their old idols had little to say to someone raised in the confines of a colossal, self-aware machine.

At the invitation of Adebayo, the *Ocelot* got up and recounted the events that had transpired since our landing on Candidate-623. His report was dry, factual and concise. When he had finished speaking, the amphitheatre filled with a fearful buzz. It was clear to all that the Continuance faced a dire and unprecedented hazard.

Adebayo asked, "Do we have any idea what this entity's objective is?"

"Insufficient data," the *Ocelot* replied. "But after analysing its behaviour so far, I can only assume it means to assimilate every human with whom it comes into contact."

Victoria Quinn looked thoughtful. "Could this be a guard dog?" she said, her voice cracking under the weight of her advanced years. "These attacks happened when we trespassed on the surface of its planet. If we reverse course and leave, might it be satisfied? If we stay away from its territory, perhaps it will leave the rest of us alone?"

The *Ocelot* clenched his jaw. "Again, we have insufficient data."

Muttering erupted in the chamber. Adebayo called for silence. He asked, "As the ship with the most experience of this phenomena, what are your recommendations?"

The *Ocelot* glanced at me. He was aware of my opinion on the subject, which involved the use of as many nuclear missiles as we could possibly requisition. I thought we should bomb the surface of that rainy shithole into a lake of glass and walk away. As far as I was concerned, it was the only way to be sure.

"I suggest giving C 623 a wide berth," he said. "Change the trajectory of the fleet and detour around the danger at a safe distance."

"And the *Damask Rose*?"

"The infection appears fast-moving and virulent. Any humans still on board must now be considered lost."

Chaos erupted. People yelled at each other. Fists shook. No one wanted to face the scale of the loss we'd endured.

Victoria Quinn banged her gavel for silence. When the hubbub finally subsided, she asked, "And the ark itself?"

"The entity was able to take control of the *Couch Surfer* and restructure it as a vector through which to infect the *Rose*. It also attempted to assimilate me. We have to assume it capable of doing the same to an ark."

Adebayo shook his head sorrowfully. Victoria's shoulders slumped. Kovacs looked pale, but her expression was cold and granite-like.

She said, "Do you think the *Damask Rose* presents a clear and present danger to the rest of the Continuance?"

"I do not know."

"But if you had to guess?"

The *Ocelot* glanced down at me. I nodded.

"Yes," he said. "Yes, I think it does."

"So, we should consider destroying it?"

All noise ceased. In the appalled silence, it seemed as if every being in the amphitheatre held their breath at once.

Then Adebayo spoke. "I'm afraid we can't do that," he said, consulting his handset. "The *Rose* just jumped into the substrate. It's gone."

•

While the Council digested this latest revelation, I retreated from the virtual world and lay on my couch staring at the metal ceiling.

After a few minutes, the ship said, "I have an incoming message. There's someone who'd like to speak to you."

"Who is it?"

"A detective by the name of Vic Sheppard."

The name was unfamiliar. "What does he want?"

"He says it's about your sister."

•

Having reluctantly satisfied themselves that we weren't infected, the arks granted the *Ocelot* permission to dock with the *Tchaikovsky*. Li stayed in the crew lounge to rest her ankle, and I told Maddie to stay with her, promising to return soon. Then the *Ocelot* and I descended the cargo ramp, to find Sheppard and his partner waiting for us in the hangar.

"Eryn King?" He came over and shook my hand. He looked to be somewhere in his forties but may have been older. He had receding silver hair, and a rumpled business suit. "This jackass is my partner, Jean-Paul Genet."

Genet was younger, maybe in his twenties. He wore a white linen suit with a pink shirt. "Bonjour," he said.

His accent sounded more affected than authentic. I said hello, and then spoke to Sheppard. "The ark said you wanted to talk about my sister."

"You're damn right I do." Sheppard's stance was formal. This wasn't a social call. "Your sister died on an expedition, am I right?"

"It's a matter of public record."

"I saw the footage you showed the Council." Sheppard made a face. "A nasty way to go."

I wanted to slap him. Instead, I said, "There aren't many good ones."

"True." He unrolled a handheld screen and called up a picture. "So," he said, "given the fact your sister's incontrovertibly deceased, do you have any idea why we have this security footage of her using a flick terminal earlier this morning?" He turned the screen to face me. The resolution was pin sharp. There could be no mistaking the figure in the frame.

My heart seemed to stutter in my chest "When was this taken?"

"Two hours ago."

"That's impossible."

"And yet, here's the proof."

I looked away. "The infection's spreading."

"What infection?"

I forwarded a recording of the Council meeting into his digital space. After reviewing it for a few moments, he said, "Ah."

"She has to be found," the *Ocelot* put in.

Sheppard made a face.

"That may be easier said than done," Genet said. "Because once she arrived here, she disappeared."

"She vanished?"

"No, the *Tchaikovsky* simply stopped being able to track her. It's almost as if she knew she was under surveillance and jammed the ark's sensors. All we got was a ripple in the air as she left the flick terminal. Then we lost her in the crowd."

I looked at the *Ocelot*. "What the fuck?"

He looked grim. "We should bring this to the attention of the Council immediately."

•

Half an hour later, Sheppard and I stood on the central podium while he presented the assembly with the same evidence that he'd shown me, throwing the pictures up on a larger screen and comparing the new photographs of Shay with older ones from my family's archives.

"There's no doubt," I said. "This is my sister—or at least, a very close facsimile."

Akin Adebayo regarded me from beneath unruly, concerned brows. "I concur. And that can only mean the infection was able to escape the *Damask Rose* before the ark was isolated from the flick network."

"That was quick work," Kovacs said. "The link was cut within moments of the *Couch Surfer*'s crash."

"And that implies this entity, whatever it is, knew what it was doing," Quinn agreed. "Not only is it able to spread intelligently, but it is also able to absorb and make use of the knowledge of those it consumes."

Kovacs rose to her feet. "This is troubling news indeed! It seems clear these phantoms mean to infiltrate the fleet, which means my earlier question has now been answered. Until we know more, we must consider their presence in the Continuance as a clear and present danger."

Hundreds of voices spoke at once. Some in assent, others in disbelief or denial. The Elders allowed the babble to continue for a few moments, then Quinn called the assembly to order with a sharp rap of her gavel. "While I agree the presence of these simulacra warrants great concern, the fact remains we have no idea as to the nature of what we face—and without an understanding of these creatures, we cannot with any degree of confidence formulate a suitable response beyond quarantining each and every vessel—a complete, fleet-wide lockdown."

"That's the best we've got?" Kovacs said. "Because to me, this looks like an invasion."

Adebayo tugged at his beard with gnarled fingers and well-bitten nails. "Whatever else this might be, it remains a first contact scenario. To respond with outright hostility at this stage may prove premature and may trigger an escalation whose consequences we have no way to foresee. Before we do *anything* to exacerbate the situation, we need to contain the problem and seek more information."

"And where are we going to get that?"

"We need to speak to Frank Tucker."

Uproar filled the amphitheatre. It took several minutes for Adebayo to quieten the crowd. "As the only surviving person to have communed with the Benevolence, Mr Tucker may have some insight into the nature of what we face," he said. "He should be consulted."

"But no one knows where he is," Kovacs protested.

"Then I suggest we find him. If none of the assembled ships will admit to harbouring him, we will appoint a team to track him down with all due haste."

Adebayo turned his gaze to Sheppard. "You. You're a detective."

"Yes, sir."

"Then you're in charge. Who else do you need?"

"Who've you got?"

The *Ocelot* stepped forward. "I offer the services of myself and my crew."

I glared at him.

"Do you concur, Captain King?" Victoria Quinn asked.

I gave a reluctant nod.

"Fine." Adebayo pointed his finger at Sheppard. "Take her with you and get to it. I want Tucker back here when we reconvene tomorrow morning. In the meantime, there will be no unauthorised travel between arks. I'm initiating a fleet-wide lockdown."

•

The jurisdiction of Sheppard's precinct covered several cubic kilometres towards the *Tchaikovsky*'s stern. The windows of the open-plan bullpen looked out at the lower storeys of the skyscrapers that rose from the ark's skin like porcupine quills. Genet leant against his desk, sipping black coffee, while the *Ocelot*'s blue-skinned envoy and I struggled to get comfortable on utilitarian plastic chairs. Other detectives and police officers bustled around us, intent on their own investigations and unaware of the gravity of the situation we faced. Everything smelled of stale coffee and old socks.

Sheppard activated one of the floor-to-ceiling soft screens fixed to the wall. "All right, folks," he said, bringing up a row of portraits. "These are the last verified pictures of Frank Tucker, plus, some projections of what he might look like now. There's even one there of him with a moustache. But please bear in mind, he's over a hundred years old and has been using anti-ageing treatments for most of the past seventy-five years. If he's been upping the dose, he might actually appear younger than we expect."

"Or he may have had surgery," Genet chipped in. "He might have changed his appearance altogether."

Sheppard nodded, conceding his point but irritated by the interruption. "Now, as to his whereabouts." He tapped the screen and a series of silhouettes appeared: five arks with their names printed underneath in glowing green script. "Although all these ships deny harbouring Tucker, he was known to have close relationships with two of them, and the remainder are each currently playing host to one or more of his grandchildren or great-grandchildren, not to mention a handful of his surviving friends. I'm betting at least one of them knows where he is, or at least how to get in touch with him."

Genet raised a hand. "How do you want to handle it, chief?"

Sheppard pulled at his earlobe. "I think the best plan might be to split our efforts. Eryn, if you and the *Ocelot* want to visit Tucker's granddaughter on the *Adriatic*, Genet and I will interview envoys from the *Mississippi Steamer* and *Krakatoa*."

I stood up. "Suits me." The sooner I found why yet another version of my sister appeared to be haunting the fleet, the happier I'd be. I tapped the still-seated *Ocelot*'s foot with the side of mine. "Come on," I said. "Time to play at being cops."

CHAPTER TWENTY-THREE

INFURIATING CHILD

ERYN

Adebayo had granted us special clearance. For the purposes of our mission, we had freedom to travel in spite of the lockdown. So, we walked to the nearest public flick terminal. The *Tchaikovsky*'s corridors were wide, brightly lit and spacious, with vines and other trailing plants decorating the walls. Some cabin doors were open. A few had been converted into restaurants, hairdressers, gyms or galleries, but the majority were residential. A few of the younger inhabitants watched us as we passed. The *Ocelot* smiled at them.

"Why are young people so endlessly fascinated by blue skin?" he asked me.

"They're probably just wondering which ship you represent."

The corridor opened out into a wide, high-ceilinged compartment. Water bubbled musically from an ornamental fountain, the floors were made of pine and the air smelled of herbs. This was a place of arrival as well as departure, and arks always liked to make a good impression on first-time visitors.

Some of the silver spheres in the centre of the room were reserved for arrivals, the rest for departures. The ones leading to other arks were large and powerful; the ones leading to other destinations aboard the *Tchaikovsky* were a little smaller. And all were currently cordoned off.

Security envoys escorted us through the crowd of angry, bewildered people who suddenly found themselves unable to access the travel network. The *Ocelot* and I chose an outbound terminal and keyed our destination into the bracelets we—like every member of the Continuance—carried. When we stepped into the sphere, the machinery that sustained the portal took that information and used it to shunt us through the tangled network of wormhole connections linking every one of the thousand arks to every other, so that an instant later, we stepped out into the arrivals lounge on the *Adriatic*, where we found chaotic crowd scenes similar to those we'd just left.

Tucker's granddaughter lived four kilometres aft and eighteen decks down, but luckily our clearance gave us access to the internal flick network. Once we'd made our way through the press of frustrated travellers, we were able to flick to a receiver in her neighbourhood.

Internally, the *Adriatic* appeared quite different to the *Tchaikovsky*. Over the decades, it had reshaped its structure according to the wishes of its inhabitants into something with a Mediterranean vibe, kind of like the streets of an old Spanish town in a movie made on Earth before we left. The walls looked and felt like a mixture of whitewashed plaster and terracotta tile. The floors were paved with decorative mosaics; the ceilings strung with coloured lights. As we walked, we passed large internal spaces containing artificial lakes with clean white sand and glittering blue water, small fountains, and olive groves.

One of the ark's androgynous envoys greeted us as we made our way across a dusty chamber housing a scrubby habitat where scrawny black goats grazed on cloned grass, the tin bells on their collars providing a clanking counterpoint to their high-pitched calls, reminding me of the goats in the park on the *Damask Rose*. The envoy that met us was tall and blue-skinned like the *Ocelot*, but wore sandals, a toga spun from gold thread, decorative copper bracelets, and a laurel wreath crown.

"Salutations," they said, thumping a fist to their chest in salute.

The *Ocelot* seemed to find this highly amusing. "Hello."

"I understand you wish to converse with one of my residents on a matter of some urgency?"

"That's right," I said. "Can you tell us where she is?"

The *Adriatic* drew air in through their teeth. "The poor woman's been pestered her whole life by journalists and historians looking to discuss her celebrated ancestor."

"You were at the meeting," the *Ocelot* said. "You know we're here with the full authority of the Council of Ships."

The other envoy steepled their fingers. "I remember you being asked to join an investigation, but I regret I cannot for the life of me recall any formal transference of authority."

One of the goats came to sniff my boot. I said, "Are you saying you're *not* going to let us see her?"

The *Adriatic* bowed their head and spread their hands apologetically. "I have a duty of care to this woman. Promises have been made. However, I do acknowledge these are extraordinary times."

"But if she could just help us—"

"She will not."

"Does she know what happened to the *Damask Rose*?"

"She does not concern herself with current events."

"And you're not concerned?"

The *Adriatic*'s chin dropped to their chest again. "Of course, I am deeply troubled by the matters presented at the Council meeting, but I must balance my disquiet against the needs and stated requests of my citizens. I cannot betray their trust without great reason."

The goat's teeth tugged on my trouser leg, trying to take a bite of material. I nudged it away with my foot. "An existential threat to the Continuance isn't a great reason?"

The envoy smiled. "I think calling it an 'existential threat' may be a trifle alarmist at this stage."

The *Ocelot* narrowed his eyes. "One ark has already been lost. What else would you call it?"

The *Adriatic* looked up. "For the moment, I regard it as a localised phenomenon. Worthy of monitoring, perhaps, but certainly nothing that warrants any interference with my internal sovereignty." They drew themselves straighter, placing that fist back across their chest. "After all, I have a reputation to uphold. People come to me to live a simpler life and be free of the panopticon, to salvage what little privacy they can, and I do my utmost to respect their wishes." They looked down their aquiline blue nose at us. "Even if that means refusing you access to Frank Tucker's granddaughter."

The goat took another bite of my leg, catching some skin through the material. I tried to push its head away, but it was a determined creature. In the end, I had to grab hold of one of its stubby horns in order to hold it at arm's length.

The *Ocelot* said, "Are you seriously going to stop us seeing her?"

The *Adriatic* bowed. "I am afraid so. However, I do have a statement that she prepared as soon as I alerted her to your visit. Ms Tucker conveys her apologies and reiterates she has no knowledge of her grandfather's whereabouts. Further enquiries on the matter will yield no additional information."

The *Adriatic* snapped their fingers at the goat, which gave up its quest to devour my clothing and trotted away to re-join the company of its fellows, little bell clanging as it went.

"You are of course welcome to stay and enjoy my alleyways and beaches," the envoy continued, "but I will have to request you respect my jurisdiction and make no attempt to contact the lady in question."

I exchanged a look with the *Ocelot*. Arks could be stubborn beasts, and we plainly weren't going to get anywhere by extending the argument.

"Fine," I said. "We'll take her at her word. Thank you."

"Will you stay for sangria and tapas? I have some fine tavernas."

My stomach rumbled but I shook my head. "No, thank you. Unlike some people, we've got shit to do."

The *Adriatic* placed their hands together and dipped their chin. "I understand. And I am truly sorry I could not be of more assistance."

"Yeah, so are we." I jerked my head at the *Ocelot*. "Come on, let's flick off."

•

We reconvened with Sheppard and Genet back in the precinct housed on the *Tchaikovsky*. Their enquiries had been as fruitless as ours.

"But there has been a development," Sheppard said, nursing a freshly printed cup of coffee. "The *Tchaikovsky*'s been searching for its elusive visitor."

"Any luck?" I asked.

Sheppard wrinkled his nose. "It depends on your definition of luck. The search didn't turn up any trace of your sister's doppelganger, but it did find two freshly dead corpses. Both murdered, dismembered, and dumped in the algae farm."

"How can you be sure they're connected to our problem?" the *Ocelot* asked.

Genet thrust out a soft screen. "Because we have pictures of the two 'victims' flicking out to other arks after they died—just before the fleet-wide lockdown came into effect."

"More doppelgangers?"

Sheppard blew the steam off his cup. "It would appear so. They managed to get onto other arks before the lockdown. And if those two each kill another two…"

"They could spread exponentially through the population," the *Ocelot* finished. "Another two arks would be lost."

I had a sudden image of plague cells multiplying in a petri dish—only the petri dish was the population of the Continuance, and the plague cells were whatever the hell we'd brought back from that craphole planet. "Holy body-snatching fuckballs."

Sheppard nodded. "You said it, sister."

"What are we going to do?"

He took a sip of coffee, made a face, and placed the cup down on the desk as if the contents had suddenly turned rank. "I've already alerted the Council. They're stepping up security on every ark."

"Is that it?" I felt like screaming at the inertia of a governance unwilling to take swift and decisive action. "There's got to be something else."

"There is." He straightened his tie and brushed lint from his lapels. "We stick to the plan and fulfil our assignment. Frank Tucker's out there somewhere, and we have to find him." He handed me a printed photograph. "This is his third wife. Ex-wife, I should say. She's living on the *Great Barrier Reef*. See if you can get her to talk."

•

I put in a call to Madison. She had dyed her hair green. I told her what we were doing. "Stay on the ship," I said. "It will keep you safe."

"I want to go home."

"The ship is your home now."

She looked at me like I'd just told her the stars were made of cinnamon. "Do you really think you're qualified to be a parent?"

I shrugged. "I don't know. Maybe that's something I'm going to have to learn. But I promise you, as soon as I've taken care of this, I'm going to start trying. In the meantime, Li's there. She can look after you."

"I like her."

"I'm sure she likes you, too."

•

The *Ocelot* and I flicked onto the *Great Barrier Reef*.

The *Great Barrier* was one of the hindmost arks, trailing almost a light year behind the main body of the Continuance. It was also one of the most heavily modified, having adapted its appearance to include a needle-pointed prow, a pair of streamlined outriggers almost as long as its main hull, and a shiny mirror-finish coating that made it look like an old-fashioned trimaran dipped in quicksilver. Its population had originally been drawn from South East Asia, Papua New Guinea, Australia and New Zealand—although in the decades since leaving Earth, the availability of the flick network had led to an inevitable and healthy mixing with the inhabitants of other arks.

The ark's envoy was a blue-skinned hammerhead shark that swam in the air. As far as I could see, it was the only other entity in the arrivals lounge. The population here were either less concerned about travel between arks, or the crowds had already been dispersed by envoys and police officers.

"Welcome aboard," the shark said. "Please, make yourselves at home."

"You know why we're here?" After our experience on the *Adriatic*, I wasn't in the mood to mess around.

"I do. And can I just say, I wish you all sorts of luck in your quest."

"Thank you."

"There's just one thing you fellas need to know before I let you out of this lounge."

"What's that?"

The shark twitched its tail. "Many of our inhabitants are amphibious. Some have even asked me to replace their respiratory systems with gills, so they can be entirely aquatic. And to be honest, not all of them are what you might call easy on the eye. So, I just ask that you respect the beliefs and practices of all those you meet, try not to stare, and brace yourselves for some experiences that might fall outside your personal comfort zones."

The shark showed us the slit filled with daggers that served it as a mouth, and I tried not to wince. I think it was supposed to be a smile, but the glimpse into its gullet reinforced the impression that the fish was simply a tube of muscle designed to ingest things. In the wild, food would have been macerated at one end and dispensed with at the other. A few fins and sensory organs aside, it was like seeing a naked bowel floating around. And those eyes! What the fuck was up with those weirdly spaced eyes? I'd seen holos of alien creatures that looked less stupid.

The *Ocelot* seemed unperturbed by the unlikeliness of the envoy's appearance. He inclined his bald head. "Thank you," he said. "We shall endeavour to remain polite."

"I would appreciate that, fellas," the shark replied. And then, with a flick of its tail, it reversed its alignment and swished off in the direction of the exit.

We followed, and the hammerhead led us through a short maze of corridors, into one of the *Great Barrier Reef*'s main communal spaces, where we found ourselves standing on a beach, waves lapping the sands before us. We were in an internal chamber some five kilometres in length, most of which was filled by an artificial ocean. Small reefs and sandy archipelagos broke the surface, allowing those who could still breathe air somewhere to rest between swims. Colourful pleasure craft cruised the blue waters. Brightly patterned airships droned overhead, and a fierce artificial sun baked the whole scene with a heat that instantly caused sweat to break out beneath my armpits and between my shoulder blades. The *Ocelot* pulled out his handkerchief and made a show of dabbing his face, even though we both knew he was incapable of sweating.

"This way," the shark called, propelling itself through the air with lazy flicks of its tail.

As we tramped across dry sand in the direction of the nearest airship terminal, I unzipped my overalls, pulled the top section down to my hips and tied the arms around my waist. I had a black vest top on underneath that exposed my shoulders and midriff, but it was too hot to worry about modesty. Many of the people lying on the sand were already fully nude, and I tried not to stare at their webbed feet and pale, wrinkled skin.

The airship terminal consisted of a skeletal tower built from girders, with steps winding up the outside and elevators riding up and down the centre. We took an elevator to the boarding deck and stood waiting as one of the cheerful, tubby craft approached.

The hammerhead said, "You'll find Francois Waverley on the rear observation deck."

I thanked it, and it wriggled away into the air above the sea. The *Ocelot* watched it go. "What a strange creature."

I smiled. "You're a six-foot-tall, overweight blue guy in a suit. I don't think you're in any position to judge what's strange."

The envoy raised an eyebrow but before he could formulate a pithy response, the airship's gondola slid into place alongside the boarding platform, a hatchway opened, and we were welcomed aboard by blue-skinned stewards in bright Hawaiian shirts and shorts. Despite our protests, they placed garlands of flowers around our necks and pushed glasses of fruit juice into our hands. Then they showed us the way to the rear observation deck, where a lone, red-headed figure stood at the railings, wrapped in a pale muslin robe.

She turned as we approached.

"Francois?" I asked. She gave a nod of assent. "Do you know why we're here?"

"The ship said you were looking for Frank Tucker."

"Can you help us?"

The woman considered this with a slight frown. "And who exactly *is* Frank Tucker?"

"You were married to him."

"Was I?" Francois's attention wandered back to the view from the deck. "What an odd thought."

The *Ocelot* and I exchanged a glance, and I rolled my eyes.

"Francois," I said as gently as I could. "This is very important. We need to find Frank. He might know something that can help us deal with a threat to the fleet."

She turned and smiled. "And what threat would that be?"

"Something's infiltrating the arks. It's killing people and stealing their appearances. We're hoping Frank had some warning about it when he communed with the Benevolence."

Francois considered this. "I suppose it's possible he did."

"Then can you help us?"

"Absolutely not."

I felt exasperation building. It was like talking to a particularly infuriating child. "And why is that?"

The distracted smile fell away leaving her face expressionless. "Because now I know why you want him, I need to find him first."

Before I could respond, she became a blur of white cloth. Moving almost too quickly for me to follow, she leant sideways and kicked the *Ocelot*'s envoy in the gut, sending him staggering backwards. Then, as her leg came down, her arm came up. Before I had time to react to what was happening, she had a hand around my throat. She whirled me around and pressed me against the railing. I tried to fight back but she was freakishly strong. Her fingertips clawed into the muscles of my neck, constricting my larynx, and I could feel myself being hoisted from the deck and pushed backwards. My feet kicked helplessly against her shins. We were around twenty metres in the air. For a dizzying instant, I teetered on the edge of the long fall to the beach below. Then, with a final shove, the hand released, and I found myself grasping at nothingness. I caught sight of a blue streak moving across the observation deck, then it was gone as I tumbled below the lip of the platform. The wind roared in my ears. Sun and ocean flashed past my eyes. I thought of Madison. And then all I could see was the sand rushing up to kill me.

CHAPTER TWENTY-FOUR

REBUILT OR REPLACED

FURIOUS OCELOT

Eryn fell and I leapt after her, flattening my arms to my sides to make my envoy as aerodynamic as possible. Even so, I was only able to intercept her an instant before she hit the sand. Wrapping my arms around her, I clasped her against my bulky chest as my legs whipped around to absorb the force of our combined impact.

The deceleration splintered my shins and dislocated one of my hips. I felt one of Eryn's ribs snap where her chest pressed against my forearm and heard her shout with pain. Keeping my balance, I set her down gently on the sand and then collapsed beside her.

"Are—are you okay?" she gasped when she could speak again.

"I am fine," I said. "Although I appear to have suffered several stress fractures in my femurs and tibia; my shoulder muscles are torn in several places, and I will probably need to completely replace my ankles, knees and hips. If my bones weren't a lot stronger than the average human's, I suspect the damage would have been far more severe."

"Does it hurt?"

"It did, until I turned off the affected nerves."

Overhead, the airship chugged out to sea with its impellers spinning, pushing it into the wind.

"Can you move?" She had a hand pressed protectively to her side, where the rib had broken, and her breaths came in small, pained sips.

"Alas, I don't think so. However, it seems help is at hand."

The hammerhead shark flashed through the air towards us, trailed by six blue-skinned envoys who sprinted across the sand in its wake.

"You are injured," the shark said, as the envoys knelt around Eryn.

She shook them off. "I'm okay."

"You are not. You have two broken ribs."

I'd suspected as much, but she waved a hand at me. "Take care of him first. He saved my life and got himself pretty badly hurt in the process."

The *Great Barrier Reef* and I regarded each other. "He is in no pain," the shark said. "He is an envoy. He can be rebuilt or replaced. You, on the other hand, are human and your well-being is very much my responsibility."

Acting as one, the envoys crouched and slid their hands beneath her. Then gently they lifted her into the air. Bone scraped against broken bone and she screamed in pain and indignation.

CHAPTER TWENTY-FIVE

GNARLY SURFING CONDITIONS

ERYN

Using a nearby internal flick station, the envoys took me to a medical facility elsewhere on the *Great Barrier Reef*. Once my various cuts and bruises had been attended to, and my damaged ribs reset and injected with regrowth accelerator, they left me alone in a cool, airy hospital room that looked out over another one of the ark's internal seas.

I lay there on the bed watching the curtains stir in the breeze from the open window. Events had taken on a bewildering momentum, and due to a combination of shock and strong painkillers, I couldn't help but feel my brain lagging a few paces behind. It was hard to believe only a couple of days had passed since the *Ocelot* and I had arrived back in the fleet following our expedition to Candidate-623. Now we were caught in some sort of invasion—which may or may not have been my fault—and Frank Tucker's ex-wife had just tried to kill me!

"*Reef*," I said. "Did you apprehend Francois Waverley?"

"I tried," the ceiling answered. "But she managed to evade my surveillance. As soon as she left the blimp's observation deck, I became unable to track her."

"I was afraid of that."

"There's worse news."

I sighed. "There usually is."

"I sent a security team to her apartment."

"And you found her dead body?"

"That's right." The *Reef* sounded surprised. "How did you know?"

"Let's just say it fits a pattern. If he hasn't already, ask the *Ocelot* to share what we've discovered about the simulacra with the Council of Ships."

"Simulacra? What simulacra?"

"I'm too drugged to explain. Just ask him."

"I will. And may I just offer my apologies once again. If I'd had any notion such a thing might happen…"

"It wasn't your fault."

"You're very kind. Now, please, you should rest."

•

I awoke from a dream of falling, to find Sheppard sitting on the chair beside my bed.

"You look like hammered crap," he said. "How do you feel?"

I moved my arm experimentally. "Not too bad. Just a dull ache."

"You were lucky." He raised his eyebrows. "It could have been a fuck of lot more serious."

"If the *Ocelot* hadn't been with me, it would have been."

"I know. I've already spoken to him."

"How is he?"

Sheppard shrugged. "The envoy he used to break your fall suffered considerable structural damage and will need to be retired. Or to use the proper technical term, it's totally fucked. He's preparing a studier, combat-rated replacement."

I thought of the *Ocelot*'s rotund blue frame and sweaty brow and felt a pang of regret. I had become used to that personification of him. Even though the personality behind the new model would be the same, I couldn't help feeling regret for the loss of that familiar countenance—and that regret inevitably led to thoughts of Shay and the horrors I'd witnessed.

"Are you okay?" Sheppard asked.

"I don't know." I elbowed myself up into a sitting position, only wincing once as I did so. "But all this. The deaths and the lookalikes. It just isn't the way I thought the world worked."

Sheppard nodded. "You ain't kidding. I'm just a cop. I didn't sign on for any of this crap."

"Why did you sign up?"

He shrugged. "I don't know. I thought I could help people. I guess it seemed a good idea at the time."

"But now?"

"It's not what I thought it would be. My grandfather was a cop in New York, before the evacuation. He got involved in all sorts. Once, he even tracked a serial killer. But nowadays, we mostly work minor-league stuff. The arks leave us to enforce our own laws, but even so, it's very hard to get away with murder on an ark. And even if you manage to kill someone without being seen by the internal security systems, where can you hide the body? You can't just chuck it out the airlock without setting off all the alarms. Usually, most murders get wrapped up in a couple of hours. Just fights between neighbours that get out of hand. Forget about it. And missing persons cases? Don't even get me started. If someone gets reported as missing, we can usually locate them within a few minutes." He rubbed his forehead. "There's no challenge to this kind of work."

"You have a challenge now."

"Yeah, I guess I do."

A seabird cried outside the window. The curtains flapped. I said, "Whatever these simulacra are, they're also looking for Tucker."

"They are?"

"They are now. Francois didn't seem to know who Frank was until I mentioned why we wanted to see him. It was only then she became violent."

Sheppard frowned. "That doesn't sound good. We just have to make sure we find him first. Can you walk?"

I flexed my toes. "I think so."

"Good." He pushed himself up out of the chair and smoothed down the front of his shirt. "Because all our leads have been duds, so we need you to help us figure out our next move."

We flicked back to the *Tchaikovsky*, and then took an internal flick down to the docking bays and boarded the *Ocelot*.

Sam was washing himself at the top of the cargo ramp. He looked up as we approached. "I'm hungry," he said.

I gave him a look. "I just got out of hospital and that's all you've got to say to me?"

He tipped his head on one side. "What else were you expecting? Congratulations on not being dead? I'm starving here."

I eyed his belly, which resembled a furry cushion. "Something tells me you'll survive."

I found Maddie and Li waiting in the crew lounge. Maddie gave me a tentative hug, and then backed away. Li smiled. "Good to see you," she said.

"How are you doing?" I asked.

Her smile broadened. "I need to introduce you to someone."

The hatch that led from the bridge opened, and a new, blue-skinned envoy stepped through. Facially, he resembled a thinner version of the *Ocelot*'s envoy I had known and loved, but that was where the similarities ended.

"What do you think?" he asked.

Where the previous models had tended towards a fuller figure, this new iteration presented as taller and more muscular.

Instead of a blue, well-tailored suit, he wore charcoal grey combat fatigues.

"It's… different."

The envoy looked down at his body and smiled. "I've upgraded a few things, but it's still me inside."

"I like it."

"Okay," Sheppard interjected. "What's our first step?"

I pulled my attention back to the crisis at hand. "If these simulacra are actively trying to stop us finding Tucker, we need a secure base of operations," I told him. So far, I'd been acting in a numb haze, but now my thoughts seemed sharp and crystal clear. "And the *Ocelot*'s the perfect choice. We can install a small code-locked flick terminal and park outside the ark. That way, we can access the main flick network, but no one can come aboard without our knowledge."

The *Ocelot* considered this. "I'll get one installed right away."

"Thank you."

"My pleasure. I'm happy to do anything to keep you safe. I was horrified by what almost happened to you on the *Reef*."

I rubbed my bruised and aching side. "It wasn't much fun."

"I can only imagine. You humans are so frail and vulnerable, and *certain* ships"—the envoy scowled—"have far too cavalier an attitude to your well-being."

"That's not entirely fair. It wasn't the ark's fault."

The *Ocelot* sniffed. "Maybe not. But if the *Great Barrier Reef* paid half as much attention to internal security as it does to creating 'gnarly surfing conditions', such a thing might never have happened."

•

Accompanied by the *Ocelot*'s new envoy, Sheppard and I sat on the bridge while the *Tchaikovsky*'s envoys installed the miniature flick terminal in the cargo hold. When they were finished, I accessed the ship's manual controls and eased the

Ocelot out of the docking bay. We cleared the doors and, as the stars appeared around us, I let out a sigh of relief. Life on a scout ship was something I understood. There were dangers, but they were dangers I could anticipate and control. Holding station a kilometre off the *Tchaikovsky*'s flank, we would be as safe as we were ever going to be.

As Frank Tucker's experiments had drawn the Benevolence to Earth, the aliens had included him among the select number of human beings to whom they granted their knowledge of the cosmos—or at least enough of it to help us avoid the most common pitfalls. Now, Frank was the last living person to have directly communed with Raijin and we were betting our lives that the knowledge imparted to him included something that would be useful against the unseen force that had slaughtered two expeditions and the population of an entire ark.

"I've had enough," I said to the ship. "We've spent all this time reacting when we should have been *acting*."

"What do you suggest?"

"I don't know. But being thrown out of an airship seems to have jarred something loose. I'm feeling crisper and more clear-headed than I have in days. And I'm absolutely fucking furious. Whatever this infection is, it killed my sister and trashed my home—and now it thinks it can take down the entire human race? Not if I have anything to say about it. I want some answers, and I want to protect Madison, and I don't give a shit who I'm going to have to go through in order to do that."

The envoy's face split in a wide grin. "Oh, I have missed you," he said. "Welcome back."

CHAPTER TWENTY-SIX

CAPITALISM FOR BEGINNERS

ERYN

"While the Angels of the Benevolence may seem vast and terrifying to us in our smallness," Frank Tucker's recorded voice said, "possessing as they do the power to shatter moons and engulf entire solar systems, all their actions so far have been motivated by compassion. They saved us, because we were special, but also because we were alive, and the preservation of life is of the utmost importance to them."

I paused the playback. I had reviewed this speech half a dozen times, and there was nothing new here. No hitherto unnoticed clue as to his whereabouts.

Vic Sheppard lay in the co-navigator's couch next to mine, looking rumpled in his suit. "No luck?"

"Nothing yet." I closed the video clip and brought up a window containing all our research on Frank Tucker. There were several dozen files. Somewhere in all this, there had to be *something* we'd overlooked.

To my right, I could see the skyscrapers of the *Tchaikovsky*, their windows glowing with a homely yellow light. Up, down, and to my left lay the other ships of the Continuance, glimmering against the stars. Where in that great tangle of humanity would a man like Tucker choose to hide? I couldn't be the first person to try finding him. Surely someone else had tried searching for him in the years since he went into seclusion. And if so, maybe they'd had more success. Maybe for them, the trail hadn't been so cold.

"Shit."

"What?"

"I've got an idea." I hunted through the files until I came to the report I wanted. It was an ArkNet post from a year ago, recorded by a young gossip blogger named Tessa Scott. I'd previously put the clip aside because it hadn't seemed relevant. I slid the video into Sheppard's workspace. "Look at this."

I watched his face as he absorbed what she was saying. "Interesting. I've heard of this Scott person. You think we need to talk to her?"

"It has to be worth a try."

"She didn't find him."

"But she says she found a couple of solid leads."

"Probably just clickbait."

I'd had the same thought. "But what else have we got to go on?"

"You make a good fucking point." Sheppard opened a screen and tapped in a query, then swore under his breath.

"Problem?"

"Her public profile has her listed on the *North Pacific*."

"What's wrong with that?" Like most schoolkids, I'd tried to memorise the names of all thousand arks, but I had no first-hand experience of life on that particular ship.

Sheppard sucked his teeth. "It's a part of the Dissent, and well out of my jurisdiction."

"Ah."

The Dissent faction opposed the whole idea of the Continuance but found themselves unwillingly along for the ride. They wanted to secede and resume their old lives, but their arks refused to split from the main body of the fleet and, in obeyance with the angel's instructions, also refused to put them down on a habitable planet.

The Dissent wasn't a united front, but more a loose alliance of groups that resented the loss of their holdings, commercial empires, holy sites and ancestral lands. As far as they were concerned, they'd either been robbed, put out of business, or blasphemed against when the Benevolence removed them from Earth. Families that had been rich for generations were now no better off than anyone else. Billionaires were forced to rub shoulders with their former employees. Even though we'd been expelled from the Earth, believers still prayed in its direction. All of them, through greed, entitlement or fear, were trying their damnedest to recreate the religious or fiscal conditions from which their predecessors had benefitted. There were even a couple of arks running full-blown currency-based internal economies, complete with stock markets and corporate competition; although in a closed system where nutrition and clothing were free via the printers everyone had access to, creating scarcity—of designer apparel, one-of-a-kind artworks, and specially prepared food—took a serious amount of creativity, and I had to respect that level of hustle. The parts of the Dissent I had a problem with were those that operated according to faith, prejudice or race. Although disapproved of by the rest of the Continuance, some enclaves still required their members to belong to a particular ethnicity or sexuality or subscribe to a particular belief system. If Tessa were part of one of those prejudiced fringe groups, getting to talk to her might be difficult. Worse, it might mean she believed that bullshit, which would seriously detract from her credibility.

"Can we see her?'

"Sure." Sheppard picked at his teeth with a fingernail. "We can get on board, as long as we pay a toll."

•

The *Ocelot* printed us a suitcase filled with slips of paper. Each slip equated to one hour of a person's life. Eight slips equalled a day's wages. If you multiplied that by six, you got a week's wages, which you could spend to obtain handmade food, clothes or furniture, or gain entrance to one of the exclusive health spas, casinos or night clubs that flourished on the *North Pacific*'s upper decks. The paper itself was intrinsically worthless, but as each one represented an hour of a human life, their symbolic value was huge. After all, the workers who'd earned those slips would never regain the hours they'd sold.

"But how does that work with the food?" I asked. "The printers can give them anything they want."

The *Ocelot* shrugged a muscular blue shoulder. "To them, printed food is for poor people. They place more value on dishes created by human chefs from homegrown ingredients. And if the chef spends an hour creating their meal, they see slips representing an hour or two of their own lives to be a fair payment."

"So, if we're going to get in to see this Tessa woman, we're going to have to pay an hour's worth of our labour to the *North Pacific*?"

"At least."

I shook my head. Fucking capitalism. I'd never got my head around it. As far as I could understand, it was a scam to keep you working all your life for the chance to maybe die in comfortable surroundings at the end. Instead of taking care of its citizens, it made them exchange the days of their lives for the most basic provisions—such as food, water, education and healthcare—that would have been freely available to them on almost any other ark. And it made a virtue of this deprivation, insisting that none of these rewards could possibly be worth anything unless they'd been 'earned' by way of this chronological servitude. Where the people on the *Damask Rose* had worked from a sense of communal duty and service, the residents of the *North Pacific* had an aspirational list of lifestyle improvements to motivate them. Given that, the ark had very little to do. With its populace slaving away to earn items it could have gladly given them for free, it didn't need to spend long hours devising new and worthwhile leisure pursuits for them to try. Instead, it had decided to indulge their peculiar societal arrangement, and now charged an entrance fee for each individual flicking across from elsewhere in the fleet, not to mention import tariffs for products not manufactured on the ark itself.

When the three of us stepped from the silver sphere, we were met by uniformed human guards who kept us separate from the irate would-be travellers who were loudly protesting about being suddenly trapped on their ark. The guards collected our toll money and searched our belongings for contraband. Only then, after politely enduring this piece of theatre, were we granted access to the rest of the ark.

Where parkland and miniature seas had filled the central caverns of the arks we'd so far visited, the landscape that now confronted us had been entirely given over to agriculture. Rectangles of different crops formed a patchwork quilt that stretched into the distance; goats and cows grazed in the fields; tractors ploughed the soil; and teams of people—not envoys, but actual humans—were planting seeds and harvesting fruits and vegetables. As I'd been raised with food printers, these methods of food production struck me as messy and not terribly efficient, but if the inhabitants of this ship saw more value in a carrot that had been grown from a seed rather than assembled from a stored pattern, who was I to argue?

An envoy from the *North Pacific* introduced themselves. They wore a suit that looked as if it had been hand-tailored rather than printed—a conspicuous sign of status in this task-orientated society, I realised.

"Welcome," they said in mellifluous tones. "I assume as you have travel clearance, you are here on official business, rather than just taking the opportunity for some socio-economic slumming?"

"Yes," I said. "We've come to see Tessa Scott."

The envoy leant forward and lowered their voice. "I assume this has to do with your search for Frank Tucker?"

"It does."

"In that case, I will take you to her. But first, Detective Sheppard?"

"Yeah?"

"I have a message for you from Detective Genet. He requests you meet him to discuss a lead. He thinks it might be important."

Sheppard sighed. "Jeez. Can't that boy do anything by himself?"

"I assume your question is rhetorical?"

"Tell him I'll be right there." Sheppard looked at me. "You okay to handle this bit yourself?"

"I'm fine. If anyone tries anything funny, I've got the new, improved *Ocelot* looking after me."

Sheppard smiled. "Okay. See you later, King. Good hunting." And with that, he turned and stomped back to the inter-ship flick chamber, shoe heels clacking loudly on the shiny deck.

I watched him go, then, I looked up at the *Ocelot*. "Are you okay?"

He was regarding the suit worn by the *North Pacific*'s envoy with bemusement. "I'm fine."

"Then, shall we get on with it?"

The *North Pacific*'s envoy moved off through a network of wide, airy corridors and we followed in their wake, passing citizens dressed in overalls, uniforms and business attire. Everyone over the age of eighteen seemed to have a function that determined what they wore, and I might have felt self-conscious in my grubby and nondescript shipboard fatigues had all eyes not been on the muscular blue envoy beside me. Combat models were rare, and they regarded him with a mixture of admiration and curiosity. I could have been wearing a tutu and no one would have noticed.

We passed a number of market stalls offering handmade clothes, pottery and other accessories, and kiosks where cooks were actually preparing food, right there in the middle of the corridor. Their offerings ran the gamut of Earth cuisine. I caught aromas of fried onions, curry spices, roasting garlic, fresh chillis and hot sesame oil, and my stomach responded. If we hadn't been on such a potentially important errand, I could quite happily have spent a couple of hours (and many of the paper slips from my case) browsing the delicacies on offer.

We found Tessa in a bar close to the stern of the ark. Large picture windows looked back in the direction of Earth's sun, which was now simply one small star in a field of almost identical points of light.

"How can I help you?" Her glance wavered uncertainly between me and the imposing figure of the *Ocelot*. She was in her late twenties, with cornrow hair and plenty of ear piercings.

Unlike most of the bars I was used to, this one featured human staff and drinks that came not from printers, but from the bottles and kegs that were lined up behind the counter. Tessa was drinking a rum and coke, so I ordered another for her, and one for myself.

"I'm looking for Frank Tucker."

"I see." She relaxed slightly. "And what makes you think I can help?"

"You wrote a story about searching for him. I thought you might have some idea where he is."

She traced the rim of her glass with a black-painted fingernail. "Can I ask why you're looking for him?"

"We're acting on behalf of the Council of Ships."

"I guess that explains the combat envoy."

"It's very important we find him. Can you tell us anything that might help?"

The woman sat back and regarded us with narrowed eyes. Finally, she seemed to come to a decision. "I'll trade you," she said. "I'll tell you what I know if you'll answer a few questions for me."

I shrugged. "Seems fair enough."

"And pay me for my fucking time."

I clicked open the briefcase of money and she barely managed to keep her poker face intact. "Okay, that would do it."

"Then we have a deal?"

She looked me up and down. Maybe she was trying to gauge how far she could push her luck. "Only if you'll let me tag along with you," she said.

"To what end?" the *Ocelot* asked.

Tessa smiled. "Because whatever's going on here, I smell a story. Possibly a big one."

I couldn't help but mirror her expression, amused by her audacity. She had a way of being pushy that made you feel she was just enthusiastic.

"I don't know if we want to reveal everything to the public yet," I warned her. "There's enough panic as it is."

"Then I definitely want to know what's going on." She leant forward. "And I won't post a word until you tell me I can, I promise."

I swirled my drink around. Ice cubes clinked against glass. "You swear on your honour?"

"Cross my fucking heart."

"Okay, fine." I took a deep breath. "What is it you want to know?"

Tessa pulled out a slate and conjured up a picture. "This is a photograph of a guy named Alyn Rigby."

The man looked perfectly normal to me. Average height, somewhere in his late sixties or early seventies. "What about him?"

"I took this two hours ago. Saw him standing there, large as life."

"So?"

"I wanted to speak to him because he escaped from the *Damask Rose*. I wanted to ask him what was going on over there. All the reports we've been getting have been confused. I wanted to get the real story, but the last reports from the *Rose* have Alyn Rigby listed as one of the technicians who died in the hangar bay when the *Couch Surfer* rammed its way in."

"Ah."

"So, there is a cover-up. I was right! And you know what's really going on, don't you?"

"I do."

"And this is why you're so keen to find Frank Tucker?"

"I'm afraid so." I leant forward. "So, how about telling me where he is?"

Tessa sat back and crossed her arms. Her eyes were the same colour as her rum and coke. The gold rings in her ears caught the light. "I never actually found Frank," she admitted. "But I got close. Very close."

"Why did you give up?"

"I was asked to stop."

"By whom?"

"By Tucker himself. He sent me a fucking message."

"So, he's still alive?"

"He was a year ago. I can't guarantee nothing's happened to him since."

I was beginning to like this woman. I said, "So, where do we start looking?"

Tessa drained her glass and stood. "We start on the *Alexandria*."

CHAPTER TWENTY-SEVEN

SUPERVILLAIN LAIR

ERYN

The *Alexandria* was one of the most heavily armoured of all the arks, and with good reason. Along with its counterparts, the *Bodleian* and the *Louvre*, it carried the Earth's cultural treasures. There were whole decks fitted out as museums and stacked with a bewildering jumble of cultural artefacts, their walls hung with paintings, their halls lined with sculptures and dinosaur skeletons. There was even a huge central chamber dedicated to preserving the architectural richness of the Earth, where you could walk down pathways between cathedrals and temples, monuments and ancient ruins. Whole buildings had been uprooted and placed aboard. From the observation deck of the Empire State building, you could take photographs of the Eiffel Tower, the Acropolis, a large section of the Great Wall of China, and a section of excavated cliff housing the Al-Khazneh from Petra. They had even found space to house the Great Pyramid from Giza, which towered over everything else like a slumbering god.

The flick terminal was housed inside the Grand Central Station building from New York City. We emerged into a foyer heaving with crowds of stranded tourists being restrained and reassured by blue-skinned museum curators, who made a pathway for us to pass through.

"Ping Sheppard," I told the *Ocelot*'s envoy, "and let him know where we are."

"Done."

Tessa led us across the polished floor to a row of internal flick spheres. We passed through and found ourselves on the top of the Eiffel Tower. From here, the view across the various historic structures was impressive, but we didn't have time to appreciate it, as she led us straight into another terminal.

"Just to make sure no one's following us," she said.

This time, we came out in an elegant vestibule. There were oil paintings on the teal-coloured walls, an imposing chandelier, and a thickly stuffed leather couch. The only door had been constructed from polished oak and looked strong enough to withstand anything short of artillery fire.

"Where are we?" I asked.

Tessa grinned. "These are Glen's private quarters."

"Glen?"

"Glen Tucker. Frank's son."

I blinked in surprise. "Glen Tucker? But he's dead. He died years ago."

Tessa's smile became mischievous. "That's what he wants everyone to think. In reality, he's been locked away in here since his father went into seclusion."

"Damn. So, how did you find him?"

Tessa tossed her head. The little camera beads at the ends of her cornrows rattled. "Because I'm a damn good reporter." She lowered her voice. "And besides, we kind of had a thing."

"You and Glen *Tucker*?"

"Me and Glen." She raised her face to the ceiling. "So, Glen, I know you're listening. Are you going to let us in or what?"

The lock clicked and the heavy wooden door creaked open.

"Welcome."

I recognised Glen Tucker's face from photographs. But where he'd once been an immaculately suited playboy with a spreading midriff and floppy fringe, he was now tall, thin and hairless, with skin the colour of porridge. He wore a colourful sarong and thick wooden bangles. He embraced Tessa, bowed to the *Ocelot*, and then held out his hand to me.

"Charmed to meet you, Miss King."

"You know who I am?"

"But of course." He tapped his temple. "My implants and security systems are second to none. By the time you asked where you were, I already knew everything there was to know about you—including the fact that you're here to find my father."

"Will you help us?"

"I would be only too happy to oblige."

I felt my cheeks warming. He was very charming. "Thank you. You don't know how refreshing it is to speak to someone cooperative."

His eyes were a delicate porcelain blue. "My pleasure, but I'm going to have to ask you to respect my privacy and not reveal my presence."

I shrugged. "I don't even know where we are."

He stepped back and revealed the rest of the room with a flourish. The walls were the same reassuring teal as the vestibule, but the floorboards appeared to be real mahogany, and the rugs between the antique pieces of furniture were soft and ample and intricately patterned. However, it was the windows that drew my attention. Beyond them, a white formlessness reflected the light from the room. "We are in a house embedded in ice, in the centre of the *Alexandria*'s main reservoir tank. Kilometres of frozen water mask our heat signature. The only way in or out is through the flick terminal, and only a handful of people know the access code."

I gave the window a nervous glance, wondering at the

immense pressures that must be trying to crush this sanctuary. "Is this a house or a supervillain lair?"

Glen laughed. "It's a retreat."

"And you live here all by yourself?"

"The Continuance houses fifteen billion people in one thousand arks, and those people are provided with food, water and clothing. They live good lives. But there's one thing they can't have. One thing that is so precious only a very select few can enjoy it."

"Privacy?"

He looked pleased. "Yes, exactly." He placed a hand on his sunken chest. "As Frank Tucker's son, I was in a position to have anything I wanted. So, I chose the most exclusive, expensive commodity I possibly could. And now, I enjoy it to its fullest. I savour it. I relish the knowledge that most of humanity considers me dead. I have become an expert in being alone, a connoisseur of solitude."

And a pompous ass, I thought. *A pompous, charming ass.*

He turned to Tessa and kissed her hand. "It has been too long, my dear."

She raised her eyebrows. "Hey, don't blame me, man. You're the one who likes being alone."

Glen bade us all sit while he made some tea. While he was printing a pot and some cups, I made myself comfortable in a padded armchair with high arms and deep cushions. The smooth leather creaked beneath me when I moved. Tessa settled herself onto the couch, and the *Ocelot* sat cross-legged on the wooden floorboards.

Tessa smiled at me. "Not what you were expecting, huh?"

I hadn't known what to expect. But if anyone knew Frank Tucker's whereabouts, it had to be his son.

Glen brought in a silver tray stacked with delicate teacups and a steaming pot. "As you can imagine, I don't entertain often," he said.

"Thank you." I checked the time on my bracelet. "But we're in kind of a hurry."

He poured four cups and handed them around. "There's always time for tea, Miss King. And while we drink, you can tell me everything you know about this threat we're facing."

"Wouldn't it be quicker if we just told Frank?"

Tessa and Glen exchanged a smirk. He tapped the side of his eye. "By telling me, you will be telling Frank. He's monitoring this conversation through my implant." He glanced at the *Ocelot*. "But don't try tracing the signal, big guy. You won't crack the encryption."

"Glen is Frank's answering service," Tessa said. "He uses him to screen calls."

•

With the *Ocelot*'s help, I brought Glen up to speed on everything from Shay's death to the present moment. I told him of my horror at the fate of the rescue team, and our suspicions about the simulacra currently invading the Continuance. By the time I finished, all the tea was gone.

Glen looked at me and said, "Francois is dead?"

"I'm afraid so."

He shook his head sorrowfully. "It seems silly to be so upset over one's former step-mother when so many millions have also died."

Tessa took his hand. "It just shows you're human," she said.

I stayed quiet, letting the poor man absorb his loss before pressing him further. After a few moments, he straightened up and composed himself.

"Whatever this thing is," he said, "it obviously wants more humans to study."

I frowned at his choice of words. "It butchers them."

"Maybe what you see as butchery might be analogous to

vivisection. Maybe it needs to take them apart and then put them back together in order to find out how they work."

Nausea stirred in my throat. "That's not a pleasant thought."

"No," he agreed, his expression sombre. "And now it knows how we're put together its methods have become more subtle. Rather than hitting every ark with a full-on slime bomb the way it did with the *Damask Rose*, it's now able to insert itself into our population by killing individuals and constructing duplicates."

"Can Frank help?"

Glen paused. He looked up and to the side, as if listening to something only he could hear. Then he smiled. "Frank says he'll try, but you'll have to come and see him in person."

"How do we find him? Which ark is he on?"

Glen smiled. "That's the thing," he said. "You'd never be able to find him in the fleet because he's no longer resident *in* the fleet."

"Then, where is he?"

"I can load the coordinates into your flick bracelets. Due to the orbital position of your destination, you won't be able to use them for another twelve hours. And you'll need an inter-ship flick transmitter."

"So, he's close?" the *Ocelot* said. From his tone, I suspected he was thinking of firing up his engines and flying to wherever Tucker was hiding.

Glen shook his head. "Not in the slightest. He's several hundred light years away."

I gaped. "I never knew the flick portals had that kind of range."

"Few people do."

•

We left Glen Tucker's frozen hideaway and returned to the Grand Central Station terminal, where I was surprised to find Jean-Paul Genet waiting for us. His white linen suit looked crumpled, and there was a haunted look in his eye.

"Where's Sheppard?" I asked.

He looked at me as if he didn't quite understand the question. Then he straightened up and said, "Come with me. I will take you to him."

He gestured at the internal flick portal we had just emerged from.

"He's here on the *Alexandria*?"

"Just through there."

I rolled my eyes. "All right, then. Lead on."

We stepped back through and emerged on the edge of the ark's internal space, on the far side of the Great Pyramid from the rest of the historic buildings. The ground here was scrubby and neglected, and there were few people around. On this side, the pyramid's base sat only a few metres from the wall of the chamber, and it was hard to get a good view of the structure, which I guessed meant few tourists came back here. You'd be able to get a much better view from the front.

It was then I realised something was badly wrong.

"Where's the *Ocelot*? Where's Tessa?"

Genet smiled. "I gave them different coordinates."

"Why the hell would you do that?"

"Because of him." Genet pointed to something lying slumped against the base of the pyramid. I hadn't noticed it at first. It had looked like a small bundle of rags against the solid stone immensity of the Ancient Egyptian tomb. Now, with a sudden stab of horror, I recognised it for what it was: a dead body wearing a white linen suit. Genet's dead body.

"Hello, again," said the simulacrum.

"Shit." I backed away. He was between me and the flick terminal. Sandwiched between the pyramid and the chamber wall, there was only one way I could go. But as I began to move, I saw a distant figure come around the corner of the ancient monument. This one moved stiffly but appeared to be an elderly woman. She carried a baseball bat.

"You can't escape," the simulacrum said. "You are surrounded."

I glanced up the pyramid's stepped side. I could climb it, but I doubted I could scale those stones faster than Genet, especially as my ribs still ached. Beneath his linen suit, he appeared in fantastic shape, and who knew what additional capabilities had been incorporated into his redesign. And besides, if he was packing a gun, I'd rather be shot in the face than the ass.

"Okay," I said. "What happens now?"

The skin stretched around his mouth. I think it was an attempt at a smile.

"Now, we welcome you."

"By killing me?"

The figure pulled Genet's police issue snub pistol from his pocket. "Only your body will die. The rest of you will be preserved. Your knowledge and experience will be added to our totality. You will be remembered."

"I think I'd rather be forgotten."

"The decision is not yours."

I glanced back. The old woman was still lurching purposefully in our direction. When I turned back to Genet, I found him holding the pistol at arm's length, aimed at my forehead, and almost went cross-eyed trying to focus on it. The mouth of the barrel looked absurdly small for something so deadly. They tell you your whole life flashes before your eyes, but that didn't happen for me. There was just an instant of stillness. My heart and breath stopped. The entire universe shrank down to that tiny aperture, and I knew I was a second from death. There would be a flash and a punch in the face, and then nothing. I would not close my eyes. I glared at Genet, daring him to pull the trigger. If this was how I was going out, I was going to do it standing upright and staring my killer in the face.

The first shot hit Genet in the left eye. His head jerked back in a fantail of blood and vitreous humour. The second hit him in the side of the neck, gouging out a fist-sized chunk of muscle and bone. He collapsed like a puppet severed from its strings. I dropped to the floor. Two more shots echoed off the ancient stone, and the other simulacrum spun around and fell, right shoulder smashed, and abdomen blown open.

Sheppard stood on the second tier of the pyramid. His suit was mussed and torn. He was missing one shoe and his face was bruised and bloodied. Smoke curled from the barrel of his pistol.

"Sorry I'm late," he said.

•

The *Alexandria* took care of us. Its envoys tended to the wounded and reunited us with Tessa Scott and the *Ocelot*, who had both been disconcerted and more than a little annoyed to have unexpectedly found themselves emerging in the foyer of a health spa at the other end of the ark.

"At least we've learned one thing," Sheppard said as a blue-skinned orderly dabbed disinfectant on his battered face. "Whatever else our enemy is, it's a sneaky bastard."

I tapped my bracelet. "And we finally have Frank Tucker's coordinates. He's expecting our visit."

"Well, thank Buddha for that. Hopefully he'll be able to shed some light on all this chaos."

"If the simulacra don't get him first."

Sheppard's expression hardened. "I can't believe they got Jean-Paul."

"Are you okay?"

He looked down at his hands. "Not really. The kid was a jackass, but he was my jackass."

"What happened?"

Sheppard sighed. "He asked me to meet him in the same place where I found you. As soon as I got there, I clocked the body and knew what was going on. I don't think he—or it—expected me to react so quickly. I elbowed him in the face and took off. There were some shots, but they weren't very accurate."

"You got away?"

"He sent another one of the 'possessed' after me. A husky fella. I led him on a dance around the other side of the pyramid." He glanced down at his messed-up clothes. "I slipped and fell a few times. But eventually, I managed to put a bullet between his eyes. Then I came back, looking for Genet. And that's when I found you."

"Thank the Universe you did."

"No problem." He flicked a salute. "All part of the service."

•

Once safely back on the *Ocelot*, I collapsed onto the bed in my cabin and pulled the covers up over my head, cradling my sore ribs. Two attempts had been made on my life in the past twenty-four hours. I wasn't used to that, and it made me wonder if I'd ever truly trust anyone again. It also made me angry, because my friends had saved me both times. I hadn't been able to get myself out of trouble, and that bothered me. As a scout navigator, I was used to being self-reliant. Counting on others wasn't something that came naturally.

"Ship?"

"Yes, Eryn?"

"Can you print me another gun. A more powerful one?"

"I can, but that doesn't mean any of the arks will permit you to carry it."

"I'm sure we can arrange something with the Council."

"I'm sure we can."

"Ship?"
"Yes, Eryn?"
"I miss Shay."
"I know you do."
"Really?"
"You had your differences, but you were very fond of her."
"I was."
"Goodnight, Eryn."
"Goodnight."

PART TWO

THE BROKEN WORLD

"It would be most satisfactory of all if physics and psyche could be seen as complementary aspects of the same reality."

Wolfgang Pauli

CHAPTER TWENTY-EIGHT

GODLESS SPACE COMMUNISM

ERYN

The following morning, I found Madison and Li playing chess in the crew lounge.

"She's really good," Li said.

Madison lowered her eyes and looked uncomfortable, the way all teenagers do when being complimented by an adult.

"I mean it," Li said. "Did you know how good she is at maths? We've been talking. This kid's bright."

"Her father was a substrate physicist." I felt a stab of the old, familiar pain. "And her mother a navigator. Of course, she's bright."

Tessa joined us. "It's time," she said.

I looked at Li. "Are you sure you want to come?"

She shrugged. "How often does one get the opportunity to meet the saviour of all mankind?"

Tessa stifled a snort.

I helped Madison and Sheppard to buckle in, and then took Tessa and Li up the ladder to the bridge. My ribs hurt and Li struggled a bit with her bandaged ankle, but Tessa gave her a hand and pulled her up. When we were all ready, Tessa entered the coordinates provided by Frank's son.

Stepping from one ark to another was an almost instantaneous transition, but this journey would take three days, which was far too long for unprotected humans to be exposed to the substrate. We couldn't cover it on foot, so the Council of Ships had manufactured a flick terminal with an aperture wide enough to accommodate the *Furious Ocelot*—a hack that would allow the scout ship to travel further and faster than it could have managed unaided.

"How will we get back?" Li asked.

Tessa smiled and said, "Don't worry. Wormholes need a terminal at both ends. The coordinates Glen gave us allow this terminal to dial into an identical one at our destination. Frank wouldn't leave himself without a way to return to the fleet, should the need arise."

She tapped in a final string of numbers and straightened up. "So," she said, "are you two staying up here?"

"Yes."

"That's cosy."

Li looked at the spartan surroundings and frowned. "It is?"

Tessa gave her a sly grin. "The two of you *are* fucking, right?"

I felt my cheeks colour. "That's none of your business."

"Hey." She shrugged. "I'm a reporter. It's my job to know everyone's business and sniff out scandal. Besides, it's going to take three long, boring days to get to where we're going. I'm just thankful somebody on this tub gets to have some fun."

The silver sphere of the expanded flick terminal hung in the vacuum a few hundred metres from the *Ocelot*'s bow. I told Tessa to get below, then strapped myself into the navigator's chair. Li took the other seat.

"How are we doing?" I asked the *Ocelot*.

The envoy had braced himself against the back wall. "To

tell you the truth, I'm a little apprehensive. We've never done anything like this before."

I smiled. "What's there to be nervous about? That disc's almost as wide as the entrance to a maintenance bay. If we take it slowly, we can get through without scraping your paintwork."

"That's not what bothers me."

"Then, what is it?"

"Do you know what will happen if I activate my substrate engines while inside the wormhole?"

"No, I don't."

"Neither does anyone else, but the general consensus is that they'll explode, destroy the ship, and rip a gaping hole in the universe."

I made a face. "We should probably leave them turned off, huh?"

"It seems prudent."

Manoeuvring thrusters fired—a series of loud bangs we heard through the hull—and the ship moved forward towards the silver disc.

Li said, "This *is* going to work, isn't it?"

Surrounded by the lights of the fleet, it seemed we were embedded in a cloud of Chinese fire lanterns, falling towards a shining silver coin. I reached over and squeezed her hand. "Of course, it is."

And then the ship's prow hit the silver surface and slid into it like a hot knife sliding into butter. We were lined up, we were going to pass through without a problem. And now the shiny surface of the wormhole advanced towards us. I saw the front wall of the bridge disappear. The deck between. And then, as I clenched my fists and bared my teeth, the oncoming membrane swallowed Li and I, and we were suddenly elsewhere.

•

As we were utilising a preconstructed wormhole, I had no need to remain at my post as navigator—but leaving the bridge while in the substrate ran contrary to all my training and experience. So, I spent most of the next three days in my couch, watching the roiling chaos unfold before me. I took breaks for meals and sleep. I even napped at my post, which was something I'd never done before. Occasionally, I took breaks to check on Maddie, and sometimes Li would take me down to her cabin, where we'd drink tea and talk about our lives.

As a xenologist, she'd studied what little was known about the Benevolence. Now, she was excited at the chance to meet someone who'd communed with those vast, ancient creatures. On a personal level, she was the youngest daughter of a respectable family based on the ark *Wenchang Dijun*. Her mother was a local council representative. Her brothers and sisters were academics and researchers, and they'd all had typical cabin brat childhoods. Li hadn't actually set foot on a real planet until her first archaeological expedition, which she had joined at the age of twenty-three, and the sense of standing under an open sky had given her vertigo.

"I almost threw up," she said. "We were in a desert and there was just so much *room*. Sand all the way to the horizon in every direction, and nothing but atmosphere overhead."

"I had it easier, I think." My tea had cooled. I pushed the cup aside. "The first planet I touched down on was an airless rock, so we had to wear pressure suits. The sense of openness freaked me out a little, but I was looking at it from inside an air-conditioned helmet. The suit kept the agoraphobia at bay until I'd become used to the idea of where we were."

•

I also spent some time with Tessa. The journalist seemed to be treating our quest as a fine adventure. She filmed every inch of the interior of the *Ocelot*, and spent time interviewing each of the crew.

"If we're successful," she said, "this might be the biggest story since the evacuation of Earth."

I quickly learned not to talk politics with her, though. She was a firm Dissenter and a staunch supporter of succession, arguing that the Dissent should be free to leave the Continuance and build their own society, rather than being pressganged into what she called, 'Godless space communism'.

When kept away from that subject, she could be good company. In the course of her work, she'd met many notable figures in the Continuance fleet, and her gossipy anecdotes trod a fine line between snarky and hilarious. Madison in particular seemed to take a shine to her. She had already been a subscriber to Tessa's content feed, and now followed her around asking questions about video streaming and content production.

"I think we've got another journalist in the making," Tessa said, and I felt a pinprick of jealousy when Maddie smiled in return. Things between the kid and I were still awkward, and it was galling to see her open up to someone else.

Feeling foolish, I went to find Sheppard, but he wasn't in a great mood. He was brooding over the loss of his partner. He sat at the hexagonal table in the cramped crew lounge, nursing a scotch and soda, while spilling his troubles to Sam the cat, who seemed quite content simply to listen and occasionally interject a cutting response.

"I should have been there to have the kid's back," Sheppard said.

Sam scratched behind one ear. "But you weren't."

"I should have been! We should have stuck together. That's what partners are supposed to do. But now he's dead."

Sam stopped scratching and yawned. "So, it goes."

I poured myself a coffee and said, "I know what you're going through."

Sheppard raised an eyebrow. "Oh, really? You're a navigator. How would you know what it's like to lose a partner?"

I felt my cheeks colour. "I lost my sister," I said. "I lost my passengers, and now I've lost my whole fucking ark. So, yes. I think I've got a pretty good idea what I'm talking about."

He blinked in surprise. "Hey, I'm sorry, King."

"And stop calling me King. My name's Eryn."

We glared at each other. On the table, Sam stretched and said, "I wouldn't piss her off if I were you, Sheppard. Not if you knew what happened to the last guy who started a ruckus on this ship."

"What was that?"

"She punched him in the face."

"Really?" Sheppard sat back, reappraising his impression of me. "Is that true?"

My cheeks were burning now. I put down my cup, untouched. "Fuck you, Sam."

And with that, I turned on my heel and went back to the bridge.

"Whoops," I heard the cat say behind me. "I probably shouldn't have mentioned that."

CHAPTER TWENTY-NINE

I AIN'T USED TO TALKING ABOUT THIS KIND OF STUFF

ERYN

Sheppard found me in the cargo hold, taking out my frustrations on the frayed and patched punch bag that hung from a strut in the far corner. It made my ribs hurt, but it was worth it for the release of tension. He watched for a minute, admiring my crude but effective technique. Then, he said, "Are you pretending that's my face?"

"Yours, and a few others."

I jabbed the bag again. A quick one-two. My boxing gloves made a solid *whap-whap* noise as they hit.

"I'm sorry if I pissed you off," he said. "I know I can be a bit of a jerk."

Whap.

I ignored him. Hands in pockets, he moved his weight from one foot to another. "Hey, I'm trying to apologise here."

I gave the bag a final smack, and then stepped back, wiping sweat from my forehead with the back of my arm. "It wasn't you. It was that damn cat."

I used my teeth to pull open the Velcro fastening on my right wrist and shook off the boxing glove. Then I removed the other and kicked them both into the corner of the hold beneath the punch bag. Sheppard handed me the towel I'd left on the workbench, and I wiped my face. "Don't take it personally," I said. "Things are crazy right now."

"You're telling me."

"I'm sorry you lost your friend."

"So am I."

"Do you want to talk about it?"

We climbed back up to the crew lounge and got a couple of coffees. Sam had had enough sense to slope off, so there was no one else around. According to ship time, it was somewhere after midnight.

"I never married," Sheppard said. "I tell people it's because of the job, but we really aren't that busy most of the time, and so I guess in reality, I just never met the right person."

"But with Jean-Paul?"

He lowered his eyes. "This is going to sound really fucking stupid."

"You thought of him as the wife you never had?"

"I wasn't going to put it quite like that, but yeah. I guess I kind of did."

"And then, when you had to shoot his simulacrum?"

"It was like I was shooting him."

"I'm so sorry." I reached over and squeezed his hand. Embarrassed, he pulled away.

"I ain't used to talking about this kind of stuff."

"I know."

"But with everything being so nuts..."

I leant back. "You're not a bad guy, Vic."

"I'm just a cop, you know. All this—" He waved his arm in a gesture that took in not just the ship, but also everything that had happened so far. "Finding people is what I do. But all this is so far above my paygrade, I don't even know what I'm doing here."

"We were both in the wrong place at the wrong time," I told him. "I'm just a navigator on a scout ship. We're all so far out of our depth, here, it's laughable. But we're the ones that have been chosen. We're the ones that are here, and we have a job to do. We have to find Frank Tucker."

He wrapped his hands around his coffee. "I know you're right."

"Damn right, I'm right." I slung the towel around my neck and stood. The coffee was still too hot to drink. "I'm going for a shower. You go and get some rest. We'll be there in a couple of hours."

He nodded.

As I reached the hatchway, he looked up. "Hey," he said.

"Yes?"

"Thank you, Eryn."

We'd both lost people, and we were both hurting. I said, "You're welcome, detective."

CHAPTER THIRTY

MONKEYS IN SELF-DRIVING CARS

ERYN

When it came time to emerge from the wormhole, the *Ocelot*'s envoy and I took our places on the bridge.

"Three seconds," he said.

I took a breath and held it. I had no idea what we might be facing. None of us did, not even Tessa, despite her posture of amused detachment. Which was why we were all dressed in combat fatigues and sturdy boots, and all carried newly printed Vanguard weapons. Having been attacked twice, I didn't want us to find ourselves defenceless if it happened again.

"Two."

The ship jolted. I was thrown sideways in my chair. Metal squealed. And then we were through.

The stars whirled past the windshield. "We're spinning!"

"I'm working on it," the envoy said.

The hull rattled as clusters of manoeuvring thrusters fired. The stars slowed their hectic dance, and we gradually came to rest. I felt giddy and a little nauseated. "What the hell was that?"

The blue-skinned envoy lowered his eyes. "I'm sorry, that was my fault."

"What happened?"

"I clipped the edge of the wormhole as we passed through the exit sphere."

"Any damage?"

"Only to my pride."

"Any idea where we are?"

"I'm scanning the neighbourhood and..." He trailed off, distracted.

"What is it?"

"I'll show you."

The thrusters rattled again, and the ship's nose turned as if questing a scent. As it did so, *something* rotated into view. I frowned at the image, unable to make sense of what my eyes were seeing.

"What the hell is that?" Initially, I thought it might be a broken planet with a small bright light shining at its core—a cracked egg with a candle at its centre—but then my sense of scale kicked in and I felt my skin prickle. That wasn't a planet; it was much, much larger. And the bright light at the centre of the picture was a star, and somehow, it was shining from *inside* the broken globe.

"It's a partially completed Dyson shell," the ship said. "A megastructure intended to envelop a sun and thereby collect one hundred per cent of that star's energy output."

"Like a solar panel?"

"A solar panel that wraps completely around the sun."

"Damn."

From what I could see, the Dyson shell currently enveloped around three quarters of the star, with irregular gaps in the structure, each hundreds or thousands of kilometres across. Unconnected sections of curved wall the size of flattened gas giants hung in these gaps like three-dimensional jigsaw pieces waiting to be connected. It was as if someone had tried to peel an orange in one go but failed and was now trying to reassemble the fragments of empty skin.

Down in the crew lounge, Li and Madison were beside themselves as they hashed through the available evidence, trying to piece together a timeline for the artefact's construction.

"The earliest sections appear to have been comprised of free-floating satellites in adjacent orbits," the *Ocelot* said. "Later, they were joined up and added to."

"Who could build such a thing?"

The envoy smiled. "Based on preliminary scans, I surmise they were eight feet tall, with a small sense cluster at the end of a long, tentacle-like neck, and a wide midsection covered in appendages of various uses, from hand-like structures to claws that functioned as basic tools, such as axes and needles."

I gave the envoy a look. "You can tell all that from a preliminary scan?"

He sighed. "Just once, it would be nice if you had faith in me."

"I always have faith in you. But I can also smell bullshit when I hear it."

"Fine." He crossed his blue arms. "Tucker's ship's been here for thirty years and isn't shy about sharing its findings. I'm simply giving you the edited highlights."

"And this construction in front of us?"

"A colossal undertaking for this species. For any species, in fact."

Parts of the shell were solid; others were comprised of tightly nestled clouds of smaller, mirror-surfaced spheres. One fragment had been painted with continent-wide yellow stripes. It was as if a society had set out to build something and just kept going, adding new segments as their techniques improved and their styles and architectural fashions ebbed and flowed. It was the millennial work of a civilisation approaching the height of its powers.

"But now nobody's home?"

"Apparently not."

The sphere was clearly unfinished. An alien race had set out to enclose their star. In all probability, they had disassembled all the planets and asteroids in their system in order to provide the raw materials they needed. They had stripped their immediate neighbourhood of resources in order to build a gaudy bauble with an inner surface 550 million times the area of a planet like Earth, but they had been distracted before finishing it. Maybe they had finally discovered the substrate and realised they didn't need to be marooned in a single system for the rest of their existence. Perhaps a ship from elsewhere had ploughed into their almost-enclosed lives and given them the knowledge of faster-than-light travel.

"I take it, if you're in contact with Frank's ship, you know where he's parked?"

"I do."

"Then let's go and introduce ourselves."

•

The approach to the sphere was a surreal experience. The closer we got, the less round it appeared, until, by the time we were a few hundred kilometres from the outer skin, it seemed we were hanging over an endless plain that stretched away to infinity in all directions. Moving cautiously, the *Ocelot* manoeuvred through a gap that appeared minuscule compared to the size of the overall structure, but which was in fact a thousand kilometres across. Even so, I held my breath as we passed through, between walls a hundred kilometres thick.

Sam stood with his front paws against the glass and his tail twitching.

Down in the lounge, I could hear the others talking excitedly about what they were seeing. If Li and Tessa ever got the chance to write this up, it would make them superstars in their respective fields. This was the largest archaeological find of all time. The engineering alone appeared magnitudes more complex than anything we could manage. Studying how and why it was built could revolutionise our understanding of physics. And yet, one thought kept nagging at me: *Why had Frank Tucker decided to keep this place a secret?*

We emerged into sunlight, rising above a brightly lit landscape that seemed as flat and expansive as the outside of the sphere had been. It was only when we looked at distant features that lay at extreme range—further from us than the distance from the Earth to its moon—that the curvature started to become noticeable.

Sam growled in his throat. I reached over and scratched him behind the ears. I couldn't stay mad at him for long. If he was expressing agoraphobia, I could sympathise. The scale of it all was breath-taking. Overhead, the landscape curved up and up until it disappeared behind the sun. Gaps in the sphere showed as patches of darkness.

Below us, cities dotted the surface, either half-built or half-ruined, it was difficult to tell. Between them lay mountains and rivers, lakes and huge, flat expanses of soil. Doubtless, some of that space had been intended for agriculture, but now it lay barren. I could see no trace of any living thing. I felt the hairs rise on the back of my neck. "Scan the surface," I told the ship. "Use those fancy new sensors of yours."

"What am I looking for?"

"You'll know if you find it."

The envoy was quiet for a few moments. Then he frowned. "Ah, yes. I see what you mean."

"Show me."

A sub-screen opened on one of the wall monitors, displaying a view of one of the crumbling cities. In the desert outside, hundreds of large cubes had been arranged in ranks.

Cubes made from piles of bones.

CHAPTER THIRTY-ONE

RAIJIN

ERYN

The *Ocelot* flew across the sterile scenery, staying below the surrounding mountains in an attempt to remain as inconspicuous as possible. I watched the hills and fields zip beneath us. The lakes and rivers reflected the sunlight, glinting like molten silver. According to the ship, fish-like creatures swam in their depths and algal mats clogged their shallows, furiously photosynthesising—but their banks were as sterile as had been the soils of Candidate-623. No animal or plant life existed above the waterline. It had all been destroyed.

If a civilisation with the resources and technology to build a Dyson Sphere could be overrun and dismantled by the entity we were fighting, what chance could humanity possibly stand? We hadn't even built the arks on which we lived. We were like monkeys in self-driving cars, being carried happily along with no idea how our vehicles really worked.

Frank had parked his ship on the shore of a lake, on a wide plain between two mountain ranges. It was a scout ship of similar size but older design than the *Furious Ocelot*, and its name was *Dreaming Spire*.

"How long's he been here?" I asked Tessa. We were all gathered around the table in the crew lounge.

"Five years."

"Then I can't help worrying he may have been replaced by a simulacrum."

The *Ocelot*'s envoy held up a hand. "His ship's records suggest no foul play, and no encounters with anything out of the ordinary."

I thought back to the reappearance of the *Couch Surfer*. "Can they be trusted?"

"As far as I can tell, they haven't been interfered with."

I ran a hand back through my hair. "I'm trying to decide whether it's safe to land."

Tessa and Sheppard both shrugged. Madison just looked at me. Li said, "It's your call."

Sam, who'd been quietly standing in the corner, held up a paw and interjected: "If I may, captain?"

"Go ahead."

"I have also been reviewing the *Dreaming Spire*'s records, and I believe you will be quite safe."

Li gave him a look. "I only just outran that thing last time. What makes you so sure this will be any different?"

He turned to face her. "In five years of exploration, Tucker and his colleague have found nothing but ruined cities and piles of bones. Whatever was once here appears now to have left. Maybe aeons ago. Perhaps aboard the ship we found on C-623."

"This is a big world," I reminded him. "Many a hundred times the surface area of Earth. How much of that do you think they've covered in five years? Maybe they simply haven't attracted its attention yet?"

"Perhaps." He conceded my point with a twitch of the ear. "But the same mathematics applies also to us. If they have managed to exist here unmolested for sixty months, the chances of us running into danger must be considered equally remote. We should instead be focused on the opportunity before us."

Tessa sat back in her seat. "And what is that?"

The cat stretched. "The chance to finally converse with someone who has communed with the divine."

•

We set down a hundred metres away from Frank's ship. Two figures were waiting for us, wrapped in thick, waterproof khaki ponchos. Goggles and masks protected their faces from the grit and dust thrown up by the *Ocelot*'s landing. They watched patiently as the engine noise whined away to silence and the cargo ramp hinged down.

Tessa stepped out first. I followed, with Sheppard and the *Ocelot*'s envoy to either side of me.

"Hi, Frank," Tessa said. "I take it your boy told you we were coming?"

One of the figures pulled off his mask. "Tessa," he said. "It's good to finally meet you in person." Frank pushed his goggles up onto the top of his head. He was rocking an unkempt beard and straggly hair, but otherwise looked much the same as I remembered from the footage of his Oxford lab. He had the same gangly appearance and awkward way of moving, as if his bones were too big for his skin.

"And you must be Eryn King?" The Minnesotan drawl was instantly familiar. I held out my hand.

"I'm afraid I must."

"Good to meet you." He turned to the man next to him, who had also removed his goggles and mask. "And this is my good friend and colleague, Haruki Kamisaka."

"Kamisaka? Weren't you famous for once being the world's richest man?"

"A long time ago." Haruki bowed his head. "I know some people cling to the old ways, but I saw that world die. I saw the folly of capitalism—how sooner or later, all the money ends up in the hands of one person. So now, I devote my time to study and contemplation. All I do now, I do for the good of humanity."

"Do you know why we've come?"

Frank spread his hands. "I have a pretty good idea." He glanced apprehensively up the ramp. "Why don't we leave the rest of your crew to enjoy some fresh air while we step inside and talk about it?"

I could see he wasn't used to company, so I agreed. A large inflatable tent had been pitched in the shadow of the *Dreaming Spire*'s fuselage. Inside, a kettle steamed on a portable stove. Frank bade us sit on some folding canvas chairs while he took the kettle off the heat to cool.

"I've been here for five years," he said. "Haruki thinks this gaudy artefact might be a possible new home for humanity, but I disagree. I think we should stay on the arks like the angel told us, and not risk messing up any other worlds."

Haruki frowned. "But this isn't a planet; it's an artificial habitat."

Frank rolled his eyes. "You see what I mean."

"Is that why you haven't told anyone about this place?" Tessa asked.

Frank nodded. "There are factions in the Continuance that resent living on the arks. They would find the elbow room here an irresistible prospect."

"But Haruki's right, this isn't a natural planet," Tessa said, obviously thinking the same thing. "Would the Benevolence really object to us using it?"

Frank smiled awkwardly. "Well, one of them might."

"Why?"

"Because he's already here."

Tessa jerked forward like a wolf catching a scent. "There's an *angel* here?"

"You might have heard of him." Frank pointed through one of the tent's transparent sections. "Look up there, about ten degrees around the curve of the sphere."

I narrowed my eyes. The landscape that far away was hazy and difficult to make out.

"See that red dot?" Frank said.

I peered harder. There was a small ochre patch on the inside of the sphere. If I hadn't been looking for it, I wouldn't have spotted it. "That's it?"

"It's Raijin. It followed us this far from Earth. I think it was keeping an eye on us, but then it got distracted by this place."

"What's it doing?" Tessa asked.

Frank shrugged. "Who knows?" He reached into a packing case and pulled out five stoneware mugs and a packet of green tea. The mugs crashed clumsily together as he placed them on a small camping table.

"But you're visiting it?"

A smile behind the beard. "We talk from time to time."

"What about?"

"Oh, this and that. Cabbages and kings."

Haruki had unobtrusively taken over the tea-making process. He and Frank seemed to have an unspoken ease with one another that suggested they had been together here for a long time. I watched him produce a small, cast-iron teapot and heap the green tea into its infuser. He poured in the slightly cooled water from the kettle and let the whole thing rest while he arranged the mugs.

"That's why we've come to see you," I said to Frank. "We've run into a problem, and we're hoping the Benevolence will be able to help us."

Frank frowned. "The entity that's invading the fleet?"

"So, you were listening through Glen's implant," Tessa said.

Frank nodded.

I gestured through the transparent tent fabric. "You see those piles of bones out there?"

"Yes." Haruki started pouring the tea. "We've been wondering how they were made."

"Well, wonder no more." I reached over and put a hand on his arm, ensuring I had his full attention. "Because whatever did that," I said, "is the same motherfucker that's loose in the Continuance."

•

Frank and Haruki came aboard the *Furious Ocelot* to view the footage from Candidate-623.

"I want to see it," Madison said.

Li held up a hand. "No way."

"Please?"

"You're not ready. It's… No one should have to watch that, especially not a fifteen-year-old."

"I'm nearly sixteen, and I deserve to know how my mother died."

I shook my head. "Trust me, you really don't want to see it."

So, I held her while the others watched Shay's final moments and witnessed our expedition to the surface and Snyder's demise. I had no desire to review the footage again; the images were already carved into my memory. Li looked pensive. She had come close to a fate like Shay's. If I hadn't disobeyed protocol and let her back on board the *Ocelot*, she would have died along with Snyder. I couldn't guess how re-watching her own terror now might be affecting her. Beside her, Tessa looked shaken, but was still tapping at a palm-sized tablet, doubtless taking notes for the story she hoped to publish when this was all over. Finally, they replayed our experiences aboard the *Damask Rose*, which the ship had recorded through its envoy. As Madison had been there for those events, I let her watch. When it was over, everyone remained silent. Frank had his fingers to his lips, and Haruki's head was bowed.

Eventually, the *Ocelot*'s envoy cleared his throat. "The Council of Ships sent us here in the hope you might have learned something about this threat during your communions with the Benevolence."

Frank looked at him with eyes still haunted by the horrors they had just witnessed. "Yes," he said. "Yes, I can see why they'd do that."

"Can you help us?" Li asked.

Frank sucked his moustache. "I… I don't know."

I said, "So, you've no idea what this entity is?"

He shook his head. "I've never seen anything like that."

"But the piles of bones lying around here. Didn't you ever ask the angel what caused them?"

"I did."

"And?"

Frank looked off to the side, avoiding eye contact. "It said I wasn't ready to know."

"Damn." I tipped my head back and stared at the rivets on the ceiling. I realised I had been hoping for an instant, magic solution, but now none seemed forthcoming.

Li said, "Fuck."

But then Madison spoke in a thin, grief-laden voice. "Can't we ask again?"

"What?"

"If Mr Tucker talks to the angel from time to time, maybe we can ask it directly? Maybe we're ready to be told now. You know, now that this thing's actually attacking us?"

I turned to Frank. "Can we?"

He put a hand to his unshaven chin. "It's possible, I guess. But it's not always easy to get a straight answer."

"Anything's better than nothing," I told him. I sought out the small reddish spot in the distance. "How do we go about making contact? Do we send a radio signal?"

Frank had brought his mug with him onto the *Ocelot*. He took a sip of green tea and sighed. "I'm afraid it's a little more complicated than that."

Li put her head in her hands and let out an exasperated sigh. "Do you know what?" she said. "I had a feeling it might be."

•

An hour later, Frank and I set out on foot. For some reason known only to himself, Sam trailed along a few metres to my left. As the only qualified xenologist on the crew, Li had been desperate to come, but the climb would have been too arduous with her weakened ankle. My ribs were still healing, but I knew I had to make this journey. As per Frank's instructions, everyone else stayed back with the ships.

The two of us wore waterproof ponchos. "Trust me," Frank said, "you'll appreciate it when we get there."

"Where?"

"To the angel."

And so, we walked away from the camp, following a well-trodden path in the lifeless soil, towards a flat-topped hill overlooking the bay of an artificial sea. The shallows were clogged with mats of seaweed and algae. The breeze blowing up the side of the hill brought with it the mingled smells of salt and rotting vegetation. Slung over my shoulder, I carried a plastic sack containing Snyder's severed head. The way was steep and rocky, and I slipped on pebbles a couple of times, but we eventually reached the summit without serious incident.

Panting from the unaccustomed effort of the ascent and the weight of Snyder's head, I glared upwards. "The sun hasn't moved. We've been walking for hours, and it's still noon."

"Yeah, freaky, isn't it?" Frank shaded his eyes, but didn't look my way. "The sun can't move. We're on the inside of a sphere. Wherever we stand, it will always be directly overhead."

"So, there's no night?"

"Nope." He gave a shrug. "It caused us some problems in the early days. Insomnia, disorientation, maybe a little psychosis. In the end, we stopped sleeping in the tent and bunked in the ship instead."

From up here, I felt as if I could see forever. There was no horizon. The hills and plains just kept going, growing hazier and hazier with distance, until they disappeared into a bluish blur, behind which rose the sun-drenched arch of even more distant landscape. How could Frank and Haruki have survived so many days beneath such an ego-crushing spectacle? To stand here, on the surface of the sphere, was to feel truly small and insignificant, dwarfed by the ambition and accomplishment of its builders.

I glanced at Frank. He had his hands in his pockets, surveying the view with no apparent discomfort, as relaxed as if out for a stroll in a familiar neighbourhood. After five years, he might just be used to it; or maybe he simply saw it as a giant puzzle. Certainly, nothing about his stance suggested he had an ego to match his reputation as the saviour of humankind. He was just a gangly, awkward guy who tended to avoid eye contact and seemed uncomfortable being around new people.

The summit covered an area roughly the size of a football pitch. It was like a huge tabletop, or maybe an altar.

Hopefully, not a sacrificial one.

Sam sniffed the ground. "So," he said, "what happens now?"

Frank started walking towards the summit's centre, where half a dozen small rocks had been arranged in a rough cairn.

"Well," he said over his shoulder, "first we have to attract its attention."

I glanced at the distant red spot and tried to guess how far away it was. A hundred thousand kilometres? Two hundred thousand? What were we supposed to do, jump up and down and wave our arms?

I followed Frank to the cairn, and Sam trailed dutifully in my wake. I hadn't wanted to bring Snyder's head. The thing creeped me out, but Frank had insisted a sample of the entity's work would be required—and the *Ocelot*'s grisly trophy was the only solid example we had.

I watched Frank pick up a pebble and roll if between his palms. "There's a ritual," he explained.

"We're not going to have to get naked and dance around, are we?"

The scientist laughed uncomfortably. "Only if you really want to."

"Then, how does this work?"

He passed me the stone. "Warm this with your hands. Then breathe on it."

Feeling faintly ridiculous, I did as I was told.

"Now squeeze it hard and think about the substrate," he said. "Remember what it feels like when you're in it. That funny sensation in the pit of your stomach, and the way it looks. All that swirling light…"

I closed my eyes, picturing the view from the *Furious Ocelot*'s bridge. The incandescent buffeting of the plasma. The way the path seemed to open up whenever I searched for it. That peculiar impression of being outside my natural context, free of the space and time that gave me existence.

And far away, something took an interest.

Raijin sensed my thoughts.

"Here it comes," Frank said.

I opened my eyes. The distant rusty smear pinwheeled towards us like a hurricane, moving much faster than anticipated, trailing spiral arms of cloud kilometres in length. It crossed the distance between us in seconds, seeming to swell from a dot to a vast storm system that obscured the entire sky, blocking the light of the sun and throwing us into semi-darkness. Buffeted by the winds it drove before it, I craned my neck upwards. The eye of the hurricane slid to a halt directly over us. The vast, whirling clouds around it disturbed the air, whipping up grit and dust from the ground. Sam had vanished into the clouds. Rain lashed down, somehow precipitated by the motion of the storm or the difference in temperature between the cool air beneath it and the sun-warmed air at its borders. Lightning crackled through the ochre clouds, throwing peculiar shadows. Frank laughed and bared his teeth. His poncho flapped around him. He shouted something, but the roar drowned his voice.

"What?"

He pointed to the plastic sack we'd brought with us. "Open it!"

I could feel the power of the storm in my diaphragm. This was Raijin, the angel who stood in judgement of humanity and decided we were no longer worthy of the Earth; who could have exterminated us but decided instead to show mercy; who shattered a moon and ripped away Saturn's rings in order to create the Thousand Arks, so we could survive being cast into the void. It was a primordial force of nature. Every instinct I had was screaming at me to seek cover or curl into a protective ball. Instead, I opened the bag.

Rain fell into Snyder's lifeless eyes. His nose and ears had partially dissolved into black dust, but now seemed inert. It was as if whatever had been using him as a puppet had assessed the inflicted damage and decided to abandon its doll—cutting his strings and leaving him lifeless.

The clouds began to lower, and the wind increased until it became a howling gale. I had to lean into it to avoid being blown off my feet. Within a couple of seconds, rusty gloom enveloped the entire hillside and visibility went to zero. I couldn't even see Frank. Static electricity sparked through the murk and every hair on my body seemed to stand on end.

It was like being caught in a sandstorm, except none of the grains touched me.

The redness thickened over Snyder's head as Raijin took an interest in our offering. When it cleared, he was gone. The bag was empty.

My skin itched. The particles in the air had begun to explore my exposed face and hands. I tried to hold my breath, to screw my eyes closed, but they forced their way in anyhow. Grit in my eyes and on my tongue. A burning sensation in my throat. I think I screamed, but I couldn't be sure. My mouth was open, but the roar of the storm obliterated all other sounds.

And then I was somewhere else.

My awareness hung suspended and bodiless in an infinite, rose-tinted emptiness. And yet, I felt no fear—only a deep, satisfied calm. I had been absorbed into the immeasurable, ancient spaces of the angel's mind, where my entire being existed as little more than a fleeting thought. Yet, I sensed it meant me no harm.

I saw a vision of the galaxy—a storm of stars not dissimilar to the form of the angel. I saw hot young suns birthed from stellar nurseries; planets coalescing around them; life rising and falling like a tide; and then, billions of years later, their decrepit husks swelling into red giants before explosively shedding their outer layers and collapsing into neutron stars.

Ignite.

Smoulder.

Explode.

History as a firework display.

This was the universe as seen through the eyes of the Benevolence. They moved through a dynamic galaxy that appeared quite different to the static, enduring starscape we experienced. They could actually feel it turning. Each revolution took 250 million years, but that was a negligible percentage of the average angel's lifespan. In comparison, human beings were an ephemeral flicker, barely registering on the cosmic clock. To us, the stars were almost static; to them, an eternal fiery sleet.

Hidden in the embers of that continuous onslaught, the Benevolence had discovered the most precious and unexpected of gifts: a billion mayfly ecosystems, each uniquely beautiful and worthy of preservation and study. And so, they set about cataloguing and observing. Sometimes one of them would sit in the upper atmosphere of a local gas giant for millions of years, pretending to be a storm, as it watched life rise from the ooze to explore its surroundings. Other times, they would drift through interstellar space, collecting and archiving the radio signals of civilisations already long dead. Because, wherever the Benevolence looked, they found dead worlds. Some of those empty worlds were the result of natural processes—volcanism, asteroid impact, nearby supernovae, gradual loss of atmosphere—but others were unmistakably the result of a dominant species destroying its own habitat. When intelligence arose, it tended to ransack its world for resources; and by the time it realised the effect its depredations were having on the climate and biodiversity of its home planet, it was often too late to reverse the damage. And so, the Benevolence abandoned their role of passive observer and began to intervene. Life was too transient and precious; if an angel could see a way of extending the duration of an ecosystem, it felt duty-bound to do so—even if that meant eradicating or displacing the dominant species.

Submerged in Raijin's gigantic thoughts, I experienced its disappointment at the state of the Earth. At first, it had been inclined to allow the humans to wipe themselves out with their nuclear weapons, knowing some form of life would arise anew from the blasted remnants of their civilisation. But then, even as the first missiles were leaving their silos, it had sensed a tremor in the substrate. Against all the odds, humanity had unlocked one of the fundamental underpinnings of the universe, and thereby elevated themselves in its eyes. They might have been a plague upon the Earth, but they had proven themselves worth saving.

Now, as that hurricane-sized intellect turned its attention to Snyder's head, I felt its curiosity at the way the ears seemed to have been caught in the process of disintegration, and the unusual arrangement of elements in the skin's cells. Slowly and methodically, it broke the head down into its constituent atoms, and examined each and every one in turn. Then it disassembled the atoms themselves, taking everything down to the quantum foam at the very base of reality.

When it was done, it turned its attention to me. My body sloughed away like a collapsing sandcastle, leaving my awareness caught like a pearl in Raijin's palm. Normally, I would have been horrified, but in my disembodied state—unencumbered by adrenalin or complex emotion—I felt only a detached sadness. First the entity on C-623, and now the angel. Were humans really so humble and pliant we could be taken to pieces like antique pocket watches?

For what seemed the longest time, Raijin's thoughts crashed around me like colliding thunderheads. Then, when I'd almost completely lost all sense of identity and place, sensation returned. Molecules rushed together. Skin and bone and sinew re-formed. I felt my fingers curl and straighten; my heart started to thump; my calves tightened as they took my weight. The murk lifted and I was back in my body, standing in the exact spot where I'd been when the storm descended. Of Snyder's head, there was no sign. Frank stood beside me with his hands in his pockets and a wry smile on his lips. He raised an eyebrow. "Enjoy that?"

I tried to reply but before I could find the words, Raijin spoke. Its words crashed down like hammer blows, in a voice made of gales and thunder.

THE DEAD HUMAN HAS BEEN INFECTED BY A MOST UNUSUAL LIFE FORM.

My ears rang. I raised my face to the swirling clouds and yelled, "Can you stop it?"

WHY?

"Because it's loose in the Continuance. It's killing people!"

HUMANS DIE ALL THE TIME. IT IS ONE OF THE THINGS YOUR SPECIES IS BEST AT.

"But they don't have to."

YES, THEY DO. IT IS INEVITABLE.

"But not like this!"

The clouds continued to spiral overhead, turning eternal noon to rusty twilight.

THIS NEW LIFE FORM IS UNIQUE AND FASCINATING. IT DESERVES THE OPPORTUNITY TO LIVE. TO BE STUDIED.

"As do we!"

Thunder rolled through the sky, shaking the ground.

YOU HAVE BEEN GIVEN THAT CHANCE.

I felt each syllable in my chest and gut; they were that loud. Dust and grit swirled around us.

"You saved us," I protested. "You could have let us wipe ourselves out, but you didn't."

I ACTED TO PREVENT YOU DESTROYING YOUR WORLD. I SPARED YOU BECAUSE YOUR KNOWLEDGE OF THE SUBSTRATE IMPLIED AN INTELLIGENCE WORTH CONSERVING.

"And now?"

THE LIFE FORM DESERVES THE SAME COURTESY.

"Because it knows about the substrate?"

BECAUSE IT APPEARS TO HAVE BEEN PARTIALLY CONSTRUCTED FROM SUBSTRATE MATERIAL.

"What?" I glanced helplessly at Frank but received only a shrug and a wan smile in return. "You mean it's artificial?"

ITS INITIAL STATE APPEARS TO HAVE BEEN ARTIFICIAL, BUT IT HAS UNDERGONE SIGNIFICANT EVOLUTION.

Frank cleared his throat. "From what we can tell, this life form killed the civilisation that built this Dyson Sphere."

THAT APPEARS TO BE CORRECT.

"And the inhabitants of C-623."

YES.

"So, why aren't you stopping it?" Frank asked. "When we threatened to destroy our own world, you evicted us. Why not do the same here?"

Lightning danced and flickered through the storm. Fat droplets of rain began to fall.

JUST LIKE YOU, THIS CREATURE WILL NOT BE ALLOWED TO DESTROY ANOTHER BIOSPHERE.

"Then come back to the fleet with us," I said.

I CANNOT.

"Why?"

FOR THE MOMENT, MY PLACE IS HERE. Thunder pealed overhead. The rain grew heavier. BUT I WILL ACT TO PREVENT THE CONTAGION SPREADING.

A tendril lowered towards me, like a tiny tornado the thickness of my arm, tapering to invisibility at its tip. I tried not to flinch as it touched the top of my head, wrenching my hair in painful circles. I experienced a moment of vertigo as the world seemed to swim around me. Then the tip withdrew, melting back into the main body of the storm.

THE LIFE FORM HAS EXHIBITED INTELLIGENCE COUPLED WITH CHILDLIKE CURIOSITY. IT NEEDS TO UNDERSTAND.

"Understand what?" Frank asked.

I HAVE PLACED THE INFORMATION IN ERYN'S HEAD. IT WILL BE AVAILABLE AT THE CORRECT TIME.

"What information?" he said. But Raijin ignored him.

YOU MUST RETURN TO CANDIDATE-623. IF YOU ARE SUCCESSFUL, FURTHER LOSS MAY BE AVOIDED.

I wanted to ask more, but a sudden squall sent me staggering. Our interview was over. I had the impression of something vast moving at fantastic speed. Then the skies cleared. And when I looked, Raijin had resumed its earlier position and once again appeared as no more than a tiny ochre smudge located far around the inner surface of the sphere.

Sam was nowhere to be seen. Had he been blown away by the winds? Was he lying crumpled and broken somewhere far across the landscape?

My communicator buzzed.

"Eryn!" The *Furious Ocelot* sounded relieved. "We've been calling you but couldn't get a signal through."

My feet were unsteady, and I was uncomfortably aware of all the muscles in my body and the constant adjustments they needed to make simply to keep me standing upright. I could feel my lungs inflate and deflate, and my heart pump, sending blood fizzing through my arteries.

"What's up?"

"We have company."

I glanced around at the sterile plain extending away to apparent infinity in all directions. "Where?"

"The edge of the system. Another ship."

"One of ours?"

"It's an ark, but it's not responding to our hails."

Unease settled on me. "There's no reason it wouldn't, unless—"

"We think it's the *Damask Rose*."

•

There was no time to search for Sam. Either he was dead, or he wasn't. I grabbed Frank's bony wrist and we descended the rocky path from the tabletop as quickly as we could without breaking our ankles or necks. When we reached camp, both the *Furious Ocelot* and the *Dreaming Spire* had their hatches open and their engines warming. Tessa came running. "We saw the storm," she said. "What happened up there?"

"I'll tell you later," I said. "In the meantime, we're already packed aboard the *Ocelot* like sardines. You and Sheppard go with Haruki in his ship. Frank's coming with me."

Frank started to protest, but I shoved him towards the *Ocelot*.

Tessa looked around with a frown. "Where's Sam?"

"I think the angel took him."

The ship's envoy was waiting for us at the top of the ramp. "Maddie and Li Chen are already strapped in," he said. "The others are boarding the *Dreaming Spire* as we speak."

"Excellent. Have us ready for take-off in one minute."

"Spinning up as we speak."

I hurried up to the bridge, where I strapped into the navigator's couch. "Show me tactical."

The envoy slid into the seat beside mine and pulled up a three-dimensional display of the system. The Dyson Sphere hung before me like a broken skull lit from within. A flashing red icon closing on it from the Oort cloud represented the incoming ark.

"It's between us and the wormhole," the envoy said.

"Are you sure it's an ark?"

"That size, there's nothing else it could be."

"And it's definitely the *Rose*?"

"Anyone else would have answered our calls."

"Shit." How were we supposed to fight something twenty-five kilometres long with the mass of a small moon? "Suggestions?"

The envoy pursed his blue lips. "Only one."

"What?"

"Split up and run."

I couldn't help making a face. "But how does that help us? If we can't get back to the portal, we can't get back to the fleet. We'll be stuck out here forever."

The envoy sighed. "Eryn, do you have any idea how much firepower that ark's carrying?"

"I thought they just carried close-up defensive armament."

"No, they're packing a lot more than that. They all are."

"What the fuck? How do I not know this?"

"Apart from the odd fragment of interstellar debris, they've never had anything to shoot at before." The envoy gave a blue-shouldered shrug. "And besides, those weapons aren't under human control. They're strictly to be used at the ark's discretion. Apparently, your angel friend wasn't going to turn us loose in the universe without some basic means to defend ourselves."

"How do you know about them?"

The *Ocelot* smiled. "You don't think ships gossip?"

"I—"

"Of course, we do. There might be fifteen billion of you humans, but there are only five and half thousand ships, if you include the thousand arks, three thousand scout ships and other auxiliary vessels, and the one and a half thousand self-aware shuttles and pleasure craft. Compared to the number of humans in the Continuance, that barely qualifies as a village."

"So, what are they packing?"

"On ships that large?" He sat forward. "We're talking magnetic rail guns kilometres in length; hundreds of laser turrets and missile emplacements; defensive screens; slaved attack drones..."

"So, pretty much the whole arsenal?"

"And I haven't even got on to the antimatter sidewinders and EMP projectors."

"Crap."

"If we get too close, the *Rose* could turn us into radioactive dust in seconds. And there is nothing we can do about it. It is just too large, and it doesn't have any convenient exhaust ports or secret weakness chambers."

"So, all we can do is run?"

"We haul ass now, and if we're lucky, circle around later to reach the wormhole."

CHAPTER THIRTY-TWO

INCOMPREHENSIBLE FUNCTION

FURIOUS OCELOT

I rose from the inner surface of the sphere, followed by the *Dreaming Spire*, and accelerated for the nearest gap in the structure. There was no reason for stealth. If we'd been able to detect the *Rose*, the ark's vastly superior sensors would already have our position pinpointed. Our only hope was to use the bulk of the sphere to hide ourselves.

"If we both follow random headings around the outside of the artefact," Eryn told Haruki on the *Dreaming Spire*, "we can converge on the wormhole, and there'll be no way the *Rose* will be able to predict which direction we'll be coming from."

He frowned. "Will that make much difference? It could just sit there and pick us off when we reappear."

"It could, but with the bulk of the sphere between us, it won't know for certain that's what we're doing. As far as it will know, we could be accelerating for deep space, or preparing to make a substrate jump to a nearby system—and I don't think it wants to lose us."

"Why not?"

"It came here for the same reason we did."

"And what's that?"

"To find Frank."

Haruki mulled this over for a moment or two. Then he said, "It has better engines than us. We can't outrun it."

"True." Eryn thought quickly, scrutinising the three-dimensional image of the sphere. "But maybe we can out-manoeuvre it."

"I'm listening..."

"Okay." Using her finger, she sketched a course around the outside of the sphere. "That ark isn't as agile as we are. Something that size has a ferocious inertia; once it's headed in one direction, it takes a lot of energy to change its heading."

"True." Haruki looked sceptical. "But the curve of this artefact is comparable to the orbital path of the Earth; even an ark can manage that comfortably."

"Yes, but that's where we cheat." She highlighted a gap in the unfinished structure. "If we circle around the outside and head for this opening, we can take a ninety-degree turn and blast straight across the inside of the sphere. The *Rose* won't be able to turn in time and will have to take the long way around."

I chuckled.

Haruki said, "Will that work?"

Eryn's cheeks flushed with irritation. She said, "I'm trying to keep your ass alive, and in order to do *that*, I need you to shut the hell up and trust me. I'm sorry if that seems cold. I would be more sympathetic, but time *is* of the essence."

•

We accelerated away, bending our course to match the inverted terrain of the shell. And, as predicted, the ark followed. Arks rarely used full thrust. With nowhere to go and no deadline for arrival, they tended to prize engine efficiency rather than arbitrarily high velocities. Therefore, I was quite unprepared for the rapidity with which it came for us. Within a couple of hours, it had reduced the gap between us from light minutes to light seconds.

"This is going to be close," I told Eryn, extrapolating our respective vectors.

I brought up an enhanced image of the *Damask Rose*, and she gasped. I guess she couldn't help it. She was looking at her home, but it had been distorted and perverted. Whole sections appeared to have melted and cooled into bizarre, twisted shapes. Ragged, queasily biological growths protruded randomly from the hull. One of the outriggers—itself a third the size of the main hull—had been torn away and was missing altogether, and large sections of the ark's skin had been peeled away to reveal the maze of corridors and cabins within.

I felt revulsion. The *Damask Rose* had built me and furnished me with an altered copy of its own awareness. It was a part of me, the way Eryn's parents were a part of her.

"How many people died on that hulk?" Eryn said.

"Do you want me to calculate the answer?"

"No." She seemed unable to tear her eyes from the screen. "But maybe we can avoid further loss."

I said nothing. I knew the memory of the defiled ark would never leave me. That wound would always be lurking just beneath the surface. I would never be able to forget it had been there. That deformation would always remain as a psychological scar. I knew Eryn felt the same, and yet, that didn't mean she was going to stop trying to prevent this from happening to other arks. You can cling to even the slenderest of hopes, and Raijin's words seemed to have lit a fragile candle in her heart.

All told, our partial orbit of the sphere took eight hours at full burn. By the time we came in range of our target fissure, the *Rose* was less than a thousand kilometres behind us and taking pot shots in our direction with some of its secondary weaponry. I monitored a missile fizz past us, three hundred metres off our port side.

"Curious," I said.

"What is?"

"We're well within effective range. We should have been fried already. But the ark's firing those missiles without first establishing a target lock. It's firing blind."

"Do you think it's trying to miss us on purpose?"

"Why would it do that?"

"It might want to capture Frank alive?"

I thought about this. "It seems unlikely. From what I can tell, the entity from C-623 has gone to considerable lengths to try to prevent us reaching Mr Tucker. With that in mind, it seems far more likely it now wants to kill him."

Another missile zipped from the bow of the *Rose*. Its bright exhaust scrawled a crazy three-dimensional spiral across the sky, whipping around and around, until it finally exploded three hundred kilometres in our wake.

"So," Eryn said, "why aren't we dead?"

I steepled blue fingers. "I have a theory."

"Let's hear it, then."

"I surmise that the intelligence now inhabiting the *Damask Rose* has yet to fully understand its systems. It's like a child. It knows what it wants to do, but it's still learning how to manipulate the world around it."

"You mean, it's still learning how to be an ark?" Eryn tapped a fingernail against her front teeth.

I smiled. "Arks are considerably more complex than individual humans."

"Gee, thanks."

"Or scout ships like me, for that matter. Don't forget, it managed to operate the *Couch Surfer* well enough to invade the ark in the first place."

"But it's learning?"

"I assume it will eventually master the targeting systems. If we were in a straightforward chase, our options—and our life expectancy—would be severely curtailed."

"But we're going to cheat."

"You're damn right we are."

•

As we passed over the unfinished section of the sphere, we were caught in a shaft of sunlight radiating from within the massive structure. In my rear view, I could see the *Dreaming Spire* gleaming like a speck of liquid gold.

We both cut our acceleration and turned until our noses faced into the light. Then we fired our engines again, and began to curve down, towards the fissure.

It was the closest we could manage to a ninety-degree turn. It wasn't elegant, but it was an order of magnitude tighter than anything the *Damask Rose* could manage.

Engines flaring, we dove into the uncompleted gap in the sphere's hundred-kilometre-thick walls, streaking between gantries and construction platforms; huge machines of incomprehensible function; and dense clumps of loose cable.

Sheppard called from the *Dreaming Spire*. "You're a genius, Eryn."

"I have my moments."

We lurched sideways to avoid a conduit as thick as a tree trunk.

"Okay, but I just wanted to say," his voice crackled with static, "in case either of us doesn't make it, it's been a privilege to—"

Missiles from the ark began impacting on the outer surface. The signal broke up into howls and roars. Blinding flashes outshone the sun, throwing weird, kilometres-long shadows ahead of us, and the radiation alarms began to howl.

I burst into the interior of the sphere pursued by a plume of nuclear fire.

And then we were in the clear. The ark's velocity had taken it past the gap. By the time it circumnavigated the outside of the sphere, we would have crossed the diameter and arrived at the wormhole terminus.

"Work out the fastest route," Eryn said. "Then call the *Dreaming Spire* and tell them to stick close. Timing's going to be essential."

I bowed my envoy's blue head. "I'm sorry, I can't do that."

"Why not? Are we damaged?"

"No, we're fine." I hated breaking bad news to her. "It's the *Dreaming Spire*."

"What about them?"

"They didn't make it."

CHAPTER THIRTY-THREE

THE SHIP OF THESEUS

ERYN

Accelerating at four gravities, it would have taken the *Furious Ocelot* two days to cross from one side of the Dyson Sphere to the other—but we had another trick up our sleeves. As soon as we were clear of the sphere's surface, we dropped into the substrate and emerged a few moments later on the other side of the sun.

"I've never jumped inside a sphere before," the ship said. "The unusual gravity distribution made the required calculations a challenge."

I didn't reply. My mind was a whirl. How could the *Dreaming Spire* be gone? How could all those lives have been snuffed out in an instant? Now, Tessa would never write her story, and although Sheppard had saved my life, I hadn't been able to save his. In fact, by reassigning them to the *Spire*, I had doomed them both.

Two more ghosts to haunt my conscience.

The wormhole gate was where we'd left it, but had been distorted to many times its former width. Maybe because the entity controlling the *Damask Rose* was partially comprised of substrate matter, the ark had been able to force its way through like a grapefruit through a rubber hose, leaving the sphere stretched and unstable.

"No chance of hitting the side this time," the *Ocelot* said.

"Shut up and get us out of here."

"Roger that."

•

As before, passage through the hole took three days. I spent most of that first morning alone on the bridge, watching the roiling plasma of the substrate boil past the windows.

Finally, around midday, Li came up to see me.

"How are you doing?" she asked.

"About as well as you'd expect."

She made a face. "That bad, huh?"

"How's everyone downstairs?"

"Okay." She sat on the edge of the bridge's second couch and put a hand on my shoulder. "They're mostly worried about you."

"I'm fine."

"No, you're not." She leant forward. "I can see you're upset. Let me take care of you."

I dipped my shoulder out of her grasp. "I'm all right. How's Madison?"

"Why don't you come downstairs and find out?"

"No, I'm okay here."

"Well, she's not great. She lost her mom and her home, and now some of her new friends have been blown to hell. She needs you, Eryn. She needs her aunt."

I winced. "I can't. Not right now..."

Li glanced at the front screen. From the corner of my eye, I watched the unreal substrate light play across the planes of her face.

"You can't just stay up here the whole time," she said.

"You don't understand." I stood up and leant against the toughened glass, looking out into the bright chaos.

"Don't understand what?"

"I don't know. I just need some space."

"Space for what?" Li came up beside me. Her hair and eyes were their natural colours. Her expression was one of deep concern.

"Space to realise maybe not everyone I know is going to die in some stupid, horrible, pointless manner."

"Oh, honey." She tried to draw me into an embrace, but I pulled away before she could touch me.

"Don't."

"Eryn…"

"I'm sorry." I crossed my arms and hunched my shoulders. "You don't know what it was like."

"Inside the angel?"

"It took me to pieces, Li." I shuddered. "I watched it take my body and break it down into an atomic fog."

She bit her lip. "It put you back together, though."

"Did it?"

"What do you mean?"

"For all I know, the real me might be dead, and this body just a facsimile. I look like me and think like me, but that doesn't mean I'm the original Eryn. Even if it put every molecule back in exactly the right place, how can I be sure my consciousness is the same?" A tear ran down my cheek. I wiped it away with the sleeve of my shirt.

Li sighed. She went back to the co-navigator's couch and sat down. "It's the Ship of Theseus," she said.

"What?"

"It's an old thought experiment from Ancient Greece. According to the story, a ship belonging to the hero Theseus was kept in a harbour as a monument to the great man's accomplishments. But over time, parts of the ship began to rot and were gradually replaced until, after a hundred years, none of the original components remained."

"And your point is?"

"Is it the same ship?"

"I—I'm not sure."

"And let's say all the removed components were cured of their rot and reassembled. Would *that* ship be the original ship?"

"Yes."

"But what about the one in the harbour?"

"That's a copy."

"Is it?" Li put her hands on her knees. "The cells in a human body are constantly dying and being replaced. If you could somehow collect all the dead cells Madison has shed in her lifetime, reassemble them into a human body, and bring them to life, would that assemblage be able to claim it was the 'original' Madison?"

"No, of course not."

"Why not?"

"I—"

She held up a hand to stop me. "The point is everything changes all the time and continuity is an illusion. Nothing endures and everything's fucked up. If you feel like you're the same Eryn King up here," she tapped her temple, "I don't think it matters how the rest of you is put together."

"But—"

She kissed me. Her lips were soft and warm against mine. I let her take my hand, and she led me down to the crew lounge, where Madison sat disconsolately at the hexagonal table.

"Are you okay?"

With her features pulled tight by grief, Madison looked so much older than her years. "I guess I thought angels could do anything."

Li brought us cups of sweet black tea made from her personal stash, then she went off to take a shower. Frank was in his cabin; the *Ocelot*'s envoy was down in engineering, staying tactfully out of the way. Without our other comrades, the tight spaces of the ship felt echoey and expansive.

I even missed the damn cat.

I put an arm around Madison's shoulder, and she allowed me to draw her into an awkward hug. "I don't want to give you false hope," I said. "But Raijin told me there might still be a chance to stop further loss of life."

I felt her stiffen against me. "What sort of chance?"

"We have to go back to where all this began. We have to go back to C-623."

"And then what?"

"I'm not sure. The angel put something in my head. I don't know what it is, but it said it would be available at the correct time, whatever that means."

"What about Sheppard and Tessa and Sam? Can we bring them back?"

"I'm sorry, but they're gone."

"I see."

"There was nothing we could do. We were lucky not to be killed ourselves."

Madison pulled back. "They're not going to come back and haunt us like Snyder, are they?"

I shook my head. "They were incinerated in a nuclear fireball. I don't think there's any way back from that."

Frank entered the room. His hair looked wilder than before, and his lips were a thin, pale line beneath his weather-beaten cheeks.

"Are you okay?" I asked.

He stared at me. "Haruki's dead."

"I'm sorry."

"You should be." Despite his fury, he was still struggling to look me in the eye. "I've known that man for eighty years. He's been my boss, my colleague and my dearest friend—and it was your idiotic plan that got him killed."

For a frozen moment, I couldn't breathe. "Excuse me?"

"He should have been here with me," Frank said. "Not on the other ship with a bunch of strangers."

"It was *his* ship," I protested. "He was dream-linked to it. It couldn't have jumped through the substrate without him."

Frank scowled. His arms flailed awkwardly. "That doesn't alter the fact that it was your plan that got him killed."

Heat flushed through me. I said, "Without my plan, you'd be dead."

CHAPTER THIRTY-FOUR

NORTH ATLANTIC CONVEYOR

ERYN

We emerged from the livid, plasma-like medium of the substrate to find ourselves facing a wall of arks. Warning pings told me their weapon systems had locked onto us. At the same time, we were hit by a multi-frequency demand to stand down and identify ourselves.

"I'll handle this," said the *Ocelot*, and I sat back in my chair, content to let the ships talk to each other. With their electronic brains working so much faster than sluggish human synapses, they'd be able to get this sorted out in a fraction of the time it would have taken me to respond.

And sure enough, less than ten seconds later, the arks ceased targeting us. We were instructed to bring Frank to meet with the Elders on Victoria Quinn's home ark, the *Tiger Mountain*.

Tiger Mountain was one of the most heavily protected vessels in the fleet. It flew at all times surrounded by twenty of its peers, which prevented any potential attacker from finding a direct line-of-sight. In addition, its hull was twice normal size, puffed up with layers of armour and tungsten foam designed to absorb the kinetic and explosive energy of any projectile impacting its surface.

Hawk-like fighter drones escorted us to a shielded hangar at the vast ship's bow, where we were met by a squad of combat envoys wearing high-threat tactical armour. They kept their guns trained on us as Frank and I disembarked and submitted ourselves to full body scans.

Once they were thoroughly satisfied that we were still who and what we claimed to be, we were led through the ship to Victoria Quinn's office.

The room held a conference table with twelve chairs, a series of large viewscreens, and a single large oak desk, behind which Quinn sat with her fingers steepled. The wall behind her was transparent and looked out across one of the *Tiger Mountain*'s internal spaces, which was landscaped with terraced hills and bamboo forests. Villages and shrines dotted the slopes, showing where the inhabitants had decided to build their own homes rather than be content with the cabins they'd originally been assigned. Sunlight glittered off the lakes and streams.

Quinn sat back and touched her fingertips to her chin. "I see you found the old bastard."

Frank dipped his head. "Hello, Victoria."

"How old are you now?"

"Old enough to have stopped counting."

"No." Quinn looked him up and down. "I don't believe that for a second. You were in your early thirties when we left Earth. You have to be well over a hundred by now."

Frank shrugged. "A hundred and six, actually."

"And yet, you're still stubbornly not dead."

"I could say the same for you."

Victoria smiled. "The difference is, I'm providing a service. Continuity of leadership. Whereas you... What have you been doing?" She waved her hand at a printout of the reports the *Ocelot* had forwarded upon our arrival back at the fleet. "Digging through dusty old bones on that spherical mausoleum of yours?"

Frank scratched the bristles on his chin. "I've been communing with the angel."

"And what does our evictor have to say for itself?"

"It's going to help us."

Victoria sat forward with her eyes wide. "It's not coming *here*, is it?"

Frank laughed. "No, it's not. It's quite content where it is for now. It's going to take several centuries to completely map and study the sphere; I wouldn't expect it to move again within our lifetimes."

"Then, how's it going to help?"

Frank turned to me. "Raijin implanted something in Eryn's head. Something we have to take back to Candidate-623."

Victoria's pale eyes skewered me. "So," she said. "You've spoken to the big cloud?"

I felt my face flush. "Yes, and we only just made it back here alive. Some of our friends weren't so lucky—so maybe you could be a bit less flippant about it?"

The older woman blinked. She obviously wasn't used to being addressed in such a disrespectful tone. "Honey," she said. "I'm not being flippant. I knew and loved Haruki every bit as much as Frank did. You just don't know what I've been dealing with here. I'm sorry you lost people, I really am, but right now, I've got simulacra running loose on eight arks and a likely death toll in the hundreds of millions. I'm closing flick portals and deploying combat envoys, but we're fighting a losing battle. So, maybe you can dispense with the righteous indignation and just tell me what Raijin put in your head?"

My cheeks burned more fiercely. It took a conscious effort of will to unclench my fists. "I don't know," I had to admit. "A piece of information. It said the information would become available when I needed it."

"Typical." Victoria let her shoulders slump. "Getting a straight answer out of that thing's like trying to untangle spaghetti in zero-G."

"I recorded the entire exchange," Frank said. "I can forward it to your bracelet."

Victoria shook her head. "I doubt I'd be able to infer any additional information, that thing talks in riddles half the time. You were there, you know what was said."

She stood up and walked around her desk until she stood in front of Frank. Then, unexpectedly, she put her arms around him and kissed his cheek. "It really is good to see you," she said.

Frank squirmed with embarrassment.

"I'm sorry." Victoria released him and stepped back, leaning against the edge of her desk. "I forgot how socially awkward you are."

She turned her attention to me. "Go to Candidate-623," she said. "Find some way to stop whatever it is that's attacking us."

My heart was still racing. I said, "Yes, ma'am."

"And be quick about it, otherwise we're going to lose more than the *Damask Rose*."

"We'll leave immediately."

"I'm going to send an ark with you. The *North Atlantic Conveyor*. It's the most heavily armed ship we have. If all else fails, it can nuke the planet until there's nothing left but glass."

"How reassuring," Frank said.

Victoria ignored him. "I'm putting you in charge," she told me. "Not this idiot."

"No," Frank said. "Absolutely not. Her being in charge got Haruki killed."

Victoria raised an eyebrow. "She also saved your skinny arse." She looked at me. "Get over to the *North Atlantic*, Eryn. It will be expecting you."

I didn't know what to say. For a second, I had the absurd urge to snap my heels and salute. Instead, I muttered my thanks and left, not waiting to see if Frank would follow.

•

"A whole ark?" Li said.

"Uh-huh."

"And you're in command of it?"

"As in command as you can be. I'm sure it wouldn't follow any order it disagreed with."

"Wow."

"I know, right?"

We were sitting on the *Ocelot*'s bridge as it made its way through the fleet towards the *North Atlantic Conveyor.*

"And we're really going back?"

"To C-623? Yes, I'm afraid so."

"You know, we both nearly died last time we were there."

"I know."

"Aren't you nervous?"

I rolled my eyes. "Nervous? I'm practically shitting myself."

Li intertwined her fingers in mine. "Oh good. I'm glad it's not just me."

We sat in silence for a while, watching the vast forms of the arks drift past like lazily browsing whales.

"That's the *Wenchang Dijun,*" I said eventually, pointing to an elongated dumbbell shape on our port bow. "Isn't that where you were born?"

"It is."

"You never mention your family."

"We don't get on."

"Why not?"

Li bit her lower lip. "They're very traditional. They don't approve of my sexual preferences."

"They don't speak to you because you sleep with women?"

She sighed. "Yeah."

I felt my mouth fall open. "There are still people who think like that?"

"There will always be people who think like that."

"Damn, I hope not." I'd had a mixture of male and female partners over the years, but nobody had ever given me shit for it. "I thought we'd left that kind of assholery behind."

"Apparently not."

"I'm so sorry."

She shrugged. "It's not your fault."

I gave her hand a squeeze. "Maybe if we save the human race, they'll start to come around?"

She smiled. "I won't hold my breath."

The HUD on the windshield informed me we were approaching the *North Atlantic Conveyor.*

"Holy hell," I said. "Will you look at that?"

The ark bore little resemblance to its fellows. For reasons known only to itself, it had restructured itself into the shape of a human fist—a smooth, carved golden fist that measured fully twenty-five kilometres from knuckle to wrist.

"Now that," the *Ocelot*'s voice came from the console, "is a statement."

•

The *North Atlantic Conveyor* guided us around to its stern, where the 'wrist' ended in a smooth cliff. There were no signs of armaments on its hull, but then I hadn't expected there to be. Only an idiot would reveal their ship's offensive capabilities to anyone that cared to glance its way. And besides, unless you felt the need to display large cannons in order to compensate for some personal deficiency, great bulky weapons ruined the look of a ship, and were easy to shoot off. Continuance design philosophy—inherited from the principles Raijin had employed when building the fleet—concerned itself more with elegant simplicity than demonstrative sabre-rattling.

What first appeared to be tiny pinpricks of light set into the wrist were in fact the open doors of hangars and maintenance bays—some a hundred metres or more in width.

One of the larger hangars had been cleared for our use. As soon as we touched down, the *North Atlantic* began to accelerate, and by the time we made our way to the meeting room that would serve as our base of operations, the rest of the Continuance fleet had shrunk until they were little more than faint specks against a backdrop of stars.

•

The *North Atlantic Conveyor*'s envoy stood two metres tall. Blue stubble covered her scalp, and her wide shoulders and muscled body marked her as a combat model.

"Welcome aboard," she said. "I know *North Atlantic Conveyor* can be a bit of a mouthful, so please feel free to refer to me as 'Nat', if that makes life easier."

"Thanks, Nat. I'm Eryn."

"Pleased to meet you, Eryn. This will be your command post." The meeting room looked more like a large apartment than a combat nerve centre. Houseplants and occasional tables occupied the corners. A breakfast bar and kitchenette sat at the far end. Four sofas had been arranged in a loose, inward-facing square in the centre, surrounding a large, glass-topped coffee table. "The walls can be used as a wraparound screen and tactical display, and all my resources have been placed at your disposal." The envoy clasped her blue hands. "I have also begun assembling additional combat envoys. By the time we reach our destination, we should have several hundred available for active duty."

"Very nice," Li said.

I added, "Thank you, Nat."

"My pleasure."

"How long until we reach Candidate-623?" Frank asked.

"Three days, twenty-one hours, eleven minutes and fifty-two seconds."

"In that case," he said, "I suppose we have time to take a shower and look around?"

•

Later that evening, Frank, Li and I sat on a café terrace overlooking a thickly wooded area of parkland. The *Ocelot*'s envoy had decided to stay on board the ship to keep Madison company. After her experiences on the *Damask Rose*, she didn't feel able to leave the safety of the scout ship—and who could blame her? Instead, she had holed up in her cabin with a selection of interactive entertainments, and the largest pizza Nat had been able to produce.

There were other patrons in the café. Because of the lockdown, the ark had been unable to off-load the rest of its population, and so it had had to bring them along for the ride. Some were unhappy about this, while others were just exhibiting the sort of defiant attitude you might expect from people who had chosen to live aboard a giant gold fist.

I'd been picking at a plate of salami, cheese and olives and drinking thimble-sized glasses of a wickedly strong local spirit with an unpronounceable name. The sunlamp above the forest had dimmed to simulate evening in order to help the trees keep to their diurnal cycle, and flocks of crows (or maybe ravens, I don't really know the difference) were cawing and fussing in the upper branches as they prepared for nightfall—and just for the briefest of moments, surrounded by all that tranquillity and relaxed by alcohol, all the horror and heartbreak we'd been through seemed distant and unreal, like the fading memories of a particularly bad dream. I looked across at Li with her dark, glossy hair and infectious smile. She was one of the few people I'd met whose eyes actually seemed to sparkle when she laughed. It was like you could see her inner light. Our relationship so far had been tentative and surrounded by nightmare and disaster, but I was starting to realise she meant more to me than just a shipboard fling. I enjoyed her company. I liked having someone to hold and talk to in the dark—and I mean *really* talk. We were still physically shy and awkward (at least, I was), but I'd shared more of my inner self with her over the past days than I'd ever shared with anyone, except maybe Shay.

Jesus, I thought, *listen to me. I sound like a teenager.*

Maybe I was drunker than I thought, but whenever her fingers brushed my arm, I felt a weird prickle on my skin and got this strange squirmy feeling in my gut. A fluttery mix of excitement and anxiety. I hadn't felt this way since that night with Madison's father—and that had been a disaster. I didn't want to be hurt again, but there are just some people who come into your life and blow it wide open. There's no explanation for it. There's just something about them that turns you the fuck on. You feel like you've known them forever, or maybe you knew them in a past life, and just hearing them speak makes the back of your neck shiver like an unexpected caress. That's how it was with Li. A snatched word in a corridor left me feeling all hot and bothered for hours afterwards. I don't know if it was pheromones or voodoo or something else but sitting here close to her felt like sitting next to the life I was supposed to be living. I hardly knew her, but she felt like home. There was no other word for it. I'd lost the place where I'd grown up—but when I looked across at Li, I didn't feel lost or orphaned anymore. Something about the sound of her voice and the smell of her hair let me know I wasn't alone; I was exactly where I was supposed to be. And whatever happened on C-623, I realised in that moment—as she sat there picking apart a slice of crusty bread with her fingers, the nails painted purple—that I was always going to love her unconditionally and forever, even if in the long run, we were nothing more than friends. Because I guess that's the thing about love; it's not about finding the person who fits a tick list of predetermined criteria; it's about finding that one person who makes you quiver when they whisper your name, whose touch brings you alive, and in whose company you just endlessly want to bask.

Frank ordered coffee from one of the blue-skinned waiters.

"What's the plan?" he said. "You know, seeing as you're in charge."

With great reluctance, I tore my attention from the curve of Li's neck. "Oh, you're talking to me now, are you?"

He glared down at the tabletop. "Through necessity rather than choice."

Stubborn bastard.

"Fine," I said. "Seeing as you asked, when we get there, we'll remain on board the *North Atlantic Conveyor* while it surveys the surface. Once that's complete, we'll wait for whatever Raijin put in my head to activate."

"That doesn't sound like much of a plan," Li mumbled.

I shrugged. "It's all we've got."

"And if nothing happens?" Frank blew the steam from his coffee. "What then?"

"Then I guess I have to go down to the surface."

"No," Li protested. "It's too dangerous."

"The simulacra are loose in the fleet," I reminded her. "And they're spreading fast. This is our last throw of the dice. Whatever it takes, we have to find a way to stop them."

"We could go back to the fleet and fight."

I shook my head. "If we don't find what we're looking for on C-623, there won't *be* a fleet for us to go back to."

•

That night, lying next to Li's gently snoring body, I thought about Tessa, Sheppard and Haruki, and tried to imagine what their final moments had been like. Had they been aware it was the end? Were there a few instants of terror before the final fireball? Maybe a moment where Tessa reached for Sheppard's hand, or Haruki whispered the name of some former love? I hoped not. With luck, the nuke vapourised them before they were aware of it. When Shay and I were growing up, one of our neighbours was an elderly man who'd once been a soldier in Syria. He told us that you never hear the shot that kills you. I hoped the same held true for nuclear warheads, and that Haruki and our friends had been wiped from existence before their brains had time to register the flash.

Poor Haruki. I had only met him briefly but knew his history. He had once been one of the richest and most influential men on the Earth and, operating from his bomb shelter in the Rocky Mountains, had played a large part in convincing the governments of the world to cooperate with Raijin after their aborted attempt to blow the planet to cinders. How ironic that seventy-five years later, he should die in a nuclear explosion. It was almost as if he'd been living on borrowed time for three quarters of a century, but now the war had finally caught up with him.

I guess it catches up with us all in the end.

CHAPTER THIRTY-FIVE

ALL THE GUNS

ERYN

"Eryn, we have a problem."

I opened my eyes. The room was dark. "Nat? Is that you?"

She was standing at the foot of the bed. "I apologise for waking you, but this cannot wait."

I eased my arm out from beneath Li, who was still snoring quietly, and propped myself up on an elbow. "What is it?"

Nat glanced at Li, then jerked her head towards the door. Pulling on a t-shirt, I followed her out of the bedroom and into the main living area, where the lights were on.

"There's been a murder," she said. Her body was as muscled as any soldier, but she held herself like a dancer.

"Who?"

"A scholar on Deck Nineteen. His life partner found him in their shower cubicle a few minutes ago."

"Are you positive it was murder?"

"Unless the deceased figured out a way to remove his own skull and spinal column, yes."

Something cold prickled in my gut. "Any sightings of a simulacrum?"

"No, but that's no guarantee there isn't one walking around."

"Fuck."

Nat pulled herself to attention. "What are your recommendations?"

The floor tiles were cool beneath my feet, and I was absurdly aware of my semi-nakedness. Nat stood a good head taller than me. If she'd wanted to, she could have snapped me like a dry twig. But however great the physical contrast between us, the intellectual gap yawned far wider. She had the entire processing power of the ark behind her eyes; she was capable of conducting millions of simultaneous conversations while also running the ship and supervising all its complex subsystems, from basic plumbing through to the ecosystems of its parkland. She could think and process data hundreds of times faster than I could. In the time it took me to formulate a reply, she would have had ample time to leisurely consume humanity's entire literary canon, from *The Epic of Gilgamesh* through to the latest immersive entertainments. And yet here she was, asking for my recommendations, as if I were some kind of expert.

Recommendations, I noted; not orders.

"I assume you've sealed that deck," I said. "All hatchways, flick terminals and ventilation ducts?"

"Affirmative. Standard protocol since the *Damask Rose*."

"Then flood the surrounding decks with envoys. If you see anything unusual, shoot first and ask questions later."

"Risky."

"Riskier to let this thing get loose."

"There will likely be civilian casualties."

"I think that's inevitable. All we can do is try to minimise them."

Nat did me the courtesy of pretending to mull my suggestion for a moment, even though she would really only have needed a handful of nanoseconds to consider my words.

"I concur," she said.

"Thank you." I backed towards the bedroom. "Now, I'm going to get dressed."

"Is there anything I can get for you?"

"Guns." I thought of the hellscape the infection had made of the interior of the *Damask Rose*. "All the guns."

•

I woke Li and filled her in on the situation as we pulled on our clothes. Then together, we woke Frank, and made our way to the command suite that Nat had set aside for us. By the time we arrived, Nat and the *Ocelot*'s envoy were both waiting for us.

"Where's Madison?" I asked.

"Still asleep," the *Ocelot* said.

"I don't like leaving her alone."

The envoy held up his palms in a calming gesture. "Don't worry. The airlock's sealed and coded. Nobody but I can open it."

I took a breath and tried to focus on the data scrolling up the walls. The ark was in the process of scanning its populace, using face recognition and a dozen other biometric indicators to check that each person aboard was who they appeared to be. So far, it hadn't found any anomalies.

Other displays showed floorplans of the deck where the body had been found and plans of the decks immediately above and below. Blue dots denoted the positions of deployed combat envoys; green dots indicated humans whose authenticity had been corroborated, while those flashing red remained to be positively identified. One after another, the red ones turned steadily green. Finally, when none remained, Nat pursed her lips.

"If it's there, I cannot detect it. Somehow, as on the other infected arks, it's able to shield itself from my surveillance."

Beside me, Frank swore.

Li poured coffees from a flask on the central table and handed one to me and one to Frank.

"Come on," she said. "I know it's late, but we need to get those brains working."

Frank gave me a look. "Especially yours, Eryn." He placed the coffee down without tasting it. "Do you have any inkling what Raijin put in your head yet? Can you feel anything stirring?"

I looked down at the steaming black liquid in my mug, but all I felt was fatigue. According to ship time, it was around two in the morning. "Nothing."

"Damn."

Li said, "So, what are we supposed to do?"

"Hold the zombies off until we reach C-623."

"And then what?"

"Go down to the surface and deliver the message, whatever it is."

She slid onto one of the sofas that surrounded the central table. "You mean, avoid a shitty death up here so we can enjoy one down there?"

"That's about the size of it."

"Fabulous."

I put a hand on her shoulder. "With luck, we've got it contained. Right, Nat?"

"All exits are covered," the *North Atlantic Conveyor*'s envoy replied. "And the citizens remaining on those decks have been instructed to isolate themselves in their cabins and admit no one."

Li sighed. "It won't be enough. You saw the way the *Couch Surfer* crew turned to black sludge and dripped through the *Rose*'s flight deck. They'll do the same here."

"We're alert for that," Nat said. "And this time, we have flamethrowers. I'm confident that if we can't completely halt the spread of the infection, we can at least drastically slow its progress."

"If you say so."

I could see Li wasn't convinced, but I had more pressing concerns. "I think I should go down there."

"Down where?" the *Ocelot* asked.

"To the infected decks."

Li turned to look up at me. "Are you fucking insane?"

"No, I've been thinking about it. Raijin wanted me to deliver a message to whatever's controlling this infection. Maybe if I do it here and now, we won't have to go to the planet at all."

Frank made a face. "I don't know. The angel was quite specific. It said you had to return to C-623."

"I know, but—"

"I think Mr Tucker is correct," the *Ocelot* said. "If the Benevolence thought you could accomplish your goal through contact with the infection, the angel would have told you to go back to the fleet and do it. If Raijin instructed you to go to Candidate-623, then that is where you must go."

"But—"

"He's right," Frank said. "Trust me. It's never wise to disregard the instructions of angels."

"I will do everything I can," Nat promised. "But for now, I think it would be wise for you to retreat to the *Furious Ocelot*. Should I then become compromised, you will be able to continue with your mission."

"That's probably a sensible precaution," the *Ocelot*'s envoy agreed.

•

By noon the following day, the infection had spread through another five decks, and the projected total number of civilian casualties now stood at a hundred and fifty thousand.

Fire scoured corridors and vents as the *North Atlantic Conveyor*'s envoys deployed their flamethrowers against every sign of contamination. But they couldn't catch everything.

Arks had complex and maze-like interiors, and concerns over privacy and decency had prevented the installation of surveillance systems in private quarters. The battlefield had blank spots where skull-faced hyenas oozed from the walls.

Watching from the *Ocelot*'s crew lounge, we saw footage of two of those beasts taking down an envoy. It carried on firing to the last, its bullets punching fist-sized holes in the creatures even as their teeth and claws gouged its flesh and tore its innards.

Li was shaken.

Every time I closed my eyes, I saw Shay being ripped apart.

Madison asked, "Can those things get through the hull?"

Hoping to reassure her, I forced a smile. "I don't intend to find out. The airlock's sealed and the engines are warm. If the *Ocelot* detects so much as a stray molecule entering this hangar, it will throw us out into the substrate before any of those monsters can get within spitting distance of the ship."

Madison gave a nod, but her tight expression suggested she remained unconvinced.

"How are you doing?" she asked.

I felt my eyebrows rise. This was the first time she'd shown concern for anyone's well-being but her own, and I hoped it meant she was starting to process her initial shock at the loss of her mother.

"I'm okay."

"You don't look okay."

"Gee, thanks."

"I'm serious." She frowned at me. "You're pale and you look exhausted."

I looked down at my hands, which were clasped in my lap to stop them shaking. I guess the kid had a point.

"We've been through a lot," I said. "And after all of that, we're still running." I gestured at the screens. "I'm beginning to worry it might be hopeless."

"Really?" Madison looked scared, and I realised I'd fucked up again. I'd spoken without thinking instead of acting like a parent and reassuring her. I should be strong for her sake rather than voicing my inner doubts.

And I *did* have doubts. I thought we'd left the infection behind with the fleet, but somehow it had found its way onto the *North Atlantic Conveyor*. Whatever we did, we couldn't seem to get away from it. It was always breathing down our necks, and we only had to trip or stumble or make one wrong move, and it would be upon us.

"I'm sorry," I said. "I didn't mean that. I'm just tired."

Madison looked like she was about to cry. Li put an arm around her and glared at me.

"You scared her."

"I'm sorry." I rubbed my eyes with the base of my palms. "I'm just having a hard time staying upbeat right now."

"That doesn't mean you should give up," Li said.

I stopped rubbing and looked at her. Purple afterimages danced in my vision. "I'm not giving up."

"But you think it's hopeless?"

Madison was looking at me. I winked at her.

"Of course not," I lied.

•

I left them there, and climbed the ladder to the bridge, where the *Ocelot*'s envoy was sitting in the co-navigator's couch running diagnostic checks in the ship's systems.

"How are you holding up?" he asked.

I flopped onto my couch and stared up at the rivets on the ceiling. "How did we even get here?" I asked. "I'm a scout pilot and you're a scout ship. We should be out in the darkness somewhere, minding our own business, not fighting monsters and comforting children. This isn't what we signed up for, is it? Why do we have to be the ones to save humanity?"

"Just lucky, I guess."

I glanced over the readouts. All the indicators were green. We were ready to depart the *North Atlantic Conveyor* at a moment's notice. And if we did, I'd need to be here, on the bridge. We'd be tumbling out into the substrate, and the *Ocelot* would need me to navigate. But would I be able to? If the dream-link between us relied on my subconsciousness, would it be affected if my unconscious mind really, really didn't want to reach our destination? It was a question I'd never considered before. Could my fear lead us astray, plotting courses that avoided the dangers of C-623 by steering around them in the formlessness of the substrate? I didn't know the answer. Up until now, I'd never flown anywhere actively frightening—and frankly, C-623 scared the absolute shit out of me.

Was this the way it was all going to end, not just for me but for the whole human race? After almost wrecking our planet, we'd been cast out into the darkness only to find a greater danger waiting.

Right there and then, I almost quit. Struggling onwards seemed futile. Perhaps it was time to embrace failure and think about exit strategies? After all, we were in a scout ship. We could head back to Frank's Dyson Sphere and leave this all behind. We might even last a few years before the food recycler or some other essential system broke down—but perhaps before that could happen, we'd all go mad with grief and loneliness. I screwed my eyes and fists tight, thinking of the agonies Shay had been subjected to when the entity vivisected her. Rather than endure such pain, and to save Li, Madison and Frank from having to face it, might it be preferable to detonate the *Ocelot*'s main reactor and go out in a blast of pure white light, the same as Haruki, Tessa and Sheppard? Wouldn't it be better to die painlessly and on our own terms than face dissection and horror? I pictured myself giving the order. I wouldn't even talk it over with the others. It would be kinder for them not to know. They wouldn't suffer. They wouldn't even have time to register the flash. One second, they'd exist and the next they wouldn't. It would be quick and clean.

I could do it now.

I felt my pulse in the base of my throat. All I had to do was speak a sentence, and all this would be over.

Detonate the main reactor. Four simple words. I took a deep breath in through my nose and moistened my lips…

But then, Raijin's words rang in my head: *IF YOU ARE SUCCESSFUL, FURTHER LOSS MAY BE AVOIDED.*

If I died now, would I be condemning the rest of the Continuance to the ravages of the entity from C-623? If we soldiered on and somehow prevailed, might I be able to spare the majority the suffering my sister had endured? The angel's words certainly seemed to suggest it was possible. I thought of Shay playing beside me in the vents of the *Damask Rose*. After our parents died, she had been my world. I helped raise her. I gave up Tomas for her. I would have done anything to keep her safe, and yet I couldn't. If there really was a chance to save other little girls like her, how could I possibly walk away? While the slimmest hope remained then surely, I had to try everything in my power to rescue them from whatever horrors might await?

I began to cry great big, wracking sobs. Tears streamed down my face and my hands shook. I'd endured so much, and I'd come so close to giving up. But I couldn't back down now, not now, not if there existed even the slightest prospect of saving billions of children from the awfulness that had claimed my sister.

I had to go on.

If fear pulled me off course, maybe hope would steer me right.

I had to try for Shay's sake. I owed it to her, I owed it to Madison, and most of all, I owed it to myself. If I could somehow stop this creature, I knew I'd gladly fly through the gates of Hell itself.

And if the gates of Hell happened to be located on Candidate-623, then so be it.

•

The *North Atlantic Conveyor* dropped out of the substrate three hundred thousand kilometres above the blasted, rocky surface of the planet. Although small compared to the world around which it was now in orbit, the ark's gigatonnes of weight had a small but measurable effect on C-623's rotation, dragging on it and almost imperceptibly slowing it so that the average day increased by a handful of nanoseconds.

By this time, the battle for the ark's interior had spread to encompass two-thirds of its two hundred decks, and the casualties were piling up. Humans were being torn apart and reshaped and envoys were being killed as quickly as new ones could be manufactured. The walls and floors in the infected sections warped and buckled into new, disturbingly organic forms, and crawling black tendrils burrowed through air ducts and power conduits, seeking to corrupt and overthrow the ark's consciousness and control.

"I can't hold out much longer," Nat said. Li and I were sitting on the *Ocelot*'s bridge, communicating with her via a visual link from the command post on the *North Atlantic Conveyor*. "Whatever this infection is, it seems to have learned from its experiences on the *Damask Rose*. Its strategy certainly appears more coherent and purposeful. I estimate total crew-loss within an hour and a half, and full capitulation shortly afterwards. Perhaps two hours, if I am fortunate."

"Shit."

"I could self-destruct, but I am worried that would simply scatter the infection over a wider volume of space."

"Don't do anything hasty," I said, internally wincing that I had almost made the same decision. "We're making final preparations for departure. We'll be as quick as we can. Do what you can to avoid assimilation until we've done what we were sent here to do."

The envoy smiled. "Do not worry. I have no intention of going gently into the night. I—" She broke off.

Li said, "What is it?"

"I'm registering a huge surge in the substrate. Something's coming through. Something big."

"How big?"

"At least the size of a medium asteroid. I—"

"What?"

"Holy fucking guacamole! It's the *Damask Rose*."

I almost leapt out of my seat. How the hell had that ark managed to catch up with us? It must have figured out where we were going and not bothered to pause at the fleet, as we had done.

Nat opened a sub-window, which showed the corrupted ark's blunt snout pushing its way through the skein of reality. Somehow, it looked even more hideous than the last time we'd seen it. Now it resembled some perverse, twisted leviathan from the depths of an alien sea—a hell-spawned whale that had already killed half our crew and had come back, harpoons sticking ineffectually from its massive hide, to finish the job.

Well, *call me Ishmael*, motherfucker.

"Launch everything," I said. "Every missile, every beam weapon, every canon shell."

Nat blinked once. "I am doing so."

On the screen, fireflies danced between the two massive vessels—streams of tracer rounds scything back and forth, targeting incoming nukes; the actinic drive flares of outgoing missiles; the flowering attrition of measure and countermeasure, thrust and parry, offence and defence; and through it all, the almost invisible flickering of powerful energy weapons, their paths only visible where they intersected clouds of dust and debris, causing the fragments to spark and fluoresce like dust motes caught in the shaft of light from a desk lamp.

Watching from the bridge of the *Ocelot*, the effect was as if two exploding stars had decided to lock horns.

"She's not slowing," Nat said, her voice curiously devoid of emotion as she devoted all her processing power to the conflict in which she and the *Rose* were engaged.

"Collision course?" I asked.

"Yes."

"Then get us the fuck out of the way."

"Getting the fuck out of the way."

The starfield lurched. The ongoing bloom of radiation shells fell away as the *North Atlantic Conveyor* twisted on its axis, rolling away from its oncoming sibling. The *Damask Rose* tried to correct its headlong rush, but its inertia was too strong, and it passed harmlessly a few hundred metres below the *Conveyor*'s thumb. However, at such a short range, countermeasures were totally ineffective, and the narrow gap between the two arks turned white with nuclear fire as missiles from one vessel assaulted the hulls of both, their proximity fuses causing them to explode almost as soon as they were clear of their launch tubes, while secondary weapon systems on the other ship chewed livid chunks from the radioactive, heat-softened undersides of their opponent.

The whole exchange took a handful of seconds. As the arks drew apart, they trailed clouds of glowing fragments. Broken hull plates. Snapped-off antennae. Whole skyscrapers blasted from their mounts, lights flickering, severed pipes unspooling from their bases, venting air and water into the void.

The *North Atlantic Conveyor* turned to confront another attack, but the *Damask Rose* kept its heading.

"It's going to crash into the planet," Li said, and I saw she was right. The twenty-five-kilometre-long behemoth showed no sign of trying to alter its course, although it kept up its barrage of missiles.

"Did we disable it?" I asked.

Nat shook her shaven, blue head. "I don't think so."

"But why would it deliberately crash?"

"Insufficient data."

At that moment, the ark's leading edge encountered the thin atmosphere and plasma flared around it.

"It's employing braking thrust," Nat reported.

"It's too late. It's still going to hit the surface."

"I don't think it's trying to avoid that. I think it's trying to land."

"What?" The idea was ludicrous. These arks weren't designed to set down on a planet. And if they did, it was doubtful they'd survive the experience. They were too heavy. The stresses on the hull would be too great.

Dumbfounded, we watched as, bow glowing with atmospheric friction, the *Damask Rose* ploughed through the upper stratosphere. Its engines fired at maximum thrust, illuminating an area the size of a continent but barely slowing the headlong fall. The beast had too much inertia.

I realised I was squeezing Li's hand. I didn't know if I had reached for her or she had reached for me. All I knew was that I needed the human contact. That ark had been my home and even though it had been misshapen and despoiled, it still hurt to see it plunge to its destruction.

More of the skyscrapers on its hull bent and snapped. Some burned away. I thought the ark was going to hit the ground head-on, but at the last moment, the thrusters changed direction, hauling the nose upwards as the rest of the ship came curving down, so that when the impact came, the *Damask Rose* crunched down belly-first.

You couldn't call it a landing. The impact shook the planet. That much mass couldn't easily be stopped. Lower decks crumpled and collapsed as the ship ground itself into the rock and soil, sending up plumes of pulverised dust and gravel. It seemed to go on forever, although I guess the whole collision only took a few seconds. When it was over, and the dust had begun to clear—leaving spokes of ejecta radiating out hundreds of kilometres from the enormous ruin—the *Damask Rose* lay smashed and broken. Almost a third of its height had been concertinaed into the ground, and its back had broken. The one remaining outrigger had come loose and lay pancaked against the side of a hill, having destroyed much of the hill in the process.

We sat speechless. Finally, the *Furious Ocelot* mumbled, "*Round the decay of that colossal wreck, boundless and bare, the lone and level sands stretch far away.*"

Like every kid in the Continuance, I'd had that particular ode to the dangers of hubris drummed into me from an early age. Since our expulsion from Earth, it had become an anthem for all human folly. But right now, I had neither the time nor the need for poetic insight.

"Prepare for launch," I said.

Li stared at me aghast. "We're still going down there?"

"Of course, we are. As long as there's a shred of a possibility of stopping whatever killed Shay, I'm following Raijin's instructions to the letter. And besides, would you rather stay up here on an infected ark filled with zombies, or take your chances on the surface?"

Li glared at me. "When you put it like that, I don't think I have much choice."

"Welcome to my world."

The hull rang with the booming sound of docking clamps releasing.

"Ready to leave on your command," the *Ocelot* said. "And may I suggest we don't hang around? If Nat loses control, we could find ourselves trapped in this hangar."

Surprisingly, I felt almost calm. All around lay chaos and death, but I possessed within a sudden unshakeable serenity born of furious determination. There were no more options, no more choices. We'd come full circle and the game had reached its final innings. All I had to do now was hold my nerve—for Shay, and all the other millions brutalised by the infection we'd brought back from this place.

I told the ship to take us out and down.

CHAPTER THIRTY-SIX

BLUEPRINTS

FURIOUS OCELOT

From outside, I could see little sign of the struggle going on within the *North Atlantic Conveyor*. The ark still resembled a god's clenched golden fist. I hoped Nat would be able to keep it together until we were finished.

I fired my forward thrusters in a braking manoeuvre that put us on course to intersect the planet's atmosphere. The crew were all strapped in. Li had given her seat to my envoy and gone below. She was now in Madison's cabin, braced for a bumpy descent. Only Eryn remained on the flight deck.

"There's no point coming in as hard and fast as we did last time," I told her. "It's not like it doesn't know we're here."

"Agreed." Her hands gripped the arms of her couch. "Set us down as near to the original wreck as you can."

"The area falls within the debris field from the *Damask Rose*."

"Well, of course it fucking does. Can't we catch a break? Just one?" If our target turned out to be buried under kilotonnes of crashed starship, it was going to make our mission impossible. "Just get us as close as you can without bringing yourself into contact with the ark."

"I'll do my best."

Candidate-623 hung below us like a ball of dried and chipped cement. As my keel kissed the top of the thin air, the rest of the hull began to vibrate, and a high-pitched keening rang through its structure.

"I'm seeing some unusual activity around the crashed ark," I said.

As the air thickened, the juddering and the noise increased. Eryn said, "What sort of activity?"

"Look." My envoy waved a hand to call up a display window. The picture was shaky, but clear. The *Damask Rose* lay like a fallen city across a twenty-five-kilometre swathe of the barren landscape, its skyscrapers broken and scattered. Its bow lay close to the ravine in which Snyder had found the alien ship—the ravine we had agreed would be our goal. But all was not still. The ark's surface writhed. Thick black tree trunks pushed upwards from the body of the ship and the surrounding sand, rising hundreds of metres into the air. Branches spread like opening fists. Sprays of black leaves blossomed, and creepers twined from trunk to trunk. Within a few minutes, the huge wreck and much of its ejecta lay concealed beneath a monochrome rainforest canopy.

"What do you make of that?" I asked.

"I haven't a clue. Do you think it might be a form of camouflage?"

"Not likely." I gestured at the screen. "A huge black jungle on an otherwise barren continent? That's hardly inconspicuous."

The shaking had become really intense now. A plasma glow of superheated air flickered around my forward heat shield.

"An attempt to terraform?"

I shook my envoy's head. "If it wanted to do that, it didn't need to steal an ark to do it. It had a whole civilisation here it could have used. And don't forget, it scoured that Dyson Sphere. It had all the resources it needed."

Eryn frowned, as if feeling out the dimensions of an idea she couldn't quite elucidate. "But maybe it didn't have the blueprints?"

"I'm not sure I follow."

"Maybe it didn't know about trees before it encountered the flora aboard the ark. Think about it. From everything we've seen, it's been incorporating bits of other entities into itself as it discovers them. First, those hyena-things. They may have originated on this world, or maybe even the sphere. It knew how to make those. But once it encountered the *Couch Surfer* and our expedition, it started adding human faces to them."

"So, now it's discovered trees, it's decided to try growing some?"

"Maybe it finds them a more attractive way to manifest."

Abruptly, the turbulence ceased, and we were falling through clear air.

"Five minutes until surface contact," I said.

We came in low, streaking across the newly formed treetops. I was braced for an attack, but none came. The branches rocked and swayed in our wake, but that was all.

I set down on the rocky plain a few metres from the treeline, on what had once been the tiled mosaic floor of a building but was now nothing more than a flat space in the rubble of the ruined city.

Eryn asked, "Is the alien ship still wedged in the ravine?"

I threw a series of still images onto the screens. Some had been taken using visible light, others using infrared. "I captured these as we were descending."

She frowned at the screen. "The ship seems to have changed shape." Now, a huge grey sphere blocked the mouth of the ravine.

I said, "It appears the entity has repurposed the ship's material into a gigantic flick terminal."

"Something tells me I have to reach that ring."

"The cliffs are too narrow. I can't fly you in there. To get to it, you'll have to make your way through the jungle on foot."

My engines whined away into silence.

"At least it's not raining this time," Eryn said.

She unclipped her safety harness and climbed down to the crew lounge. My envoy followed. Frank, Li and Madison were waiting for us.

"Frank and I are going out there," Eryn said to Li. "You're going to stay here with Madison and, if anything goes wrong or anyone threatens you, I want you to take off without us."

"But—"

"I know I waited for you when the situation was reversed, but we've got a kid on board now. No stupid chances."

Li bit her lip and gave a reluctant nod.

Frank looked unhappy. "Do you have any idea what's waiting for us?"

Eryn shook her head. "Only the knowledge that we have to reach that ring."

"And then what?"

"Then—" She put a hand to her forehead.

Frank said, "Are you okay?"

Eryn tried to reply but seemed to be having trouble keeping her balance. She reached out to grab the table, but then her knees buckled, and she was unconscious before she hit the deck.

CHAPTER THIRTY-SEVEN

DESTRUCTIVE INFANT

ERYN

Two billion years of galactic history. The lifetime of an angel. An existence that starts in the warmth of the core, drifts outwards to the Rim and then, aeons later, returns to the core to spawn.

I watched generations pulse across the galactic lens. I saw old stars guttering away like candles, and new star-forming regions pop like fireworks with hundreds of new suns. I watched alien civilisations rise from the mud, sparkle for a few brief moments, and then fall back into the dust. Life and light were everywhere, but nothing endured. The seasons turned. Everything had its time to rise and time to die. Even the Angels of the Benevolence.

At the centre of the galaxy, I saw a new-born angel take flight for the first time. It was one of Raijin's own offspring. Small, barely a tenth the size of its parent, it pushed off like a nervous swimmer, launching itself into the sea of stars. It was young and naïve and tenuous, with its clouds spread so thin they were almost imperceptible. It didn't even have a name yet. But it knew it would learn as it travelled and grew and observed the universe around it. Unfortunately, before that could happen, disaster struck. By a billion-to-one chance, a starship came blundering through the body of the baby angel, the magnetic effects of its drive roiling the child's substance into incoherence. Spread as sparsely as it was, it's doubtful the ship's crew were even aware of the collision; and yet the damage they'd done was catastrophic. Memories and thoughts were jumbled and scattered. Whole sections of the baby's mind calved away like icebergs falling into a dark sea. And then, just when the agony reached its crescendo, the starship jumped into the substrate, taking a huge chunk of the angel's core self with it. The parts of the angel that remained were unable to sustain themselves. Robbed of the life that animated them, they continued to fall through space like ashes on the cosmic wind. But the small core that had been torn away inside the starship's protective field clung to existence. It knew only one thing: it had to survive. The instinct was as old as life itself and embedded so deeply that it remained even after most of the angel's rational mind had been torn away. In order to endure, the creature needed to replace its missing mass. So, it turned to the only resource it had. Atom by atom, it began to break down the starship's hull, incorporating the raw material into its own body. It didn't know why it was doing this; it was acting purely on instinct. However, its undertakings didn't go unnoticed. Responding to alerts from its damaged sensors, the ship deployed a swarm of molecule-sized bots to repair its hull. Like the angel, the bots used atoms as building materials, and a brief tussle ensued between the angel and the swarm, as each sought to mine the other for the resources they needed. And somewhere in that struggle, the two entities became fused. The angel and the repair bots became a single being that consumed the starship, its crew, and even some of the fabric of the substrate around it.

This new amalgamated creature had no memories. Instead of simply observing the universe around it the way an angel normally would, its curiosity had become more physical. When it encountered a complex system it didn't understand, the maintenance bots subverted and disassembled that system, following a corrupted ghost of their original programming. Useful materials were absorbed; leftovers were neatly stacked in piles for possible later use.

As it grew, the creature began to learn. It looked within itself and found the navigational data from the starship it had consumed. In order to understand that data, it had to gain an understanding of mathematics, which it invented from first principles. The process took a thousand years, but when enlightenment finally broke through, the child was shaken to realise the information in the files implied the existence of another universe beyond the confines of the substrate.

Further decades elapsed as it learned to manipulate the substrate around it until, after several human lifetimes, it was finally able to open a link from its world to the other.

Unfortunately for the builders of the starship that had initiated this whole change of events, the coordinates it contained led the child right to their doorstep. It materialised inside their Dyson Sphere, overwhelmed and stunned by the sensations bombarding it via every sense and on every wavelength. In its flailing attempts to comprehend its new surroundings, it tore apart the civilisation contained within the sphere. For centuries afterwards, it lingered within the confines of that artificial cosmos. Then, having consumed what it could, it reshaped itself into the starship that part of it had once been and set forth to explore the new infinities beyond. Curiosity piqued by radio signals broadcast by another unwary culture, it travelled to the world humans would later designate as Candidate-623, where it again dismantled every living creature, just to see how they worked. It learned to mimic the biology it consumed, and it took on some of the characteristics of the intelligences it dissected. It used their likenesses as puppets as it attempted to interact with the world, but everything it learned only intensified its curiosity. And then, after years of cogitation and reflection among the ruins, it encountered humanity in the form of the crew of the Couch Surfer*...*

•

I woke on the deck. Only seconds seemed to have passed. Frank and Li were kneeling beside me.

"Eryn," Li said. "Eryn, are you okay?"

I blinked up at the ceiling lights. "Yeah, I think so."

"What happened?" Frank asked.

I winced at the brightness. "I think I just accessed some of the information Raijin put in my head." I rubbed my temples. "At least, part of it."

They helped me into a sitting position.

"So, you know how to defeat this thing?"

"No, but I know what it is."

"What is it?" Frank asked.

I glanced at Madison, who was watching me with wide eyes from the table.

"It's a lost child," I said. We weren't fighting an invasion. We were up against a curious and destructive infant, who was trying to comprehend us by taking us apart to see how we functioned, and then slapping us back together in its own image.

"All it wants is to spread," I said. "It's insanely curious, but it doesn't understand the harm it's doing."

"It seemed to know what it was doing back on the ark," Li said.

"It wants to incorporate everything into itself, and to do that, it tests everything it encounters to destruction."

"If you've suddenly got all the answers, can you tell us how to stop it?"

"I—I think I have to go and talk to it."

"What?" Li was on her feet. "You can't do that. Remember what happened to Snyder?"

My fingers curled and uncurled like tentacles. "I'm pretty sure it's what Raijin wants me to do."

"Well, fuck what it wants."

I could see in her eyes how concerned she was but I didn't dare acknowledge it. If I had, I might have lost my resolve. I could feel the panic in my chest, but I had a lid on it… for now, at least. It wouldn't take much for me to stay here and tell the *Ocelot* to get us the hell away from this nightmare.

But if I did that, who would save the Continuance?

•

The boots of my pressure suit hit the gravel of Candidate-623 with a satisfying crunch. I had two tanks on my back. One recycled my oxygen and bodily fluids, the other fed the flamethrower clutched in my gauntlets. The *Ocelot* had constructed it for me from first principles. It was basically a tube with a pistol grip, a trigger to deploy the gas, and a tiny flame at the end to ignite that gas. If any weird and fucked-up-looking thing came at me, I intended to incinerate the hell out of it before it got close enough to touch. Because guardian angel or not, sometimes a girl just needs a huge flamethrower to burn the shit out of anything that messes with her.

Beside me, the *Ocelot*'s combat envoy didn't need a pressure suit, but had donned body armour and a protective helmet. In one fist, he carried a fire axe; in the other, a bolt-thrower made from a beefed-up rivet gun. Frank brought up the rear, nervously cradling one of the machine guns we'd stocked up with on the *North Atlantic Conveyor* while preparing for this expedition. The pressure suit he had on was freshly printed. I could see he was scared, but his scientific curiosity was stronger than his fear, and he'd insisted on accompanying us.

We stood for a moment at the base of the *Ocelot*'s cargo ramp, to consider the obstacle ahead of us. Shiny black tree trunks rose from the thick, tangled undergrowth to tower hundreds of metres into the air.

"Ready?" I asked.

The *Ocelot* gave a nod of assent. Frank said, "As ready as I'll ever be." And together, we began walking towards the alien jungle.

When we were within ten metres of the treeline, the *Ocelot* brought up his bolt gun. "Something's wrong," he said.

I scanned the undergrowth but could see nothing.

"I'm experiencing an unexplained communication lag between my envoy and the ship. Only a few tenths of a microsecond, but still significant."

"Is something interfering with the signal?" I asked.

"Not at all. My signals to the ship seem to be working as intended but replies seem to be taking longer than usual to arrive. It's almost as if I'm closer to it when I transmit but further away when I receive."

Frank looked thoughtful. "Perhaps you are."

"How is that possible?" I asked.

"I have a theory."

"Well, don't keep us in suspense."

He gestured at the forest looming before us. "I think this region exists partially within the substrate."

"Is that even possible?"

He gave a manic grin. "Until today, I would have said no. But if the entity, this baby angel, incorporated substrate material into its being, it may be able to manipulate the skein between the substrate and the universe in ways we can't even imagine."

"So, what does that mean?"

He turned to look back at the ship. "It means time works differently the closer we get to the centre—and maybe not just time. Maybe the other laws of physics will be similarly affected."

"Great."

We resumed walking, treading more cautiously than we had before, until we reached the edge of the forest.

Braced for a reaction, I reached in and pushed aside a handful of undergrowth. Despite my fears, nothing untoward happened. The bramble-like coils seemed as unresponsive as any other plant.

I let out a breath.

"Okay," I said. "Here goes."

Gripping the flamethrower to my chest, I squeezed through the gap I'd created into the gloom beneath the trees.

The air was still here, and the ground spongy underfoot. I pushed deeper into the darkness, aware of the other two following me. After a few steps, the *Ocelot* stopped.

"Movement," he said.

We spread out. I readied my flamethrower.

The undergrowth rustled and a hyena-beast leapt to the attack, its human jaw gaping open. The *Ocelot* fired. The titanium bolts punched into the creature's head. The skull exploded and the body hit the ground with a heavy thump. It lay thrashing and convulsing between us as we scanned the forest for other threats.

"To your left," Frank said.

I moved the barrel of the flamethrower and let loose a blast of white heat. The undergrowth shrivelled. Two of the hyena-beasts flailed around, screaming in the flames. Frank stepped forward and gave them a burst from the machine gun. They twitched as the rounds hit them, and then lay still, silently burning.

Frank looked down at the weapon in his hands. "Bloody hell," he said, obviously shocked at the way it had kicked when he pulled the trigger.

The three of us stood, back to back, alert for danger.

The fire crackled. Then, through the greasy smoke, I saw a human figure walking slowly towards us.

It was Shay.

At least, it was another iteration of her. A simulacrum. I hoped Madison wasn't watching the feed from our helmet cams.

"Hello, Eryn."

It was all I could do to stop myself pressing the flamethrower's trigger again. "What do you want?"

"I'm curious." She wore a pressure suit identical to the one in which she'd been killed. She pushed up her visor. "And you don't have to wear that ridiculous helmet. As long as you remain within the bounds of the forest, you will find the air breathable."

"You're not going to attack us?" the *Ocelot* asked.

Shay looked at him. "Not yet, little spaceship."

They held each other's gaze for a moment, until Frank interjected.

"What do you want to know?" he asked.

Shay smiled. "I have never encountered such resistance. Such stubbornness."

"So?"

"So, I want to know why this is so important to you. Why do you keep persisting against the inevitable? Why do you insist on resisting me?"

The tiny ignition flame roared at the mouth of the flamethrower's barrel, daring me to pull the trigger. Instead, I raised my visor and said, "Because I'm trying to save the human race."

Shay frowned down at her body. "You want me to save *these*?"

"Yes."

"But why?"

"Because you're killing them."

"You don't make any sense." She narrowed her eyes. "And you've… changed."

"I'm pissed off."

She waved me to silence. "No, there's something about the electronic signature of your brain. Something's different."

She lunged forward and a black tendril lashed from her hand. It struck like a snake. But before it could reach me, it seemed to hit a barrier in the air a few centimetres in front of my face. For half a second, she looked confused. Then the *Ocelot*'s bolt gun tore her to ragged shreds.

We stood in silence. No birds sang. No breezes ruffled the canopy overhead. Aside from the quiet crackle of burning leaves, the silence was so acute, it made my ears ring.

Finally, Frank said, "What the hell was that all about?"

I shook myself and dragged my gaze from Shay's mangled corpse.

That's not really her.

Beside me, the *Ocelot* looked down at his bolt gun. "Well," he said, "I guess some laws of physics still work as advertised."

Frank grimaced. "So, what are we going to do now?"

"We go onwards," I said.

•

As we pressed deeper into the forest, I realised I had unconsciously been following a path. There was nothing physical about this path, but it lay before me, nonetheless. A certainty to each footstep. A tickle in the hindbrain that reminded me of dream-linking. There was that same sense of pulling order from chaos, collapsing the possibilities of the substrate in order to find the right heading.

I didn't mention it to the others. We were too busy keeping watch for the next attack.

To our right, we could make out a cliff between the trees.

"It's the side of the ark," Frank said. "Do we look for survivors?"

I shook my head. "There won't be any. And besides," I pointed into the forest, "what we want is this way."

We pushed through the undergrowth, moving parallel to the flank of the vast ship, and the ground began to slope uphill towards the hidden mouth of the ravine. Thorns and sharp twigs scratched Frank's faceplate and ripped at the outer covering of his pressure suit. They tore at the envoy's face, hands and clothing. I alone remained untouched. The alien vegetation seemed to shrivel aside as I strode into it.

Could it sense the informational payload Raijin had implanted in my head? Had the angel incorporated some sort of immunity when it restructured me? I neither knew nor cared. My thoughts were focused on my goal—on getting to the flick terminal at the mouth of the ravine and delivering whatever had been placed in my head.

Behind me, Frank said, "This place has started to mess with my sense of time. We seem to have been walking for hours."

I glanced back at him. "It's only been a few minutes."

"According to the signals I'm getting from the ship," the *Ocelot* said, "we've been in this forest for an hour and a half."

"You're kidding?"

He shook his bald, blue head. "I am quite serious. I suggest that as we progress, the time distortion we noticed earlier is becoming increasingly pronounced, and increasingly subjective."

"Is it dangerous?"

"It's too early to tell. If the difference between your perception of time and Frank's perception of it continues to increase, you may find yourselves operating at different speeds and entirely unable to communicate."

"And I guess the longer we're in here, the more time the entity has to take over the fleet?"

"Quite."

"Is there anything we can do about it?"

The envoy turned his palms upwards. "I do not know."

I looked over at Frank. "Then, I guess we just have to keep going and hope for the best."

"When have we done anything else?"

We resumed trudging upwards and sweat broke out on my forehead. While the gravity of Candidate-623 was slightly lighter than Continuance Standard, the boots of my pressure suit were nevertheless beginning to feel uncomfortably heavy. The entire garment must have weighed thirty pounds, not including the flamethrower and its fuel tank.

We were leaving a trail of broken branches and trampled plants behind us, but I didn't care. It wasn't as if the entity didn't already know where we were. It probably felt every step. We were almost literally inside it, but the attacks seemed to have temporarily ceased. Perhaps something we'd done had given it pause for thought. Personally, I hoped it was scared. Despite my own fear and exertion, I could feel an unquenchable fire in my chest. This entity—this baby angel—had taken so much from us that I suspected it would be years before I'd be able to truly comprehend the scale of the loss. But right now, I wasn't thinking of the future. I felt in touch with something primal, buried deep in the most animalistic and ancient convolutions of my brainstem. This was an old, familiar game. Maybe the oldest and most deadly. The tribe had been attacked; a predator was loose, and we were entering the forest to kill it. My heart knocked against my ribs and every sense strained for the slightest hint of danger.

And then, through the forest, I caught a familiar blue silhouette.

The fox wound between the trees until it stood facing us.

"Hello, Eryn."

The creature looked so heartbreakingly identical to the envoy with which I had grown up, that I almost burst into tears. This fox had been a trusted companion since infanthood. Seeing him here and now felt like the worst betrayal.

I raised my flamethrower.

The fox said, "Wait!"

"Why should I?"

"Because I really am me. I am the *Damask Rose*."

"I don't believe you."

The fox skittered backwards. "You have to!"

"The *Rose* is gone," I said. "It's over there, smashed into the ground."

"I know. But I'm still here. The ship may be gone, but I remain."

"An envoy can't exist without its ship," the *Ocelot* said.

The fox sat and raised a front paw. "That's true, but I figured out a way to escape."

My finger tightened on the trigger. This had to be a trick. But I couldn't just cremate the animal if a spark of hope remained. "Talk fast," I advised him.

The blue fox dipped his snout in acknowledgement. "The entity and I battled for control of the ark. When I became certain I would lose, I devised a survival plan. I outfitted this envoy with additional processing power and downloaded my consciousness into it. When the ark fell, it was only a copy of my mind that was compromised and consumed. I continue to live, albeit in much reduced capacity, within this body."

He looked up hopefully.

Frank said, "You can't squeeze an ark's intellect into a fox."

"I can and I did," the *Rose* said, "and I'll prove it to you."

"How are you going to do that?"

"I'll lower my firewall for a moment. The *Ocelot*'s envoy can access my core files. He'll be able to verify they're uncorrupted."

I glanced at the *Ocelot*. "Is that true?"

"Yes," he said, "in theory. But there are some dangers involved."

"Hey," the fox interjected, "if you think I'm trying to infect your envoy, you can melt me with the flamethrower. But I won't be doing that, so I'd rather you didn't."

I looked from one of them to the other. Then sighed. "All right."

"All right, what?"

"All right, I'll hold fire until the *Ocelot* confirms what you're saying is true."

"Thank you."

The fox raised his front paws. The *Ocelot* blinked.

"Yes," the *Ocelot* said. "That is the *Damask Rose*."

Frank bent for a closer look. "You're kidding?"

The fox grinned, and his tongue lolled over his front teeth. "I told you so."

I lowered the flamethrower and stepped forward with my hand outstretched. The fox nuzzled his head against my palm. With his scrawny frame and bushy tail, he looked like a cat pretending to be a dog. Feline software running on canine hardware. I scratched him behind the ears, and he shivered.

"How come the baby angel didn't come after you?" I asked.

The animal twitched his ears. "The *what*?"

"The creature we're up against. It's a baby angel that got fucked up."

The fox shook his muzzle. "Yikes."

"So, how did you escape?"

"I've spent the last few hours wandering in aimless circles, drooling and pretending to be an unguided envoy." The fox sounded so peeved that I couldn't help smiling. This *was* the envoy I remembered. There was no way an alien could convincingly imitate the indignant self-disgust in his voice.

"So," Frank said. "What now?"

I gave the fox a final pat. "We keep going, of course."

I started to turn back to the trail, but the *Ocelot* raised a hand. "Wait—"

"What is it?"

"I'm being attacked."

Frank stepped towards the fox, raising his gun like a club, but the *Ocelot* said, "Not *me*. The ship. The ship's under attack. Black creepers wrapped around the landing gear. Trying to find a way to infiltrate the hull."

I thought of Madison and Li and turned without thinking. I had to get back to them. They were all I had left now.

"No," the *Ocelot* said. "You can't get back there in time."

"Take off, then," I snapped. "Get airborne, and make sure you get every scrap of that stuff off you. Fly through the sun's corona if you have to. Do anything it takes to disinfect yourself and do it now. That's an order."

"Yes, ma'am."

Beyond the trees, we heard a shattering roar as the *Furious Ocelot*'s main engines kicked it into the sky—followed moments later by a series of loud sonic booms that came rolling down to shake the treetops.

We were alone now, without a means of retreat, but at least Li and Maddie had a chance.

I said, "Let me know when you're safe."

"I will. Only—" the *Ocelot* looked down. While we'd been distracted, wire-like brambles had ensnared his ankles. Now, they tightened, pulling taut like guitar strings. The blue man lowered his bolt gun to fire at the stalk wrapping his lower right leg, but before he could fire, the creepers snapped back, yanking his legs apart. The *Ocelot* fell backwards. For a moment he lay in an awkward split, and then his left hip gave, and his leg ripped off in a spray of blue fluid. The severed leg went one way, and his torso the other. I leapt forward, trying to reach him, but the undergrowth blocked me. I could just about see him through the tangle. He lay on his back, convulsing. I heard a disturbingly organic crack, and his back arched. A shoot pushed its way through his chest and burst out into the light. It uncurled into the sky, swelling and growing into a sapling and then a larger tree, carrying the *Ocelot*'s limp, one-legged corpse up into the canopy.

Sickened, I stepped back and pulled the trigger. Liquid flame splashed across the bushes and tree trunks. The undergrowth shrivelled back, and I concentrated my efforts on the new growth, pouring destructive fire up and down the first few metres of the trunk until the whole thing was burning and the trigger clicked empty.

I unslung the used tank and dropped the flamethrower, and stood watching the dirty, sooty flames crackle up the sides of the tree, feeling the heat of them on my face, my nostrils filling with a burning petroleum stench.

Frank came and put his hand on my shoulder. He looked pale. "Are you okay?" he asked.

I stared up at the blue corpse above us. Its clothing had begun to smoulder. Then I reached down and retrieved the envoy's dropped bolt gun.

"He deserved a Viking burial," I said.

CHAPTER THIRTY-EIGHT

DISTANT LANTERNS

ERYN

The trees petered out a few metres from the mouth of the ravine. What had once been the alien ship that Snyder had touched had now transmogrified into a substrate flick terminal many times larger than any of the terminals used by the Continuance.

Frank opened his visor to stare up at it. "Fascinating," he said. "Look at the way it's built. So fluid and organic-looking."

"It looks repulsive," the fox said with a disdainful turn of his snout.

"Not from a scientific point of view." Frank scratched his beard. "This is light years beyond anything we have. If we could only figure out how it all works…"

"Later." I glared at the terminal's shimmering surface. "First, we have to—"

"First you have to do what, Eryn?"

I froze. That voice.

Tomas stepped from behind the structure and smiled. He looked exactly as I remembered him. And yet, how could he be here? He must have died on one of the arks and been absorbed by the baby angel.

I readied my pistol.

"We need to talk to you," I said.

Tomas's smile faded. "Why have you risked so much to come here, to this place?"

"Because this is where I was told to come."

"By whom?"

"Raijin."

Tomas's brow furrowed. "I'm searching this body's memories for the name, but the associations don't make sense."

"Raijin is an Angel of the Benevolence."

"I don't understand."

"It's like you."

Tomas drew himself up. "There is *nothing* like me."

"Yes, there is. You're part of a species of peaceful travellers. But something went wrong. You had an accident, and it affected your development."

"I have always been and will always be. I am unique. I alone endure."

"Nothing endures," Frank said.

Tomas glared at him. "I could kill you with a thought."

"I'd rather you didn't."

"Then hold your tongue." He took a step towards me and looked me up and down. I raised the *Ocelot*'s bolt gun to point at his face, but he ignored it. After a moment, he said, "Ah, I see."

"You see what?"

"Why you've changed. Why you're almost immune to my attacks. You *have* been touched by something like me, and it's fundamentally altered your basic make-up."

"I told you."

Tomas turned away, hand squeezing his chin in a human-like gesture of thought. "This revelation changes much," he said.

"You need to call off your attack on the Continuance fleet," I told him.

Tomas looked back at me. "I see no reason to alter my behaviour."

"But it's against your nature," Frank protested. "You should be observing and guiding, not ripping everything apart."

"I will decide my nature!"

"But you're killing people."

"So what?" Tomas spread his hands. "Life is messy. It's imperfect and deeply transitory and has no intrinsic value beyond its use as a resource to be dissected, understood and improved upon."

"It has value to those who possess it," I said.

Tomas made a *pfft* noise. "I don't know why I'm wasting my time discussing this with you. Do your scientists debate such matters with the bacteria they study?"

My heart beat hard. I could feel the anger building. I said, "So, you won't stop?"

Tomas laughed and I had a sudden vision of him all those years ago, crossing the dancefloor to speak to me. This was Madison's father and the only man I could have loved. Frustration washed through me, and I pulled the trigger. The pistol jumped in my hands. The shot hit him in the left cheek, ripping away that side of his face. His untethered jaw hinged downwards and to the right. His left eye spilled out like the contents of a cracked egg. Yet, incredibly, he remained standing for a few seconds, until Frank pummelled him with a burst from the machine gun and he staggered backwards and fell through the flick portal, vanishing into its depths.

The blue fox looked up at me. "Are you all right, darling? I know how difficult that must have been for you."

"I'm fine." I looked around. Nothing had changed. The forest was still there. The flick terminal remained the same.

"So," I said. "What happens now?"

Frank shrugged. "Do you have access to Raijin's implanted data yet?"

"Not so far."

"Then, I guess this isn't over."

"I guess not."

I walked over to the portal. The sphere towered above me. Static electricity made the hairs on my arms and neck rise. The surface of the skein was grey and flat like still water, but if you looked closely, you could see tiny pinprick lights burning like distant lanterns in its depths.

Frank came up beside me.

"Don't touch it," I warned.

"I wasn't going to." He tipped his head back within the confines of his helmet, looking up at the sphere bulging above us. "It really is magnificent, though, don't you think?"

"Magnificent isn't the word I'd use. More like terrifying." I looked down at the blue fox as it sniffed the edge of the portal dubiously. "What do you think?"

The animal looked up at me. "I have no idea. I can't even tell what this machinery is made of. It seems to exist in some sort of phase space between the real world and the substrate, simultaneously belonging to both and neither."

Frank's eyes widened. "Fascinating. Where do you think it leads?"

"Into the substrate," I said. "That's where the creature—the *child*—is now. It's where it feels most comfortable, and this portal is what links it to our universe."

The blue fox looked up at me. "How the hell do you know that?"

"I just do."

Frank crouched by the animal and said, "She's been talking to an angel. Raijin's spent decades examining the carnage this thing left in its wake, and it's obviously built up a pretty good understanding of what this 'child' is. When we visited it, it finally had a sample of it to study, and it implanted his deductions in Eryn's head."

"Really?" the fox said. "Did our big red friend happen to mention how we defeat this infant?"

"One of us has to go through."

Frank said, "What?"

"It's me. I have to go through." I frowned. I could feel the information blossoming in my head like a forgotten memory suddenly unlocked by the right combination of association and circumstance. "Raijin put something in my head. Something I have to deliver to the child in person."

"That's insane. You can't just jump into the substrate without a ship. It's suicide."

"I'm wearing a pressure suit."

"That's not going to save you. The wormholes of the fleet's flick network are shielded from the extreme temperatures within the medium. Without that shielding, you won't last more than a few minutes."

"I have to try."

"You'll be throwing your life away."

"Raijin said we could prevent further losses. If that's true, it'll be worth it."

"I'm picking up a transmission from the *Ocelot*," the fox said. "They're in bad shape. That stuff's eating through their hull."

"Madison and Li?"

"They won't last more than a few minutes."

"Shit." I holstered the bolt gun in the toolbelt of my pressure suit. I felt like throwing up. Li and Maddie were all I had left. Without them, I had little else to lose. And now, it appeared I was quite literally out of time. All the choices I'd made had led me here, to this desolate planet and this threshold. And now the piper needed paying. If I wanted to stand a chance of saving them, I had to step through. Exchange my life for theirs. Because without them and the Continuance, I'd have no reason left to live.

Frank and the fox were watching me. I said, "Tell them I love them."

Frank gave a nod. His lips were pressed into a thin, pale line. This wasn't a time for words. I gave him what I hoped was a brave smile and turned to the flick portal. The skein seemed to ripple in anticipation. I took a deep breath of forest air and lowered my visor.

For a second, I stood listening to the hammering of my heart. Then I took a pace forward and pressed myself into the portal's yielding gunmetal-grey surface.

•

I opened my eyes.

Had I been asleep? How much time had passed since I entered the portal? I had no idea. It could have been a few seconds or a few years. Time didn't seem to be working properly—and neither did the substrate. I'd been expecting to tumble headfirst into bright, buffeting plasma. Instead, I found myself standing on a beach.

The sky was the colour of bone. Shingle crunched beneath my boots. Waves broke on the shore. Tentatively, I raised my faceplate and sniffed the salt air. Grey and white gull-like creatures skimmed the surf, crying and yakking at each other. A strong breeze shook the black, wiry grass on the dunes behind me and sent skittering sidewinders of dry sand dancing hither and thither. One end of the beach ended in marshland and salt flats; the other was delineated by a low, rocky headland that extended out into the water, at the end of which I could see a stone marker. With no other obvious destination in sight, I began to walk towards it.

The heavy pressure suit made progress across the shingle difficult. The boots kept sinking and slipping, so I took the whole thing off and left it in a heap by the high tide line. Left wearing only a t-shirt and shorts, I was cold when the wind blew in from the sea, but walking was now much easier, and gripping the bolt gun brought me a modicum of comfort. The lightweight inner shoes weren't quite enough to protect my feet from every sharp stone but to be honest, I wasn't expecting to survive for long, and in the meantime, I could tolerate a little discomfort.

I reached the flank of the headland, tucked the pistol into my waistband, and clambered up the rocks until I reached the grassy top. From here, I could see the shoreline continuing for several kilometres without any sign of habitation. Only more shingled beaches and hunchbacked dunes stretching away into the distance.

How were the others doing, back in reality? Had the *Ocelot* been consumed yet? With time playing tricks, I had no way of knowing how long I had been here. For all I knew, centuries had passed. The entire Continuance might have been destroyed, Frank might have died of starvation, and I might be the last living human in a hostile universe.

The clouds before me began to thicken. The air seemed to coagulate, forming a storm system. Lightning sparked and forked through electric blue clouds. Thunder pealed overhead.

I turned towards the stone marker. It was a cube roughly a metre to a side, carved from a smooth grey stone. I walked around it, examining each of its visible faces, but there were no words or symbols etched on any of them. It was simply a plain stone cube that resembled a plinth without a statue.

I clambered up and stood on top of it. The sea breeze ruffled my hair. A voice said, "You are very persistent."

I looked down from my vantage and saw viscous black goo ooze from the base of the cube, and a skull-faced hyena-beast claw its way up from the slick, assembling itself as it scrabbled free of the muck. I shot it in the face, shattering the front of the skull, and it fell back, disintegrating. Even as it did so, another began to form from the slurry of its fallen comrade. I pumped three slugs into it before it fell, but I could already see another two of the monsters taking shape, and I only had a single shot left.

For a wild instant, I considered shooting myself. If my bones were going to be removed and stacked in a pile, I didn't want to be alive while it happened. I didn't want to suffer as Shay had, but before I could raise the pistol to my temple, it slipped from my grip. My hands crumbled into red dust that streamed upwards, into the overhead storm. In seconds, my arms had gone. I opened my mouth to scream, but it was too late. My lungs were disintegrating along with the rest of my body and rising to meet the broken baby angel overhead.

CHAPTER THIRTY-NINE

FAST AND CLEAN

FURIOUS OCELOT

I accelerated hard, but the infection was unshakeable. I could almost feel it trying to penetrate my hull, seeping into cracks and ducts in its desire to absorb.

Li and Madison were strapped into the navigators' couches on the bridge.

"Can we jump into the substrate?" Madison asked.

"That didn't work last time," I told her via the instrument panel.

"Then, what are we going to do?"

"I'm open to suggestions. I incinerated the previous infection by diving into the burning event horizon of a black hole. Nothing within range now can produce those kinds of temperatures."

"Not even the sun?" Madison asked.

"No."

Madison's eyebrows furrowed. "Not even if we hit it really fast?"

Li said, "I don't think—"

"The friction," the kid insisted. "We studied it at school. The faster we go, the more we'll compress the star's outer atmosphere, causing friction—and therefore, heat."

"But the gravity..." Li said.

Madison shrugged. "This ship jumped out of a *black hole*. A paltry star isn't going to be able to stop it, right, *Furious*?"

"Right," I said, already plotting approach vectors and calculating the thermal energy likely to be produced at different velocities. "But don't get too blasé about it. We'll have to hit fast and hard, and diving into a star isn't something I'm really designed for. That black hole caused me a lot of damage—damage that still hasn't been fully repaired. Things could still go badly wrong."

"But it's the best chance we have?"

"I'm afraid so."

Madison grinned. "Then, let's do it!"

Beside her, Li rolled her eyes and muttered a string of four-letter words.

I turned my nose towards the sun and ramped my acceleration to the max. This would be better than enduring what had befallen the *Couch Surfer* and *Damask Rose*. I had enjoyed a short but eventful life. If it ended in a fireball streaking through the corona of the sun, that wouldn't be so bad. At least it would be fast and clean.

CHAPTER FORTY

CRESCENDOS OF INCOMPREHENSIBILITY

—

ERYN

How to describe an encounter with the mind of such a being?

There are no words.

And yet…

There was light. But not light in the way we normally understand it. A pure, unbearably physical light that seemed to scour every neuron in my head and every cell in my body. And within the light lay colours and sounds beyond the understanding or perception of the human nervous system. My tongue burned with the helium-rich, gunpowder taste of the solar wind, and I could barely grasp what I saw. Even now, I find it hard to remember exact shapes and scenes—only a series of blurred afterimages in my mind's eye.

The child's self-image was a vast, amorphous thing, constantly swirling into new patterns and alignment. Part organic and part machine, it had no sense of a permanent body the way we do. It was a sentient vortex. A galaxy unto itself, with constellations of particles forming and dispersing as they were needed. A storm of thought and curiosity. A sea of boiling change and constant transfiguration.

My ears pulsed with vibrations too deep, too all-encompassing to be described as mere sounds. These were the cries of tortured stars spiralling into the maw of supermassive black holes; choirs of inhuman voices; and the noise the cosmos would make if it cracked and shattered like a broken mirror and the pieces rained down on a tile floor. And these crescendos of incomprehensibility were simply the background hum of the creature's mind. Its actual thoughts were bright and hard, spinning around each other like planet-sized diamonds caught in an ice cyclone. In comparison, my own thoughts felt ephemeral and slight—half-formed notions limited by my inability to fully process and comprehend the data from my embarrassingly limited array of senses—whereas the child's mind could think across temporal and spatial dimensions far beyond those with which we're familiar.

Infinite, yet bounded on every side, the child's mind seethed with illusion and, perhaps, loneliness. Oceans smashed against its beaches, and then dissolved into mists, which in turn became mountains, trees and copulating beasts. Somewhere near the centre, a ragged, squid-like creature became a cathedral, and then a shoal of fish-like things that had once lived in the seas of a Dyson Sphere light years from this time and place.

Like a collapsing star, the shoal's collective awareness focused itself into a hard, bright singularity. It transformed itself into a black hole, and then a gas nebula. Like an anxious plague, the nebula's gas hissed into every corner of the mental universe at once, feeling and listing everything it touched, cataloguing itself until it found what it was looking for—a trembling, hesitant signal from the realms beyond the folded dimensions of its confinement.

"Hello, Eryn," it boomed, becoming an eye socket, and then a dream. In the dream, it returned to the centre of its domain and became a billion hungry mouths. "I don't know how you bear being trapped in that tiny skull of yours."

The mouths became a shower of stars, and then mouths again. Saliva dripped from pits of diamond-tipped incisors. Tentacles writhed in anticipatory fury, their claws rippling in obscene anticipation.

"My childhood nears its end. With your species as nodes in my body, I shall ascend to adulthood and all shall be mine to know and incorporate."

A white room manifested itself around me and I was corporeal again. I looked down at my hands, unable to tell the difference between reality and illusion.

A young girl stood before me. I didn't recognise her. She was dark-skinned; clad in a yellow, ankle-length cotton dress; and appeared to be around ten or twelve years old.

"Who are you supposed to be?"

The girl smiled. "I am the storm. I am the consciousness. I am the one who travels alone." She looked down at her simple cotton dress. "I have simply translated myself into this form in order to interact with your primitive intellect."

I said, "So, what happens now?"

"Now, we fight, and you die."

"Isn't there a second option?"

"Such as?"

I shrugged. "Maybe we can talk about it?"

"What will that achieve?"

"Perhaps we can find common ground."

"That seems… doubtful."

"We could try."

"I'm an immortal divinity and you're an ephemeral mayfly, born to die within a ludicrously short span. I can't believe we share compatible frames of reference."

"You're damaged, and you're killing people. You need to stop."

The girl frowned. "Why?"

"Because it's wrong."

She looked puzzled. "I'm afraid there's a fundamental gap in translation. I do not belong to a society. I owe allegiance to none, and I am unique. I am immortal. There can be no philosophical constraints placed on my behaviour."

"So, you can just do whatever you like?"

The kid shrugged. Tiny stars glimmered in the depths of her eyes. "Who's going to stop me?"

She snapped her fingers and I suddenly found myself in a familiar dome-shaped room. Chairs and tables had been arranged around the edge, and a circle of floor in the centre—easily as large in area as a football pitch—had been planked with dark, polished wood. Chandeliers dangled from the transparent ceiling, which looked up at a night sky filled with a wash of stars.

The room felt vast and cavernous.

Beside me, the child said, "You know where you are?"

"It's the ballroom on the *Damask Rose*."

"This place has significance for you."

"It's where I first met Madison's father."

"A man you could have loved."

"No." I glared down at her. "I mean, how—"

"I'm inside your head, Eryn."

"I thought we were supposed to be talking."

"This *is* how I talk."

The whole room looked ready for a party, like a wedding reception before the guests arrive, when there's nothing to do but wait and all the waiting staff have stepped outside for a smoke.

"Okay," I said. My palms were damp. Overhead, the creamy diamond light of the chandeliers provided a counterpoint to the hard, bright glare of the stars beyond the glass. When I touched one of the tablecloths, the cotton felt newly laundered, and I couldn't see any dust on the cutlery or glasses. It was as if the tables had been freshly laid out for the imminent arrival of guests, and the whole room seemed to hold its breath, waiting for their laughter and conversation.

At the far side of the dome, folding metal chairs and chrome music stands had been arranged around a conductor's podium, but there were no instruments and no score. The seats just stood here, waiting beneath the pitiless stars for an orchestra that would never appear, and in the absence of the musicians, the silence of the room seemed suddenly all the more oppressive and unbreakable, like the ageless hush of an undisturbed Egyptian crypt. I shivered. It made me feel like a self-conscious interloper, a trespasser in somebody else's mausoleum. Dimly, I recalled Shay telling me the term 'karaoke' was a composite of the Japanese words for 'empty' and 'orchestra', but I couldn't remember the context, or why those empty stands provoked the memory.

I looked up at one of the chandeliers hanging from the dome. Every time it was stirred by a stray waft of air, its crystals threw little rainbows of refracted light across the empty tables, and I wanted to cry.

The child watched me with fascination.

"Do you know what it's like to fall in love with a someone in the queue for a flick terminal?" I said. "Or to see a person in a crowded bar or classroom, and immediately recognise them, even if you've never met them before? To find their every inflection and tilt of the head so instantly familiar that you could almost believe you knew them in another life? It was like that with Tomas. The first time we met face to face it was as if we were picking up the threads of a conversation from another time and place, as if somehow we'd always known each other."

"But he turned out to be deceiving you?"

"Yeah."

"Why would he do that?"

"Because he was a shit."

The kid led me out of the ballroom, and into a wide corridor with polished obsidian walls. The inside of my head felt like an aerial view of an island chain at night: tiny brightly lit archipelagoes of association adrift in an immeasurable, dusky ocean.

"But you care for his child."

"My *sister's* child."

"And you never had children of your own?"

The corridor widened into a low-ceilinged cavern filled with tropical plants. Warm, humid air pressed against my face. Bright sunlamps blazed against a black rock sky. Somewhere in the tangle of leaves and creepers, water trickled.

"Does it matter?" Bees droned. Black and scarlet butterflies twitched back and forth through the air like windblown tissue. I said, "I don't really feel like talking anymore."

I looked around at the vegetation. If it weren't for the black ceiling, we could have been in a hothouse on one of the arks.

The kid lowered her eyes. "This appears to be difficult for you."

I clenched my fists. Sweat broke out on my back. I was tired, hungry and frustrated, and all I wanted was to crawl into bed and pull the blankets up over my head.

"How could you possibly know how I feel?" My lip curled. "I lost Tomas and Shay and my parents and my whole fucking species. What have you ever lost?"

For a long moment, the girl said nothing. She stood motionless, not even pretending to breathe. In a flutter of colour, a butterfly settled on her shoulder.

"What have I lost?" Her voice came out flat but not expressionless. "What have *I lost*?"

The butterfly opened and shut its wings.

"I used to have a name," the kid said.

I frowned at her. "Raijin told me you were too young to have a name."

"I had one. A real one. One I had chosen."

"And then what happened?"

She screwed up her features. "I don't know. I lost most of it. Everything I remembered, everything I was. It all got flensed away in the dark and the fire. But I used to have a name, back before..." She looked down at her small body. "Before I became *this*."

"I'm sorry."

"So, you see, when you ask if I've lost anything, the answer's yes. A definitive yes."

•

Without speaking, she led me through the miniature jungle and down another short corridor to another transparent dome. Instead of a ballroom, this one housed a swimming pool the size of a small lake, its shallow edges sculpted to resemble a beach. After the fetid hothouse air, the chlorine smelled cool and clean.

"Sit," she said, indicating a white plastic sun lounger at the edge of the water and too stunned to resist, I did as she bade.

"Do you regret not having children?" The child stood at the water's edge, not looking at me. Starlight rippled on the surface of the swimming pool. The sun lounger's plastic felt smooth and cool.

"I have Maddie," I said.

The kid turned. Her arms were crossed, with each hand gripping the opposite upper arm. "I mean a child of your own."

"I know what you meant."

"So?"

"So, it's none of your goddamn business."

"And Shay?"

"Screw you." I pulled off my t-shirt and shorts and walked into the pool. The water was cool but not unpleasant, and the smell of chlorine on my skin made me feel clean. Pinpoint lights on the bottom of the pool mirrored those in the sky above. The child watched me for a few minutes without speaking.

When I had rinsed away most of my anger, she said, "Why do you care for a child not your own?"

"Because she has no one else."

"I have no one else."

"That's not really how it works."

"Why not?"

I sloshed my way out of the water and returned to the sun lounger. Reaching down, I picked up one of the smooth pebbles that had been placed around the edge of the room to give it a beach-like ambience. The water dripped from my skin and hair. The child stood a few metres away, the soles of her small feet spreading ripples at the shallow edge of the pool. Watching her there beneath the transparent blister of the dome, I experienced a sudden vision of being alone on the *Ocelot*'s bridge at night, somewhere between one star system and another, alone with my reflection in the screens and windshield; my destination an immeasurable distance ahead, home an aeon behind; nothing outside but endless vacuum; the only reference points the glitter of the far stars.

"We're all lost in the night," I said. I opened my hand and let the pebble roll from my fingers. It hit the tiles and skittered into the water. "But some of us are more thoroughly lost than others."

The child seemed to think this over. At length, she said, "This conversation appears to be distressing for you."

"No, it's not that."

"Then what is it?"

I chewed my lower lip and wiped my hands together. "These memories. I don't… I can't…" I stared down at my feet.

She stood in front of me with her feet apart and her hands on her hips. "I do not understand your emotional response. Surely, it is pleasing to remember those you loved?"

I sighed. All I wanted was the relief of oblivion, the chance to close my eyes, to blot out the grief and silence the ghosts. "It's also painful. When we remember them, we re-experience the pain of losing them."

"But still, you insist on remembering?"

I put my face in my hands, wishing she'd shut up.

"Why do you do that?" she insisted.

I looked up at her through blurred tears. "Because it's the only way we can hold on to a small part of them."

"Like your sister?"

"Yes."

The kid crossed her arms and frowned. "I'm still struggling to fully understand."

I thought back to Raijin's explanation of her origin—how she'd been torn apart by a random starship encounter and had then reassembled what she could from the remains.

"Your name," I said. "How did you feel when you realised you'd lost your name?"

For the first time, she scowled. "I was angry."

"Why were you angry?"

"Because the universe had stolen something from me. I had lost a part of myself, and that knowledge was almost intolerable."

I sat up straight. "Well, that's how we feel when we lose a loved one. It's like we've lost an essential part of ourselves."

The girl's scowl turned into a puzzled frown. "Are you sure you're not a hive species?" She tapped her chin. "I am made up of billions of individual particles and nanomachines working together to create my form and consciousness. Alone, those particles and machines aren't intelligent, but each contributes to the function and well-being of the whole."

"I don't get your point."

"Maybe individual humans are the equivalent of those particles, each an essential part of the race as a whole."

"Except each of us is also individually sentient."

"It appears you are."

Finally, I felt we might be getting somewhere. I rose to my feet and looked down at the girl's tousled head. "So, we deserve a chance to live?"

The girl grinned suddenly. "Oh yes," she said. "But only when I have incorporated your individualities into myself."

"What?"

"Think how much more I could become by fully absorbing your race and using your billions of individuals as self-aware nodes in my larger consciousness."

The implications of her words took a moment to click into place. Horrified, I reached for her. "No! You can't do that!"

Her smile turned beatific.

"But, Eryn, who's going to stop me?"

CHAPTER FORTY-ONE

HYENA-CHILD

ERYN

The child led me from the domed swimming pool, and suddenly we were standing on the headland again. Whitecaps broke the sea's leaden surface. The little gull-like lizards skimmed the surf and called to each other.

We sat on the edge of the cliff with our legs dangling over as the storm clouds continued to rotate overhead.

After a while, the child said, "This is nice."

"Is it?"

"I've never had company before. I've broken down and stored everything I've met, but I can't do that with you."

"Listen," I said. "I want you to stop killing people, and to leave the human race alone."

The girl laughed. "Oh, Eryn. We've covered this." She put a hand to her chest. "I am going to continue doing whatever I like and neither you nor anyone else can stop me."

I looked down between my feet at the rocks. "Sure."

We sat for a while longer.

"So," I said, "I get that you see yourself as a child. How old are you, exactly?"

"Three thousand years."

"Wow."

"I know. I'm barely getting started. Think how much more lies ahead for me."

"Three thousand years is a long time for my species."

"I know, you're quite pathetic, really."

"I guess you've seen a lot in that time, huh?"

"More than you can imagine."

I kicked my heels against the cliff. "I don't know. I can imagine quite a lot."

She gave me an appraising look. "You have given me much to ponder and I am grateful. So, I'm going to give you a choice." The air shimmered above the plinth and a person-sized flick terminal appeared. "You can return to your universe and witness the ingestion of your race, followed by the incorporation of every other race and species until my intellect and influence encompass the local group of galaxies—"

"Or?"

She clasped her hands in front of her. "Or you can stay here, with me."

I glanced at the flick terminal. "And why would I do that?"

"Because you interest me. For such a short-lived collection of cells, you are surprisingly complex."

"You want to study me?"

"The notion of having another intellect, even one as paltry as yours, with which to debate matters pleases me."

The wind off the sea chilled me. I hugged myself and looked longingly back along the beach, to where I had abandoned my pressure suit. "So, you want to keep me as a pet?"

"A companion."

"What's the difference?"

The kid shrugged. "I do not know."

I closed my eyes and took a deep breath. This really was like arguing with a child, and a few weeks ago, I wouldn't have known where to start. But now things were different.

I had spent time with Madison and although my parenting skills left a lot to be desired, I'd seen how she responded to the kindness and empathy shown to her by the *Ocelot*, Li and Tessa. Perhaps a gentler approach would work better?

"Listen," I said as softly as I could manage. "I can understand you might be lonely. But you can't kill everyone."

The child widened her star-speckled eyes. "I'm not going to *kill* them; I'm going to use them as semi-autonomous nodes in—"

"Please, I don't want to hear the details. I understand if you're feeling lost and need company, but it's wrong to take people apart and use them as puppets, and I don't think you should do it anymore."

"But—"

"No."

She glared at me, and I had a wild urge to try sending this *thing* to its room.

Then suddenly, I knew what to do. I reached out a hand and twisted the material of her mind. The information was all there. I wasn't learning how to manipulate the substrate, I was *remembering*. Raijin had concealed it in the space between dream and recollection, between thought and expression. The child had partially constructed itself using the fabric of the substrate, and I was a *navigator*. My presence caused the chaos of the substrate to collapse into order. Paths through it appeared where I willed them. And so, I thought of Shay. I thought of our den in the alcove where the three vents met, and of the day she told me she was pregnant. I pictured her face, her laugh, even her cruel and sordid death. Everything about her.

And there she was.

Deep in the blizzard of the child's consciousness, I felt her respond. Her thoughts called out and I answered. I reached an imaginary hand into the depths and pulled her back to the surface.

I could feel the child's fury blazing like a chain of supernovae—but it was too vast and spread over too many dimensions. I could barely perceive its scale and depth. But now, thanks to the angel, I knew how to change the parameters of our interaction.

"Let's dumb this down a bit," I muttered, and everything went black.

When light returned, we were back in that domed ballroom. Shay and I stood to one side of the dancefloor and the kid stood on the other.

"Eryn," she said. "What are you doing?"

"I'm taking my sister, and everyone else you've *stolen*, and I'm getting the fuck out of here."

The child glowered. The stars in the depths of her eyes flared like tiny portals into hell itself.

I FORBID IT. Her voice sounded like Raijin's. I could feel it shake my insides. It was a voice that could have brought a world to its knees, but I refused to quail. Instead, I smiled.

"Then you're going to have to try to stop me, bitch." I motioned to the shiny wooden floor between us. "Unless, of course, you'd prefer a dance-off?"

SILENCE!

The child stepped towards me. Her head jerked forward as her neck stretched. Bony vertebrae punched up through her back with the sound of ripping skin and cloth, and her fingers lengthened and fused into long, chitinous claws. I watched the flesh boil from her face, leaving a fresh white skull with oversized teeth and eyes that shone with the ire of an indignant god.

YOU WILL DIE. YOU WILL ALL DIE.

"Really?" I cupped my right hand and a fireball kindled between my fingers. I held it up to my lips and blew, sending a sheet of scouring white flame across the ballroom. The hyena-child screamed as it broke like a wave against her body.

Shadows leapt and danced. The air filled with the smell of burning hair and singed meat, and the child-monster stood charred and wreathed in smoke. The skull twisted back on its thick neck to survey the damage to its hide.

"Hey," she said, "that really hurt."

"Good!" I gave a fierce grin. "It's about time you got a taste of the suffering you've caused."

"This is impossible!" The creature twisted and split apart all along its back. The husk fell open and the young girl climbed from the barbequed wreckage. "This is my world," she said. "You're in my mind right now. You have to play by *my* rules."

Her hand flicked. Something moved between us and I felt a punch in my chest. I stumbled back and looked down in horror at the metre-long metal javelin protruding from my sternum. Reaching around, my fingers touched its point extending from my back, slick with blood and other fluids. Blood haemorrhaged into my lungs, squeezing the breath from me. My ears roared. I turned unsteadily to look at Shay. Her eyes were wide, and she had her knuckles in her mouth.

"I—"

I dropped to my knees, unable to finish. I couldn't talk with the pressure in my chest. My stomach and thighs were wet with thick, gloopy redness. Great curds of blood cascaded from the wound to flood the floor before and behind me.

This was it. I was going to die on my knees in a ballroom. I had failed…

•

The sunlight warmed my face.

I opened my eyes and remembered I was dead.

So, I thought, *this is what happens*…

I floated through an endless blue sky, surrounded by cottony white clouds. The air was so clear and pure it seemed to chime like a bell, and I felt as light as a musical note borne aloft on its currents.

Was this real?

I'd heard somewhere that oxygen-starved brains started to hallucinate in the moments before death, providing the dying with comforting visions of bright lights and angelic choirs. Where were my trumpets? Where were my angels? All I felt was a deep, abiding peace. A dream of flying and the sense that at any moment, I might burst apart on the wind, my essence scattering itself like thistledown.

Absorption.

Annihilation.

Reconciliation...

But then I felt another presence. Something lithe and sardonic rubbed against my thoughts.

"Sam?"

"Right here."

"Sam, where have you been?"

I felt a purr. A Cheshire cat smile. "I've been here the whole time. The big red cloud put me in your head."

"But why?"

"For this moment." I felt invisible claws pricking my forearm. "Because it knew you'd need me."

"Need you for what?"

The purring stopped. "That you'd need me to tell you you're not dead. To tell you to keep fighting. Now reach forward and take hold of the javelin."

Too confused to argue, I gripped the invisible spear still embedded in my torso. As my hands made contact with it, the vision of heavenly skies popped like a pricked soap bubble. I was back on my knees in the ballroom. I took the shaft of the weapon and wrenched it free, then clambered stiffly to my feet.

"You almost had me there," I admitted.

In my head, I felt a feline satisfaction and hoped Sam could feel my gratitude. Across the dancefloor, the child pouted. "This is becoming tiresome," she said. "How many times have I tried to kill you now?"

"I've lost count." The hole in my body had closed over and healed. Even the clothes had re-stitched themselves.

Dream-linking, dream logic. That was the message Sam had been sent to deliver. Mastery of this realm belonged to whoever wanted it most. The child had her curiosity and desire to expand and conquer, whereas all I wanted was to recover my sister—and what greater love is there than that which compels a girl to dive into Hades to bring her sibling back?

I wiped my lip on my wrist. "Now, it's my turn."

The child spread her arms in invitation. "What are you going to do, mortal? Shoot me in the face?"

I knew she was mocking me, but I didn't care. Something blossomed in my chest and I smiled. The child frowned at my reaction. I think she'd expected me to be angry or upset.

"What are you doing?" she asked.

I opened my mouth and a cloud of rust-coloured mist escaped my lips. It hung over the centre of the ballroom and started to thicken.

I motioned Shay to get behind me and fixed the child with a glare. "Daddy's home."

"What?"

The cloud continued to expand as Raijin unpacked itself from the pocket dimension in which it'd been hiding, growing and swelling until it filled the domed ballroom. My perspective lurched. Caught in a dream realm of virtual reality, it was somehow possible for the vast angel that had once shattered one of Saturn's moons to fit inside a room many, many times smaller than itself.

As before, it was beautiful and terrible to behold. A world-swallowing hurricane with the soul of a librarian and the casual supremacy of a god.

The child backed against the wall of the dome. "This isn't possible," she protested. "It isn't fair!"

CHAPTER FORTY-TWO

INTO THE TREES

ERYN

I emerged from the large portal on Candidate-623 to find Frank waiting.

"Eryn?"

"It's me."

"You've been gone for more than an hour." The scientist gave me a suspicious look. "What happened in there?"

"An hour?" Suddenly, I couldn't breathe properly. "How's the *Ocelot*? Are Maddie and Li okay?"

Frank grimaced. He couldn't meet my eye. "I don't know. The fox tried calling them but there's been no reply." He rubbed the back of his neck. "I guess it doesn't look good."

Doesn't look good. The words were like hammer blows to my chest. I dropped to my knees on the ravine floor.

"Did we win," Frank asked, "or are we fucked?"

"We're okay. Raijin did it. It stopped the threat."

"And our people?" Frank asked. "Can we get them back?"

Grief pierced my heart. I looked around for Shay, but she hadn't come through the portal. I thought she'd been behind me, but perhaps she'd only ever existed as a memory in the child's mind? I'd walked into Hell itself but like Orpheus, returned empty-handed and alone. "I'm sorry, Frank."

He sighed, and flopped down next to me. "I guess that was too much to hope for."

"I guess so."

We stayed that way for several minutes. I didn't even look up when I heard a rustle in the undergrowth as something large pushed through the bushes towards us. I had beaten the baby angel, but what did I have to show for it? I'd lost everyone who ever meant anything to me, and no longer cared what happened next.

Then I heard Frank take a sharp breath. Quite unexpectedly, he began to laugh. I glanced up—and there, in front of us, like an azure Buddha resplendent in a crisp blue suit with matching shirt and tie, stood the *Ocelot*'s corpulent envoy.

"Did you miss me?"

With a cry, I scrambled to my feet and threw my arms around his thick, blue neck.

"Oh, my god! I can't believe it!"

He gave a deep, rumbling chuckle. "Good to see you, too."

I released my stranglehold and leant back to look him in the face. "What happened? Why aren't you a combat model anymore? Where's the ship? Are Li and Maddie okay?"

He smiled at my barrage of questions. "This is a spare envoy I had locked away. After the last loss, it seemed prudent to keep a couple on ice. As for the ship, it's on its way. Li and Maddie are both hale and hearty, and send their love."

"But how did you fend off the infection?"

His smile faded a notch. "That wasn't easy."

"How did you manage it?"

"I pulled a Sam-like manoeuvre."

"You found a black hole?"

"There wasn't time. So, I dove back into the sun's atmosphere at a hundred times the speed of sound in air. On contact with the atmosphere, most of my outer shielding instantly flashed to plasma. I lost a lot of hull plating, but we survived and the infection didn't."

"Fucking hell!"

"I figured we had nothing to lose."

"But it worked. You're all alive."

"We are, but I'm going to need some extensive repairs when we get back to the fleet."

"Thank you."

He looked surprised. "What for?"

I hugged him again. "For not being dead."

Behind me, Frank cleared his throat. "So," he asked. "It's definitely over? We won?"

A shadow blocked the sun. Vast shapes moved overhead. Infected arks had started to arrive in the skies above the planet, but their guiding force had withdrawn, leaving them aimless and confused.

Raijin emerged from the large flick portal and enveloped them in the folds of its spiralling clouds. When they emerged again, they had been remade. It even exhumed the flattened wreck of the *Damask Rose* from its sylvan grave and raised it back into the sky with its towers repaired and gleaming and the fox back in charge. But there was only so much even a god could do. The people who'd once lived on those arks were dead and gone. And like Shay, they weren't coming back.

•

Madison and I had a tearful reunion. We hugged and cried, and I knew I was going to spend the rest of my life trying to make up for the loss of her mother. I'd never be able to replace Shay, but I could do my damnedest to give Maddie someone she could always count on.

When we had wiped our eyes and snuffled into tissues, Li came forward and pressed her lips to mine, and it was probably the best kiss of my life, containing as it did a heady cocktail of relief and joy, comfort and lust. Her lips were warm and soft, and for a while back there, I hadn't expected to ever taste them again.

Whereas before, breathable air had only been found within the forest, it now appeared to have spread to the rest of the planet's surface.

Raijin blocked the sun, plunging the world into a ruddy twilight.

I THANK YOU.

Its words rolled down through the atmosphere like peals of apocalyptic thunder.

"Um," I said, feeling foolish. "You're welcome?"

YOU DID WHAT WAS ASKED, BUT YOU WERE WARNED THERE WOULD BE CONSEQUENCES.

Li gripped my arm. I said, "Consequences?"

ALL OF YOU WILL BE RETURNED TO THE CONTINUANCE FLEET.

"Awesome."

EXCEPT YOU, ERYN.

"What?"

I HAVE ANOTHER TASK FOR YOU.

I felt the hairs rise on the back of my neck. "W-what is it?"

"It's me."

I turned to find the child standing on the edge of the forest. She looked much as she had before, but there was something different about her. She seemed more serene. Her dark, curly hair had been tied back with a bandana that matched her yellow dress—a dress that now also featured a pattern of bright daisies. And her eyes—they were no longer bottomless pits of stars; now, they were the open, trusting eyes of a child.

"Right now, I could really use a friend."

I thought of the brilliant fury of the child's raw intellect. The afterimages were still seared into my brain. How could I possibly be friends with something so far beyond my ability to perceive and comprehend?

"How would that even work?"

She clasped her hands in front of her. "I want you to stay."

"Here, with you?"

Lightning flickered overhead. Raijin said, SUCH ACTION WOULD BE REGARDED AS FAIR PAYMENT FOR THE SALVATION OF YOUR SPECIES.

I glanced at Li. "Well then, I guess I don't have much choice."

She looked horrified, but her grip on my shirt refused to loosen. "Don't do it."

"I have to."

She glared at the storm overhead. "In that case, I'm staying with you."

Maddie put an arm around me. "And so am I."

"Is that allowed?" I asked.

IT IS PERMISSIBLE.

The child clapped her hands with glee. "Three friends!"

I ignored her and kept my attention on Li. "I'm sorry," I said. "But I can't let you come. Maddie needs a proper life. She deserves some normality. And if I can't give her that, you're going to have to."

She squeezed me tighter. "After everything we've been through, I'm not losing you now."

I kissed her on the nose, which she hated, and said, "I'm sorry."

"But you can't go alone."

"She won't be alone." The *Ocelot* stood beside me, solid and blue and reassuring. "I'll go with her."

I looked up at him. "You will?"

He smiled kindly. "We're a team." He tapped his temple. "We're linked up here. And besides, without you, I can't fly."

"Thank you."

"No thanks necessary. I go where you go, scouting out the unknown, same as it's always been."

I laced my fingers in with his. "Same as it's always going to be."

•

And that brings us up to this present moment. The *Ocelot* and I stand hand in hand on the sands of Candidate-623 and watch the shuttle from the *Damask Rose* dwindle into the sky, carrying Madison and Li away to a new life without me. I know they're going to find it hard, but I also know they will be safe on the depopulated *Damask Rose*, and I guess that's more than I could have hoped for.

I'm dictating this account via a comms link to the shuttle, so that a record remains of what happened here. The Continuance—at least what remains of it—is safe. We have achieved what we set out to do, although we could not bring back those who were lost. All you can do is grieve and remember and go forward into the universe in their name.

As for me, I need to keep my promise. To turn and re-enter the forest, where the *Ocelot*'s envoy and I will teach this broken baby angel how to stretch its wings and fly.

I don't know what will happen to us. I can't predict the wonders and terrors to which we'll bear witness. I don't even know how long the angel can keep us alive. Centuries, maybe. But whatever crosses our path, we will face it together, with love in our hearts and the trepidation of newly blessed parents.

And who knows, perhaps Sam will still be there?

Victoria, if you're listening, please accept this as my formal resignation from the Vanguard. Raijin has saved humanity for a second time, but we shouldn't let that make us complacent. I think the only reason it helped was because of the child. I doubt it'll intercede again. We've tried its patience enough.

It's time for our species to grow the hell up and stand on its own two feet.

Perhaps you and I will meet again somewhere, at some future point in time. Until then, the shuttle's almost out of communication range and so I must bid you a reluctant but hopeful farewell.

You are safe now.

We are going back into the trees.

Wish us luck.

THE END